THE HONGKONG AIRBASE MURDERS

Van Wyck Mason

THE HONGKONG AIRBASE MURDERS

*"Will bear comparison with the best of Oppenheim's
tales of international intrigue."*—NEW YORK TIMES

WILDSIDE PRESS

For
PHIL CONNORS
of the Regulars

THE HONGKONG AIRBASE MURDERS

CHAPTER I

YIELDING TO THE PRESSURE of a stout screw driver, the window rose gently, but Captain Hugh North suddenly tensed into immobility for, directly below, two chair coolies in palm-leaf raincoats had halted to indulge in a shrill altercation. He held his breath. If either of those Charley boys saw him they'd raise a row and, like as not, spoil any chance of finding out just how much G. Travers had had to do with Trans-Pacific Airways' long siege of hard luck.

A bank of mist, however, came ghosting in from the China Sea to smother the Native Quarter in a sour-smelling pall and prompt foghorns out in Tathong Channel to ask mournful questions of the night. Eventually the coolies reset their round blue hats and moved off, their clogs clicking dully on Shameen Street's rain-lashed cobbles. Once they were gone the man in the sodden trench coat raised the window, threw a leg over its sill and relowered the sash with care.

Then, recalling the burglar's truism that "a crook can always dispense with getting in but never with getting out", he muffled a flashlight with his hand and played it about a living room which was neat save for a magazine lying neglected on the floor, some empty highball glasses and an overflowing ash tray. The rug, Captain North perceived, was of excellent quality, harmonizing with several fine old Chinese paintings and rattan furniture of a Peking design.

By the dim glow of rays escaping amber-red between his fingers the visitor discerned a long settee ranged before a window which must in daytime afford a view of Hongkong's busy, ever-colorful harbor.

Keeping an ear cocked for any untoward sound, North searched the drawers of a desk with practiced thoroughness until he came upon a box of note paper which he opened immediately and examined. Shifting the light, he delved into an inner pocket, pulled out a folded square of paper upon which was typewritten:

12 Shameen

BEANIE:

Just talked with Melhorne. Maybe we can do business. He'll see you tomorrow at eleven in Macao.

G. TRAVERS
6–10

"Allee samee." The intruder, after a swift comparison, heaved a small sigh of satisfaction, then continued a search so silent that the febrile drumming of rain on the windowpanes was distinctly audible. Who, he was wondering, would G. Travers be? And what? Male or female? British, Eurasian, American, German?

The groping beam of Captain North's light afforded at least half the answer in revealing a fingernail buffer on a nearby table. If Travers was a man, some fair caller might have left behind a lipstick, but a buffer?

Ergo! Travers must be a woman. Pretty? Middle aged? Sallow? Probably sallow. What with the perpetual dust, wind and blazing sun of China, it was no wonder most women lost their looks in a hurry.

Standing in the center of the room, he deliberated. Should he search the living room thoroughly or first take a look-see into G. Travers' bureau drawers? He inclined towards the latter course, experience having taught that women were given to concealing valuables among their lingerie, perhaps arguing that one set of secrets might remain secure with another.

Before North could move, however, a faint rapping caused him precipitately to merge with the shadows behind a horrendous spirit screen inaccurately placed across the nearest corner. A faint gleam of metal showing in his hand, the intruder peered through an aperture in the screen's elaborately carved teak and was astonished because a shadowy figure had risen from the settee and was hurriedly smoothing sleep-rumpled hair. The person outside tried the lock and commenced an impatient knocking.

"Don't, Beanie!" sharply warned the apparition. "You'll draw attention."

A light switch clicked, then a table lamp's golden glow revealed, bending over it, a slim young woman clad in a brown sweater and tweed skirt. Above her forehead a fugitive lock of chestnut-brown hair glowed, giving off bronze hues near its tip when, obviously pulling herself together, she hurried to the door and turned a snap lock to admit a tall young man who entered quickly, flicking the wet from his hat onto the beige and blue rug.

"Land sakes, honey," he complained, "did you enjoy the six-day bike races?"

"How did you make out?" G. Travers demanded in breathless expectancy. "Did you——"

"Tell you later. Give us a kiss." He tried to take her in his arms, but, making a little face, she backed away.

"Don't, Beanie! You're wet and cold as a pup's nose!" Prettily the girl yawned. "Oh-h-h! I was *so* sound asleep!"

Once the young man's burberry, heavy with water, had been cast aside G. Travers slipped into his arms easily, like a crisp young moon into a cloud.

"Whew," she sighed presently. "Separation seems to make the heart grow fonder."

"Sure does. Slip us a skag, honeybunch. I'm played out." He hesitated, serious all in an instant. "Everythin' okay? A.W. didn't tumble?"

The girl pulled a package of cigarettes from a red lacquer box. "He thinks you went to Canton." One eyebrow raised, she shot him an appraising glance. "Pretty rotten crossing from Macao?"

Wet, easygoing features glistened above a match flame as the new arrival jerked an emphatic nod, then shivered and nervously looked about.

"Lousy trip—got any liquor?"

She examined dubiously a silver and crystal carafe. "'Most out of bourbon, but Alex Lebov sent over a couple of quarts of scotch."

"Lebov!" The man called Beanie flushed, started to speak out, but faltered. "Say, honey, didn't you promise me you wouldn't fool round with that no-count Russian any more?"

"Jealous, Beanie?" The girl smiled over her shoulder, then quite calmly splashed a quantity of liquor into two tall tumblers. "Well, you needn't be. I've been handling his kind of playboy these many years. What did Stag Melhorne say?"

The visitor grimaced and rubbed a chin which, had it been more powerful, would have made him much handsomer.

"Plenty! After beating round the bush a while he sure enough came through with an offer. $250,000 Mex."

Eyes intent, G. Travers leaned forward and asked in her slightly husky voice, "You didn't take it?"

"No. Like you said, I held out for $350,000."

"Bet we could have gotten $400,000," the girl remarked with a tight smile. "And then what?"

Beanie shivered once more and drank thirstily. "Melhorne got mighty tough, and I don't mean maybe! Warned me he would have me watched and if I didn't do exactly what I was told"—the speaker paused, unhappily looking G. Travers in the eyes—"he said perfectly casual-like, he'd have me bumped off."

Some of G. Travers' lightness departed. "Oh, Beanie, you're kidding. He didn't really say that!"

"He sho' did, honey, and I reckon he meant it too. You should see the port they're building in Macao! Air Oriental must be expectin' to fly some mighty big boats—thirty-six tons, likely. Their hangar's half again as big as ours." Beanie's voice began to assume new energy and life. "One of their G-38 Junkers was in. One sweet job, what I mean! J.U. 52/3m motors. The Heinies are smart, they figure on octane value——"

"Oh, Beanie, don't get started on engines again."

"Okay. Well, Melhorne had me demonstrate the E.F. carburetor adjustment to a bunch of tough-looking Russian and German mechanics. Then he told me to give 'em the efficiency and performance tables we'd figured for the emergency fuel. Just as if he'd already got the stuff——"

"Speaking of the stuff"—the girl took a nervous gulp from her highball—"what did Melhorne say? How are you going about getting it?"

"Can't tell you that, honey," came the unhappy reply. "Honestly, I'd be afraid to."

"Why not?" The girl sat up. Her mouth become a scarlet ruler mark. "Why can't you tell me?"

"Gave my word I wouldn't." The tall young man looked as happy as a fish being taken off a hook. "In my family a man's word means somethin'."

"I don't see why you had to give your word."

"So long's we're in on this, honey, I'm set to do just what I'm told until—we get our chance."

In hurt silence G. Travers took a sip.

"You wouldn't blame me if you'd seen the look in that old soldier of fortune's eyes."

"Oh, I'm not blaming you," the girl murmured abstractedly. "Only I'm worried. Things aren't going the way I thought."

"I'm wonderin' if you really understand Melhorne as well as you think? How many times you seen him?"

In a masked voice the girl replied, "Oh, we've had maybe half a dozen dates at Repulse, Fan Ling and

Happy Valley. The gallant ex-colonel amuses me, and that torn ear of his kind of makes him sort of picturesque. You've no idea how people turn and stare."

Beanie grinned mechanically, but his soft brown eyes held a baffled gleam. "Sho', hon, I reckon you're what the profs back in Charlottesville would call a sadist."

Again he gathered G. Travers into his arms, and for a long interval the only sound in the room was that of wind gasping about the roof's corner tiles and the slobbery swash of rain in the gutters.

"Gee, honey," the young man sighed, "that sho' was worth a lousy trip across the bay. How about a real get-together tomorrow? I—oh, honey, I'm awful hungry for you."

Her hand crept up, touching his wavy dark hair. "Oh, dear, I'm afraid it can't be managed. What with the new operations manager and Captain North both just arrived, Dad and I will be playing the heavy host and hostess."

"North? Who's Captain North?"

"Captain Hugh North is the U.S. Army Intelligence's *tajên*—which is Chink for big shot."

"Yes, but what's he doin' here?" The other seemed startled and uneasy.

Winged eyebrows expressed sardonic incredulity. "Bean-ie! You really didn't imagine Dick Donaldson's suicide would get by without some sort of hell being raised?"

"I reckon not," he admitted. "You don't think this North fellow will maybe try to cramp our style?"

"He'd better not," came the prompt reply.

Over the top of his glass Beanie anxiously studied his companion. "Tell me some more 'bout him."

"Think back. You *must* have heard about the 'Guardsman'* case—you know, it was in Washington. Why, up in Shanghai they still tell how he soft-pedaled a big *tuchun* war,** and that was *years* ago!"

Nervously the man from Macao rubbed his palms together. "Well, he'll find Hongkong's different from North China. I'm tellin' you, honey, things are comin' to a head—fast." He hesitated, stared emptily at his glass. "And if it weren't for you I'd——"

Infinitely caressing was the gesture made by G. Travers in slipping an arm through his and the lovely oval of her carefully made-up face became provocatively tilted.

"Now, don't go getting all worried, darling. What we're after is worth running some risks for." She tilted her head sidewise, a speculative hand pressed to her cheek. "Somewhere I've heard North's good looking."

"Don't kid yourself," drawled the visitor. "Bet you a buck he plays pinochle in his shirt sleeves."

G. Travers shook her neat chestnut head. "Take you! From what I've heard he's nothing of the sort. Bet you he's one of the charm boys with a Harvard accent."

"Charm or not," grunted the caller, draining the last of his highball, "he'd better check up on his insurance premiums."

"Suppose I develop a yen for the gallant captain?" suggested the girl in the revealingly tight brown sweater.

The Washington Legation Murders.
**The Shanghai Bund Murders.*

"If he butts in or gets in the way it'll be just too bad." Beanie's manner grew strangely detached. "There's too much money and international jealousy in this . . ." The speaker sighed and heaved himself to his feet. "It's right cozy here. Wish I didn't have to beat it and check in at the airport, sugar."

"It's just as well. Even if I dress like a fireman I'm going to be late for dinner." Suddenly G. Travers' arms slid up about his neck, pulling down his dark, tanned face. "Beanie, you really *do* love me, don't you?"

"You know I'm crazy about you." Almost frightened was the voice of this big young man with the too good-natured expression as he muttered, "You'll never let me down, will you? I—I couldn't face it!" Fiercely he strained her lithe body to him. "I'd do anything, *anything* in the world for you! Honest I would."

"I believe you, dearest." The watcher saw her expression soften. "Things won't be easy these next few days, but we'll stick together, and when they're over, why, we'll have each other and all the world for our own backyard!"

Long after her caller had gone she remained in the center of the floor, absently twisting a bracelet adorned with many little golden charms. At last a slow sigh escaped her, and, turning, she caught up her highball. "The silly fool," she cried in impatient contempt.

Among the shadows beyond the spirit screen Captain Hugh North gathered himself together, for, in changing her clothes, G. Travers would inevitably turn on more lights, move around. Accordingly he drew from his pocket and donned a band of wire gauze, skillfully tinted to counterfeit a face. This type of mask he had found to possess the advantage of effectively disguising his features while remaining barely noticeable at any distance.

"Bon soir, mademoiselle."

"Oh!" The girl gasped and spun about; her eyes become enormous blue pools ringed with alarm. "Get out right away, or I—I'll scream!"

North jerked a little bow. "I'm sure you scream most charmingly." He waited a full minute, then went on. "Why do you not cry out?"

"Wh-what do you want?" the girl demanded and shrank away from this supple man in the sodden raincoat.

"Your pardon, mademoiselle. I am jus' curious to learn why a girl of your social importance should find it necessary to maintain *garçonnières* under an assumed name?"

"That doesn't concern you," she stated in a cool, still voice. "If I choose to do something I generally do it. Who are you?"

Again a deprecatory little bow and shrug. "Suppose, mademoiselle, we again consider the question: why do you do this thing?"

G. Travers attempted nonchalance, but a watchful glint in her eyes gave her away. "Because it amuses me."

Casually North perched himself on an arm of the couch, remarking, "It does not seem to amuse your—er—gentleman friend as much."

"Perhaps not. But there is a good reason for our being friends. A very good reason."

Frank curiosity became evident in G. Travers' expression as she deliberately surveyed the man before her. Hat, gloves and a length of trouser leg visible beneath the trench coat—all were of a neutral gray. His hands, long and wiry, alone gave her a clue. They were not large but suggested, nonetheless, that they might become cruelly powerful.

Her pink little chin went up a trifle. "You don't believe me?"

"To doubt the word of so charming a lady would be unpardonable. Yet, a pied-à-terre in the Native Quarter? What a droll whim!"

North chuckled, and behind the mask's vapid, unvarying grin his teeth glinted.

G. Travers sauntered over to the sideboard, poured another drink and over her shoulder said sweetly, "Will you please leave? I want to dress for dinner."

"Why did you send your ami to Macao?"

"*Send* him?" G. Travers summoned an amused smile, but for all that, he thought he could read her anxiety. "Whatever gave you such a weird idea?"

"One will not pretend to be clever." Captain North fished from his pocket the slip of paper and held it up. "This was, er—found in your gentleman friend's pocket."

On recognizing the note, the girl paled a little. "I see. You're just a common pickpocket."

"Not a common one, I hope," came the amused reply. "And now, mademoiselle, please answer my question."

"I won't!"

"Then"—the other did not raise his voice, but it was as if a knife had left its sheath—"one advises you to cease meddling in this affair. Else you may get hurt, and your ami may be killed."

G. Travers reddened, but her veneer of assurance remained unflawed. "I won't! You can't stop us."

"*Hélas!* I'm afraid I cannot." North shrugged with a lift of his hands to denote helplessness. "Pardon me if I look about."

Rapidly, methodically, the masked man resumed his search where it had been interrupted, and all the while G. Travers watched him so calmly that he guessed no further information from Macao was to be found.

"You're very quick," remarked G. Travers, fluffing a coronal of chestnut hair. "Funny, in some ways you remind me of a samurai's sword."

"*Comment?*" The painted mask loomed over his shoulder.

"Lean, deadly and—and graceful."

"Graceful!" North chuckled. "Mon Dieu! It is to you the adjective applies."

"You're really too kind to me," she drawled, raised her glass an inch or so in acknowledgement and was silent as if listening for something. But only the patter of the rain and the distant whine of a native lute met the ear.

"Here you shamelessly burgle my flat—is 'burgle' a real verb?"

"It serves, *au moins.*"

"I should be furious; and yet, I'm not."

"Am I not already punished?" queried the intruder. "Have I not been forced to watch another man make love to you?"

She stood straight as a candle flame. "I don't think I like you after all."

"I feared that, mademoiselle." He sighed, then continued in a faintly mocking tone, "One imagines you only tolerate people you can dominate."

"Do I?" She bit her lip and came closer, her squarish, very red mouth tinder to draw flame from any man. "Maybe you're right." She offered the lacquer box, and Captain North reached to take one but ended by intercepting her lightning grab at his mask. Emitting a low, wicked chuckle, he struck a match for her cigarette.

"Mademoiselle does not appreciate my mask?"

"I think it makes you look rather silly." Breathing quickly, G. Travers stepped back, lips parted in a half-amused, half-frightened smile. "But maybe you've got buck teeth or something. . . ."

"Gallantry forbids my leaving you to worry."

North's arm went about her quickly, but even more rapidly she hooked a finger over the mask's elastic and jerked hard. Her little gasp of triumph died because, simultaneously, the light flickered out, leaving her to struggle with an increasing sense of futility. She smelled such masculine odors as pipe tobacco, shaving soap and damp wool. Then a cool hard mouth pressed her cheek. She ended by meeting the kiss in an inexplicable uprush of response. Promptly he let her go.

In the darkness her voice sounded shaken. "Oh dear, I—I didn't mean to let——"

"Au revoir, ma chère," murmured Hugh North, then added in a suddenly effective voice, "Remember my warning—your friend is courting death!"

She heard the door shut and surprisingly light footsteps fade down the stairs. Only then did she rouse herself, and, leaning far out of the window, she watched

North's trench-coated figure become lost amid the mist and driving rain of Shameen Street.

On her way to the bedroom she paused and slowly, curiously passed the tips of her fingers over her lips, then back again.

"Silly fool yourself," she murmured.

CHAPTER II

"A MOST miserable evening, monsieur," observed the large gentleman who stood waiting in Commander Tipton's doorway between a pair of stone Fo dogs which, snarling on either side of him, seemed also to resent the wind-driven rain.

"Isn't it?" agreed the newcomer as a gust of wind made him clutch convulsively at his top hat. "Rickshas seem to dissolve with the first shower."

In response to persistent rapping the door opened at last, loosing a broad band of yellow light which revealed a pair of porters in straw raincoats and wide blue hats who were plodding by, bent beneath their jiggling carry poles.

In a brilliantly lighted hallway a very fat number one boy took their things, whereupon the pudgy guest vigorously wiped the wet from his cheek in almost feline irritation.

"*Zut!* This means delayed mail," he complained, and a bracelet of heavy gold links gleamed when, using his palms, he reached up to smooth thinning blond hair. His eyes were of a pallid blue which one instinctively felt would not stand washing or boiling well. "One does

15

not suppose the American ship will depart either."

"Oh, I don't agree with you. Wouldn't it take much more of a blow to hold a liner in port?"

"One refers to the Hongkong Clipper, a flying boat of the Trans-Pacific Airways."

"Oh! Then I guess you're right. They would be foolish to take off in the face of typhoon warnings. The Trans-Pacific's been playing in hard luck lately, too, I hear."

"Indeed yes. The American line has suffered some most unfortunate incidents," blandly agreed the other, slipping an eyeglass into place. "You permit that I introduce myself? I am Alexis Lebov from Canton— à vôtre service." He offered a hand on which a diamond winked at two others decorating his immaculate dress-shirt bosom.

"A pleasure, M. Lebov. You are to be on the island long?"

"One hopes so," that gentleman murmured. "I am interested—one might say ver' much—in aviation. I own land near Canton so suitable for an airport. The Americans and the Air Oriental Company are both trying to buy it."

"Nothing like competition to run up prices, is there?"

"I ask only a fair price." The other smiled, then hesitated. "Pardon, I am so ver' stupid—I did not catch your name?"

Beneath the taller man's close-clipped black mustache appeared a smile. "Sorry, my name's North; Hugh North."

M. Lebov gargled faintly, then murmured, "An honor

of the highest, I am sure, mon capitaine. If you plan a long stay I shall be delighted to offer the privileges of my club, and if you have need of an airplane I can arrange for it. Chinese trains are mos' uncomfortable."

"That's extremely kind," North declared but made no comment on M. Lebov's evident knowledge of his rank. "Are you always so obliging?"

Alexis Lebov's teeth flashed, and he shrugged just a little. "When a gentleman is a friend of Commander Tipton and also wears the ribbon of Congressional Medal of Honor it is a privilege to be of assistance."

From the depths of the house appeared a brisk young woman in evening clothes who carried a shorthand notebook instead of an evening bag. Captain North watched her approach with rising interest for, although not out-and-out pretty, she was really handsome. Her chief asset, he decided, was ash-blond hair, skillfully dressed to emphasize the perfect oval of features that had been largely untampered with; indeed, her complexion was so pallidly translucent as to need only a dash of carmine on firm, disillusioned-looking lips.

"Good evening. It's good of you to come out on such a miserable night." Her eyes of dark brown quickly appraised both guests and showed tiny little splinters of gold in their irises when the light of a candelabrum struck them. "Is either of you Captain North?"

Captain North hesitated, occupied in attempting to place this young women whose vigorous figure was sheathed in a white evening gown which escaped being risqué by a scant margin. About her shoulders a magnificent Chinese shawl glowed like a vast emerald.

M. Lebov's whitish brows rose a trifle. "You are sure?

It was I who was to have a small talk with the commander—about some land near Canton."

"Sorry. So you must be Captain North." Her look came to rest upon his long body, which all but filled the door frame, then flitted over prominent cheekbones, narrow jaw and straight, high-bridged nose.

"Good evening." Captain North bowed a little. "You are Miss Tipton?"

"Oh no! I'm Trina Sinclair, the commander's secretary."

"Miss Sinclair, may I present M. Lebov?"

Captain North kept his eyes on the secretary and noted her faint flush when the Russian deliberately removed his monocle, polished it, and, restoring it to its place, again swept her with a look which was nothing if not appraising.

"You'll find the other guests are in the living room, M. Lebov," the Sinclair girl explained. "You don't mind?"

The White Russian wafted away the suggestion, but his eyes clung to Miss Sinclair's ankles when, trim as a yacht in her white evening gown, she turned away.

Leaving in her wake a faint suggestion of perfume, Commander Tipton's secretary led North down a corridor, her small, neat heels darting in and out of sight with a distinctive little flutter. Presently she paused before a door marked "Study."

"Who is in there?" inquired the guest.

"The commander and Mr Swazey." In answer to North's interrogative look she amplified, "He's our new operations manager."

"New?"

Her soft brown eyes sought the floor. "Yes. Mr Donaldson—er, died last month."

"Killed himself, didn't he?"

"Yes," she replied and hurried off.

When North knocked the door was opened by a florid, well-set-up individual whose flat back and drilled shoulders suggested a military background.

"I'm Tipton," said he succinctly. "This is Mr Swazey." His glance indicated a bony, greyhound sort of man wearing a wrinkled dinner coat, old-fashioned pumps and steel-rimmed spectacles.

After locking the door the base superintendent heaved a little sigh.

"Damned glad to see you aboard, Captain. It's been rough sailing these past few weeks."

"Hope the worst is past," smiled Captain North, accepting a cigarette and considering a fascinating array of model seaplanes and flying boats. To one side was a desk swamped beneath shoals of mimeographed orders, reports and interoffice communications. A tray of pipes, an empty glass of milk and a tide mark of ashes testified that this study was in constant use.

"Wish I could think it was past," Tipton said, "but I'm afraid it's the contrary. You see, Donaldson's suicide drew public attention to our having this emergency fuel. No, the situation's critical."

"Critical?" Swazey queried and ground out his cigarette on a small bronze tray cast in the shape of a propeller. "Isn't that putting it kind of strong?"

Tipton's sandy red head shook slowly. "Not when you think of Donaldson's death and the other attempts to bribe T.P.A. employees."

"What about Donaldson?" North demanded, looking at a photo of a very pretty girl christening a flying boat.

"You'll have heard the story plenty of times. Some 'Coaster' got her claws into Dick. He spent plenty on her and went bust, so he went to the *compradors*. Pretty soon they had him in so deep he was desperate." Tipton began speaking more rapidly, prompted by the distant voices of newly arrived guests. "Somebody, we don't know who, contacted him and offered a young fortune if he'd deliver a copy of our emergency fuel formula." The base superintendent glanced up quizzically. "See how it goes? Well, by sheer luck I caught Donaldson drafting a copy."

"What did you do?" Swazey inquired quickly.

"He'd a fairly good explanation, and we'd come out here together to establish the base, so I only bawled Dick out. But when I heard about this girl of his—no, we don't know her name—I investigated. When I found he'd deposited fifty thousand in a Kowloon bank I called him in and told him to explain or quit as operations manager." Tipton passed a harassed hand over eyes bloodshot with fatigue. "He wouldn't answer me, and before the police could nail him he wrote me a note and —and shot himself in some third-rate hotel over on Tong Kai Street.

"It was a damned stupid shame! Dick could get more out of the service crew than anybody I've ever seen. . . . Regular shark, too, when it came to doping out what was wrong with a bum motor. He could smell a loose hoist shackle a block away. . . . Poor old Dick!"

"You said Donaldson left a note?" North reminded.

Nodding, Tipton produced a bunch of keys, unlocked a desk drawer and in silence offered a sheet of cheap letter paper splashed with a couple of grim reddish-brown spots.

DEAR ARCHIE: [The note read.]

Guess this is about the only out. Sorry on your acct, old horse. Don't blame Eve. She's one swell kid, and we'd a good time while it lasted.

In a way I'd like to stick round and watch the Clippers go to town. You've a swell line, Archie, and it's going to boom. Say, weren't the old survey days swell?

Listen, Archie, tell Cupid to recheck the H.K. for Condition "B"—index weight should be about 10,719-255 unless you get a lot of mail at the last min.

I'd have copied the E.F. 371 if you hadn't come back when you did, so you'd better keep your eye on it. Some people would do anything to grab stuff that can give ship a base free range of 6,000 mi. One outfit's figuring on having it by Saturday; another one's got to have it or go bust—figure it out for yourself.

So long, old Pilot, and keep your tail up.

DICK

More than a little touched by the tragedy written between the lines, Captain North returned the letter and asked, "That's why T.P.A. asked for government help?"

Tipton summoned a wan smile. "Yes. Some fool reporter published Dick's note and threw the fat in the fire. Up till then we'd kept the E.F. business pretty dark. Inside the last few days various people have offered me everything from yachts to twin red-haired mistresses."

"Naturally," North said with a sympathetic smile.

The base superintendent had a desperate look in one eye and impatience in the other. "I don't mind so much about myself, Captain; but it interferes with efficient operation, and it's giving the line a lot of adverse publicity. Thank the good Lord we won't have the E.F. to worry about much longer."

Mr Swazey leaned forward, deeply interested. "Sorry, Commander, I don't understand."

The base superintendent absently fingered Donaldson's letter. "Well, it's this way. Because the emergency fuel in its present form is workable our clippers always carry a cannister along as an extra margin of safety. But the fuel isn't perfected yet—not by a long shot."

Swazey leaned further forward, shrewd features attentive. "You must forgive me, Commander. I've a lot to learn, but what is this chemical and how is it used?"

The base superintendent glanced at his watch, frowned, then hurriedly described E.F. 371 as a combination of chemicals which, on being mixed with either fresh or salt water, would form a combustible substitute for gasoline.

"Um. A light compact fuel . . ." Captain North's eyes narrowed, and a low whistle escaped his lips as he considered various types of aircraft and some of the chancelleries which were grooming bombers for long-range activity. He felt a little dizzy—this meant increased range for submarines, torpedo launches; in short, a supremacy!

"No wonder he's been having trouble, eh, Mr Swazey?"

The new operations manager arose, a wiry, hard-bitten fellow with a silent-looking mouth, and commenced pacing nervously. "I'd no idea the stuff was so useful. Its possibilities are staggering—colossal! Did you say, Commander, it's not perfected?"

"In its present form E.F. 371 deteriorates rapidly," Tipton explained. "I'm no chemist, but the instructions Davenport sent out say that because some of the chemicals react to each other the stuff is only good for a week; after that it won't ignite properly." He sighed. "This blasted formula's been dynamite for us. But not for much longer, thank God!"

"Why?" quickly demanded Swazey.

"We've just been advised that the E.F. has recently been improved enough to keep for at least three months."

"Which means you won't have to mix the salts at this end of the run?" North suggested.

"Yes. In another week I'll have this responsibility off my hands. Good God, you'd think the home office would realize a foreign base isn't equipped to protect a confidential matter of such importance! Try to tell 'em anything, though!"

"Suppose," suggested Mr Swazey, casting North an oblique look, "you go ahead and give us the rest of the story? Being fresh in from Lima, I don't know beans about this mess."

Over a sudden squall of Chinese voices in the not-distant kitchen the host raised his voice. "If you read the papers you'll know Trans-Pacific Airways has spent millions to prove it's safe to fly the Pacific. Well, we've done it. We've got the Department of Commerce's okay; we've landed mail subsidies and sold the public! We've got a monopoly on Trans-Pacific air traffic. . . . But here's what I'm coming to: Air Oriental's planning a Pacific line."

"Who are they?"

"Nobody knows much about them yet, but there's a pretty authentic rumor that some big bug got the idea of buying all the minor airlines in the Far East and consolidating them."

"Who is this interesting gent?"

To North's query Tipton could only reply that no one knew—some said he was a German, others an American, and still others a Japanese. Almost at once, the superintendent explained, it became evident that the new company's policy was to be an aggressive one. In short order Air Oriental's airports had commenced to dot the interior and the coast of China, and far from the least elaborate of these was the base under construction at Macao.

"But why should they try for the Pacific run?" Swazey demanded in his quick, precise fashion. "The only practical route is ours—T.P.A.'s. Any other would call for impossibly long ocean hops."

"Would it?" Face brushed with harrying knowledge, Tipton swung to face his colleague. "Suppose Air Oriental could refuel at sea by simply sitting down and pumping the ocean into her tanks?"

"Oh!"

A grimace flitted over Tipton's features. "I'll complete the picture. Air Oriental's registered as a Chinese corporation, but they use German pilots and equipment."

"Then they're operating?"

"Only in China. Just now they're running survey flights along their Pacific route."

"And that route is?"

Both Swazey and North glanced at an oceanographic chart papering one whole side of Tipton's study.

"Take-off's from Macao, then it's Tainan to Formosa, Formosa to Saipan to Jaluit in the Marshalls. Hiva Oa in the Marquesas comes next, then Clipperton and Acapulco, Mexico.

"Mail and passengers for the eastern United States wouldn't have to change planes," Tipton continued, "because the route crosses Mexico at its narrowest part, jumps the Gulf and climbs our Atlantic seaboard."

"Which lets them tap all the great coast ports," Swazey acidly pointed out.

"But *only if* they can get the E.F. formula?" demanded the intelligence officer.

"Yes. I guess Air Oriental would pay lots of money for it, eh, Captain?"

"Since they must have it or abandon their Trans-Pacific project, one would presume so." He hesitated, undecided. "How many people have access to this formula?"

Only two, Tipton informed the tall figure in immaculate evening clothes. The chief engineering officer at the terminal and himself.

Miss Sinclair knocked, then thrust her head in the door.

"They're all here now, Commander, except Miss

Holden," she said, but her eyes sought North. "And Tuck Fat has been in twice, very much upset because the cook is beginning to weep for fear the ducks will dry up."

"Thank you, Miss Sinclair." Tipton nodded heavily like a porcelain Chinaman. "Well, shall we finish this now or later?"

"Makes no odds to me," Swazey drawled.

"Why not later? Any cook who'd cry over a dry duck is worth keeping," North amiably suggested.

Palpably ill at ease, Miss Sinclair rewarded him with a grateful glance.

"My daughter isn't home yet?" Tipton glanced petulantly at his wrist watch.

"She phoned to say she'll be here any minute. Is there anything more?"

The base superintendent glanced up from locking the drawer. "Are Louis Martin and his wife here yet?"

The Martins had arrived, it seemed, and North asked who they were.

"Friends of Connie's. He's an inventor of sorts; wants to sell me a fog-piercing light beam, but it's no good. All right, Miss Sinclair; that's all. Be sure to get those letters off—wouldn't do to miss the Dollar boat. Have a good time."

"Oh, I'm sorry you're going on, Miss Sinclair," North lamented.

Gravely her eyes met his. "So am I. I—I've been so thrilled to meet so famous a man, but I'm staying till Miss Holden comes if she's not too late."

Tipton led the way into a living room in which M. Lebov, a remarkably tall Japanese and the inventor and his wife, a smartly dressed couple, were standing. Another girl who markedly resembled a rabbit hovered uncertainly in a far corner.

A moment later North drew the secretary aside.

"Was I mistaken, or did Commander Tipton refer to Miss Holden as his daughter?"

She looked at him a long instant before she explained that Consuelo Holden was a stepdaughter; theoretically she kept house for the twice-widowed commander, but Tuck Fat, the cook, and a wash amah really ran the establishment with the help of a "small pigeon" and a very lazy chair coolie.

Suggestive of a Buddha unexpectedly attired in starched linens, the number one boy was circulating a tray of martinis when the front door banged and a laughing young woman burst in, stripping off a gay orange evening wrap trimmed with white fox as she came.

CHAPTER III

"HELLO, VALERIE! Hi there, Jill!" she greeted, eyes flitting from one face to another. "How are you, Louis? Evening, Mr Tashima."

"Really, Connie, you're inexcusably late. I'm afraid you owe our——"

"Awfully sorry, really, so don't scold, Dad," Miss Holden pleaded and left a faint ellipse of scarlet on Tipton's cheek. "It was such a lousy night Do Wellington let me change my rags at her place."

Consuelo Holden's voice was rich and just a little husky, a fact which appealed to North, who had long since gotten infernally weary of clear, brooky and tinkling female voices. Tipton's stepdaughter, he decided, was more than commonly pretty despite rather prominent cheekbones, which were compensated for by singularly lovely and alert eyes of dark blue. At odd variance to her animated manner was her squarish, lazy-looking mouth.

Under the stimulation of his cocktail the host commenced to lose his preoccupied manner while performing various introductions. "Connie, this is Mr Swazey, our new operations manager."

"Oh, it's so nice to meet you," the girl declared with an air of genuine enthusiasm. "I was hoping they'd send out somebody nice. Here in Hongkong T.P.A.'s like a big family."

Mr Swazey's manner thawed, and he looked disappointed when her stepfather led her over to the Russian.

"And this is M. Lebov, who wants to sell us half of Canton. Ha-ha!"

Hugh North, while accepting a dividend from the cocktail shaker, intercepted a glance of more than casual recognition passing between the two. The White Russian murmured a compliment, bowed and kissed her hand with all formality.

The base superintendent passed an arm through North's and led him out to face the majority of the guests.

"Mr and Mrs Martin—all of you—listen please," he called. "I want you to meet the famous Captain North of G-2!"

Under cover of excited exclamations North silently damned his host. In Baron Tashima's heavy-lidded eyes shone a sudden animation; Mr Martin started, checked the progress of an hors d'œuvre to his mouth. Beaming, Tipton turned to his stepdaughter.

"Well, I told you I'd have a surprise for you tonight."

In mounting approval the Holden girl's dark eyes took North in from bronzed features to patent leather dancing shoes.

"Surely, Connie, you've heard about Captain North?"

"He's awfully nice looking," she pronounced judiciously. "But I'm afraid I haven't. I suppose I should, though?"

Miss Sinclair acidly intimated that Captain North was only known in both Americas, Europe, China and parts of Africa.

Consuelo eyed her father's secretary with no visible enthusiasm and drained a cocktail ere she drawled, "How very well informed you keep yourself, Miss Sinclair. Bet you already know whether Captain North goes in for moonlight swimming parties at Sywan Bay."

"Aren't you giving me credit which should go to you, Miss Holden? I'm pretty sure Captain North wouldn't enjoy one of your, er—p-poker p-parties."

"Connie, *deah*." Mrs Martin fluttered up to gaze rapturously upon the Intelligence officer's face. "You *must* bring Captain North in for cocktails tomorrow. Now I simply *won't* take no for an answer."

"Yes, do," urged her husband, a dark, bitter-looking individual with a small moon-shaped blemish marring one cheek. He smiled with mechanical impartiality in answer to every remark. "If you go in for that depraved sort of tipple."

Coolly Consuelo slipped an arm through North's and, throwing back her head a little, cried, "Oh, no you don't, Louis! He's going to be mine, all mine if I have to fight half the females in Hongkong. When did you arrive, Captain?"

"This afternoon from Shanghai."

"I thought the P. & O. boat docked this morning," Martin commented.

"I came by plane."

"Please," Tashima begged, "tell us about the ships of the new line. Air Oriental, iss it not?"

"They're built by Junkers, very comfortable and solid, and you can scarcely hear their motors. They were made by Klemm, Siemens, I think someone said."

"He was wrong about that, Captain," came Mr Swazey's unexpected correction. "The Junkers are at present using Y.B. 10 Wrights."

Mr Tashima hissed softly to express his appreciation.

"Do you like Hongkong, Miss Holden?" North queried.

"I'm *crazy* about it! You will be, too, because it's the most romantic and colorful port in all the world. Wait till you go up to the Peak and see the bay by moonlight! The Bund will interest you too. The Sikh police, the funny smells . . . And you rub elbows with every race in Asia. Tell you what: tomorrow we'll have dinner and dance at Repulse Bay. Louis has a mat shed there— it 'll be simply elegant!"

She ran over to the Martin man and threatened him with the devastating battery of her eyes. "Do be an angel and round up Ted and Beanie. They have the divinest music there, don't they, M. Lebov?"

The Russian nodded vigorously. "And what lovely women! But in Hongkong I do not like the climate. Mon Dieu! Every morning one has to scrape the mildew off one's shoes."

"Oh, nonsense," cried Martin. "You'll enjoy Hongkong, Captain, especially after you meet Sam Patterson, our genial host's C.E.O.* Sam's a regular Baedeker

*Chief Engineering Officer.

on the local hot spots." Then carelessly he inquired of
Consuelo, "By the way, where's the old bean been keeping himself lately?"

"Don't know." Copper hues shone in Consuelo's bob
when she shook her head. "Out of town somewhere.
Where is he, Dad?"

"Ran up to Canton to look over our friend Lebov's
property on the q.t.," Tipton replied. "He ought to be
back tomorrow, though."

"Ah," Mr Tashima sighed. "We can talk about the
mail connections then. I am most anxious to make a
favorable report to postal imperial authorities."

Just then the dining-room doors were opened, and
Tuck Fat appeared, clasping both hands over a stomach so rotund as to render ludicrous his attempted
ceremonious bow. Simultaneously in the front of the
house a telephone bell commenced to ring.

"Suppose I take it on my way out, Commander?"
Trina Sinclair suggested.

The guests had barely seated themselves when the
secretary came hurrying back. She was ashen, and her
lips were compressed into such a tight, frightened line
that a hush fell upon the crystal- and silver-laden table.

"What is it?" Tipton demanded sharply.

"It's Mr Patterson, sir. He's b-back at the office. He
says"—the secretary's voice shook like a taut cable—
"says your s-safe's been opened and do you want to
c-call in the police?"

"*What!*" The base superintendent sprang up, and
Mr Tashima's jet eyes began glittering, but not so
much as those of Mr Martin. More color rushed into

Tipton's blunt and ruddy features, then ebbed suddenly, leaving them an ugly, mottled red gray.

"No!" he choked as he sprang up. "Good God, no!"

Consuelo, conscious of M. Lebov's interested gaze, turned eagerly. "Isn't it too exciting for words!"

"Is Patterson still on the phone?" Captain North spoke succinctly and was answered in the affirmative by Miss Sinclair. "Then tell him to wait there."

Jerking a nod, Tipton's secretary flew back to the phone while North drew the gray-faced superintendent aside.

"It's in there? The E.F. formula?"

"Yes. But it's well hidden. I'm sure they can't have found it."

North was puzzled. Surely Tipton must have known of safer places for such an enormously valuable formula. Why risk it in so vulnerable a repository as an ordinary office safe? He wondered whether he had not begun to comprehend Tipton's previous nervousness.

In leaving he managed a quick, comprehensive look at the guests and registered an impression of the Martins talking in whispers and not in English either—any halfway competent lip reader could tell so at a glance. All of a sudden Consuelo seemed to perceive less amusing aspects to the news.

"Oh, Dad," she cried. "Please don't worry! Everything's all right!" But she blinked as if to shut out a startling train of thought.

As for Alexis Lebov, he was repeatedly wiping his monocle and saying rather foolishly, "What a nuisance! What a great shame!"

The new operations manager's reaction interested North; that angular fellow seemed to be trying to make up his mind about something while intently studying his host through narrowed eyes.

In the hallway the guests gathered, all talking loudly. By contrast Tipton and Swazey were deadly silent; so was Mr Martin.

"Come on, Captain," Tipton rasped, jerking on his coat. "You too, Swazey. The rest of you please go on with dinner. Very sorry—can't be helped."

North was settling a neatly monogrammed muffler of white silk when he felt a little tug at his cuff and, turning, looked into the beautiful but distraught features of Trina Sinclair.

"Please," she implored in a low voice, "can't I come along? *Please*. Probably nothing's happened, but I know the office from A to Z, and the c-commander is s-so upset he mightn't notice d-details."

Only a fraction of an instant the Intelligence officer hesitated before yielding to the logic of her suggestion. "Yes. Come along. Keep your eyes open."

"Oh dear," Consuelo wailed. "Now *wouldn't* something like this have to happen? Oh, Jill, what *are* we going to do about dinner?"

"Never mind," Mrs Martin said. "We left-behinds can go out somewhere. It'll be lots of fun. Then Captain North and the rest can join us later."

"Yess, a good idea," Mr Tashima's teeth gleamed. "Perhaps you will be my guests?"

"But no." M. Lebov raised pudgy hands in protest. "It must be my party. Dear Miss Holden, I insist . . ."

They were still squabbling when Captain North

handed Trina across the streaming sidewalk into a taxi Swazey had had the presence of mind to run out and find.

Tipton, his face a wooden mask, rapped to the driver. "Three dollars if you get us to 330 Zetland Street in a big rush!"

It was a comparatively short run to the T.P.A. office, but the driver was out to earn his money and drove like a maniac down Arbuthnot Road and along the upper end of Ice House Road. Through glistening, deserted streets whirled the conveyance, its tires whining and its lights but ineffectively piercing the dimness.

"There it is—where the lights are!" Trina cried with a little catch in her breath. "Don't worry so, Commander; probably everything's all right."

In a further effort to lend the harassed superintendent a measure of composure North drily suggested that since the robbery was all over nothing was to be gained by headlong tactics. Tipton, however, seemed not to hear, and when the taxi halted he sprang out as if projected from a cannon. Snatching open double doors bearing the T.P.A. insignia, he raced up a short flight of steps.

The necessity of keeping abreast was obvious, so North whipped off his top hat and bounded up in the superintendent's wake, callously deserting the secretary to Mr Swazey's attention. Charging through a ground-glass door as if he would break it down, Tipton skirted a heavy railing designed to keep the public at a distance ere he plunged into a large dim room cluttered by the outlines of sleeping typewriters, computing machines, filing cabinets and other office paraphernalia. The deathly stillness of this normally noisy place struck North, but his eyes remained on a rectangle of light beating through a door at the far end of the main office. Framed in it, a long-legged, rather ungainly figure in a light-colored burberry called out:

"That you, Skipper?"

"Yes!" Tipton panted. "Is everything all right? For God's sake, tell me, Patterson. It *is*, isn't it?"

The man in the raincoat shrugged. "Reckon so, but we can't be sure because we haven't touched anythin'."

"We? Who else is here?"

"Fuzzy Carleton of the Traffic Bureau."

When Tipton pushed past Patterson, North, over his shoulder, glimpsed a nervous-looking young man with very curly black hair and a jaunty little mustache like a pilot's insignia. Revealed by a bright overhead light in the superintendent's office, he seemed hemmed in by dozens of brightly colored posters, renderings and diagrams of T.P.A.'s ships and airports.

"Across 4,000 miles of ocean you fly *secure* in the knowledge that T.P.A. ships are *safe!*" screamed one of them, picturing a great flying boat.

Amid overwhelming suspense Commander Tipton stalked across the floor of his private office, set his hat on the desk and halted before a safe the sight of which gave Hugh North a moderate attack of heart failure. Though very tastefully decorated with T.P.A.'s trademark—a leaping sailfish rendered in scarlet—it was only a cheap Japanese imitation of a well-known British make.

North's eye, in following the superintendent's progress, had registered a screw of tinfoil and pink paper lying crumpled near the center of the office's blue carpet, and he would have salvaged it then and there had not Swazey and Trina Sinclair made a breathless appearance. The smartly dressed secretary's glance flew to Sam Patterson's sunburned features and then to the safe, a fact which Hugh North noticed along with the manner in which the chief engineering officer flushed and turned his back.

Distinctly audible was the whisper made by Tipton's shoes on the carpet when he knelt to squint at double doors standing perhaps an inch apart. He would have grasped a pair of nickel handles had not the Intelligence officer snapped, "Don't! Please use a handkerchief."

"Fingerprints," Swazey said as if to himself.

"Aw, what's the use?" demanded Carleton. "Nowadays nobody's dumb enough to go round leaving fingerprints."

"Shut up!" Patterson growled. "Well, Skipper, that's just the way she was when we found her."

"We're probably getting all excited over nothing." Tipton made a ghastly attempt to force a laugh. "I— I— Would you mind opening the safe, Captain?"

Slipping on dress gloves of white kid, the Intelligence officer bent and, though the witnesses were forming a tense semicircle in his rear, slowly forced open the safe's dark red enameled doors.

Trina stifled a little scream. "My God! The formula's gone!"

"Shut up!" Patterson warned savagely. "Maybe it's not!"

Swallowing convulsively, Tipton threw himself onto

his knees and after casting a dreadful look into the detective's impassive features pulled out a little drawer. Reaching far inside, he fumbled at the back of the aperture, and his nails, scraping the safe's lining, made a minute sound North would long remember.

CHAPTER IV

"IT'S NOT THERE!" Tipton broke into spasmodic curses, then fell silent, as if sensing their impotence. "My God, what am I going to do?"

"Try the next drawer—it's got to be there," Patterson urged. "Maybe you've made a mistake?"

From beneath the brim of his top hat Captain North treated the young man to a swift but penetrating look and noted that this brown-faced chap with perspiration on his forehead was a good-looking sort, athletic, but a bit weak about the mouth.

"Oh, God, it *must* be there!" Tipton's stubby, trembling fingers snatched out adjoining drawers in rapid succession until an untidy little pile lay beside him. When the last container was out the superintendent's body went slack, his knees striking the floor with a distinct bump far more eloquent of despair than his cry of, "It's gone! They've stolen it! North! Swazey! Oh, my God, Patterson, what are we going to do?"

"This looks pretty fishy," Swazey said slowly. "What's been going on in this office?"

"Quiet please!" North's voice flicked like a lash.

Kneeling, he thrust a narrow iron-gray head into the safe and surveyed several presumably untouched canvas currency sacks bearing the Hongkong & Shanghai Bank's chop. But a row of ledgers and confidential reports were in wild disorder. Just then his eyes, in dropping, glimpsed a small triangle of something like egg-shell lodged in a crack before the safe. This he secured by pretending to drop his handkerchief.

"I—I can't understand this," Tipton was groaning. "I took every precaution, didn't I, Patterson? Even had a special burglar alarm installed last month!"

Confidently North straightened, brushed pale dust from his knees and faced Patterson. Perhaps this was going to be easier than he had imagined. A person so incautious as the C.E.O. might be capable of anything. Anticipating possible violent objection, he drew himself up, distributed his balance on the balls of his feet.

"I don't suppose you would object to being searched?"

Patterson flushed, glanced dubiously at Carleton but ended by nodding. From hat to shoes, testing every inch of cloth, feeling for any substance secured to the body by adhesive, North searched the engineering officer and, finding absolutely nothing suspicious, promptly revised certain estimates.

The Traffic Bureau man also submitted, albeit ungraciously, to a fruitless search, but during the course of it North managed to pick up, unnoticed, the piece of tinfoil and paper. It turned out to be a chewing-gum wrapper.

"By the way, Commander," remarked the man from G-2, "didn't you say Mr Patterson was in Canton?"

"Why, yes," Tipton admitted. "How is it you're here, Sam?"

The tall young man nodded easily. "Went up early this mornin' and looked over the land. It's a pretty good site, so I hunted up the real estate broker and took him down to the magistrate's *yamen* to search the title. It was okay, so, having finished the job, I caught the five-thirty down. Never have seen Canton hotter or smellier."

"I see. But how did you happen in here?"

"I was goin' by and noticed the front door was open," Patterson explained readily. "I reckoned that was queer 'cause the office windows were dark, so I came upstairs and was turnin' on the lights when Carleton showed up. Tell 'em the rest of it, Fuzzy."

The Traffic Bureau man nodded vigorously. "A copper on the street thought he heard a little ting! of the safe's burglar alarm, but he wasn't sure, so he stopped in to ask if anybody would be working late at the office. I only live around the corner."

"And then?" North's voice was an effective anodyne to alarm.

"When that bell really goes off she sure raises the dead. But I got to thinking," Carleton continued, "and I figgered maybe I'd better drop over and see. That's when I met Sam. We looked about, and when we found your safe open, Skipper, Sam called you right away."

The C.E.O. started to say something, but North checked him with raised hand.

"Mr Carleton, when did the policeman say he heard that single ting?"

"About half-past eight, he said, but I didn't get over here until around nine."

"So then the robbery must have been taking place about eight-thirty," Trina Sinclair observed slowly. "A time when most all of us were at your house, Commander."

"Who wasn't?" Swazey inquired.

"Mr Tashima and Miss Holden were the last ones to appear."

Captain North suddenly felt like a small boy at a six ring circus; so much was going on he couldn't possibly devote his attention to any one point of interest. Yes. Five persons in a good-sized office were too many to observe with any hope of consistency, so he decided on a rapid dismissal of several people.

Of Trina Sinclair he inquired a trifle maliciously, "Do you chew gum?"

"*Gum!* Mercy, no!" She gasped and could not have looked more insulted had her legitimacy been questioned. "Do I look as if I did?"

"No, not really, but I found a piece of gum wrapping on the floor and thought I'd ask. We all have our weakness—mine's dunking toast," he confessed sadly.

Her expression lighted. "Good. I felt all along you were very human. But about the gum wrapper. I don't know who could have dropped it because I know Sam—I mean Mr Patterson—doesn't use it, and I never remember having seen Fuzzy chewing." Fathomless and very appealing brown eyes claimed his further attention. "If there isn't anything I can do to help I'm going to clear out," she announced. "I've always believed that during a crisis a useless person's room is more welcome than her company."

His look expressed both admiration and gratitude—in large quantities. "Who knows the combination?"

"Only the department heads. A.W. and Mr Patterson. I presume Mr Swazey will be given it soon's he gets settled."

Addressing to her stunned and vacant-eyed employer a warm word of sympathy, Miss Sinclair gave a nod to the others and gathered a black velvet evening wrap about her.

"Wait a minute, Trina," Patterson urged. "Let me find you a chair."

"Don't bother, Mr Patterson." Her reply was quite natural, but somehow North had a feeling that she was thinking hard and trying not to show it. "I don't imagine Captain North has finished with you."

"Perhaps Mr Carleton will find you one?" North suggested. "You'll ruin your gown."

Scarcely had the two disappeared when North commenced a cross-questioning of Patterson as tactful as it was subtle.

Patterson stated he had come directly from the ferry to the office. Yes. He was planning to go out later; Miss Holden had said something about his joining a supper party at the Pinnacle if he got back from Canton in time. Yes. The window had been just like that when he came in. Didn't Mr Patterson think it odd that the thief should have entered by the window, only to leave by the front door? It *was* queer, he admitted, but he'd no good explanation. No. He'd no idea who else might have known the combination; of course Donaldson might have given it away.

At this item of news the Intelligence officer's mouth

tightened, and he turned on Tipton a rather searching look. "Do you mean to say, Commander, that you *didn't* have the combination of the safe changed after the suicide?"

The superintendent nodded miserably, his face looking old and bleached like the upholstery of porch furniture exposed too long to the weather.

"I—I'm afraid not. What with the scandal and doing Donaldson's work on top of my own, I didn't order the safe people to change it until last week. They should have been here long ago." He sighed and seemed to beg for understanding. "You've been in China long enough to know that it's always mañana, mañana out here."

So the combination hadn't been changed! North sensed new pitfalls in the ground he was treading, but no one would have guessed it when he suggested that he and Commander Tipton would like to talk in private.

"Right. I'll scram. I'm hungry as a wolf," Patterson confessed with an engaging smile. "If you want me, Captain, I'll be in my room at the Pinnacle Hotel for the next hour or so." He lingered uncertainly. "I—I'd like a talk with you later on, Captain. You aren't going to be at the Pinnacle after twelve, are you?"

"I might be. Why?"

"Just been gettin' a hunch," said the C.E.O. in his soft Southern voice. "Maybe it's no good, but I—well, I'd give a lot to see our E.F. formula safe."

Buttoning his damp burberry about him, Patterson murmured a sober, "Good night," and swung out of sight. Briefly his footfalls echoed through the empty main office but paused momentarily at the top of the steps as if the C.E.O. were debating a return. In the end, however, they went on again and presently the front door banged.

Swazey, who had said not a word during the last fifteen or twenty minutes, aroused himself from what must have been some serious thinking.

"Well, if you'll excuse me, Commander, I'll be going too. I want to unpack. Tomorrow I'll tell you about some dodges we tried out in South America. Good night, Captain, and please give me a buzz at the Métropole if anything breaks."

North lit a cigarette and, turning to the superintendent, beheld a haggard, desperately uncertain man, torn by forces too great for him. The base superintendent said nothing, only licked his lips, ran a finger inside his wilted dress collar and walked stiffly over to his desk. He collapsed rather than seated himself behind it and buried his face in his hands.

Mercifully tolerant of the other's necessity for a breathing spell, the Intelligence officer crossed to examine the window, which, half open, gave access to a regular burglar's dream of a ledge and admitted a damp, sour-smelling breeze. Hugh North drew a deep breath and smiled; blindfolded, he could have told where he was. China. Nowhere else could just such a reek exist— a blend of unclean streets, open sewers, highly spiced foods, rice steamings and laundry forever hanging in sunless alleys. Peering out, the Intelligence officer found he could just make out a ghostlike pattern of distant masts, spars and rigging looming above the housetops. Gratefully he noted a lessening of the rain and an increase in the plaintive wails of "Ricksha, wanchee?" "Ch'eh, wanchee?"

After seven years it was pleasant to be revisiting this restless city of paradoxes. Odd, at first one expected everything to be old and Chinese, yet despite Hongkong's oriental mask the "Tight Little Island's" coldly practical influence was dominant, all pervasive.

North's straight dark brows merged when he considered the sum of his evidence: only a bit of eggshell and a chewing gum wrapper. The last *was* evidence, he decided, because the office had obviously been thoroughly cleaned and swept after Tipton's departure. An explanation for the eggshell eluded him. Why the devil should a thief about to commit a robbery of terrific consequence pause *to eat an egg* on the scene of his crime? The question tantalized him, and only reluctantly did he shut the window and face about.

"Well, Commander, have you any suspects?"

Visibly Tipton pulled himself together, sat up straight like the naval officer he once had been. "No. Because, well, I've gradually come to trust nobody. You see, Hongkong does things to men. Too many race tracks, I suppose, Eurasian girls and luxuries most of us could never afford at home. I'd have trusted Dick Donaldson with my life, yet he tried to sell me out. How do I know you're really Captain North?"

"You don't. You could have seen my credentials had you asked," grimly replied the tall figure in evening clothes. "And out here you should have, you know."

"Well . . ." Tipton floundered. "I was going to as soon as I could. Damn it, man, you've no idea the strain I've been under this last month."

"Perhaps I have." North's manner remained unrelenting. "But why were you so criminally stupid or

careless as to keep the E.F. formula in a safe the combination of which probably was no longer a secret? You
knew Donaldson might have given it away!"

Stung, Andrew Tipton leaped to his feet, heavy
features crimsoning. "God damn it! I won't stand for
such insinuations from you or anybody else!"

"You won't have to," came the unperturbed reply,
"provided you answer my questions."

The ex-naval officer choked off a furious outburst
and, dropping big capable hands spotted with brown
freckles, stepped back from the desk.

"Sorry, Captain. I—I don't often lose my temper.
Guess this business is getting me. You're wrong too.
The E.F. formula, unless it's necessary to mix a fresh
cannister of the salts, is always kept in a safe deposit
box at the bank."

Upon considering the perishable nature of the mix-
ture and the fact that the Hongkong Clipper was not
scheduled to take off until the second day following,
North found himself perplexed as to why Tipton had
decided to prepare the chemical so far ahead. Having
long since learned that to say nothing is often to learn
much, he remained silent, and Tipton continued in the
deep, resonant voice he might once have used on a
quarter-deck.

"I got it out early this time because today the home
office cabled a change in the proportions." Tipton's eyes
sought the safe and wavered aside. "I intended taking
it back to the bank but got tied up here past closing
time."

"How?" Glimmerings of light played on the horizon

of North's understanding. Or was it only witch fire? he wondered.

"Discussing the land proposition with Alexis Lebov. He was late for his appointment, and it was half-past four before we knew it. By that time our negotiations for the day were over. The bank was closed, so"—he shrugged—"I was fool enough to take a chance and lock the formula in our safe. The rest you know."

Slowly the Intelligence officer's dark head shook. "I wish I did, Commander. Please answer this question—and don't think me quite crazy. Do you ever eat your lunch in this room?"

"Heavens, no. I go to the club."

North took no chances. "What about the employees?"

"It's against the rules. They'd not come in here anyhow."

"You closed and locked the safe *yourself?*"

"Yes," was the superintendent's prompt rejoinder. In a rising voice eloquent of crackling nerves he continued. "After asking Lebov to wait outside I put the formula in a heavy manila envelope and sealed it with this ring. Nobody else touched it," he added with a belligerent air, "so hold me responsible and be damned to you!"

"Oh, come now, Commander." Captain North spoke definitely but was at pains to soothe the unhappy man. "I'm here solely because the War and Navy departments dread any possibility of your formula's falling into unfriendly hands. You must have had communications in respect to that?"

Tipton replied that ever since Donaldson's death both departments had bombarded him with queries, ad-

vice and requests. What would Captain North suggest
he do?

The Intelligence officer slowly brushed a speck of
dust from his top hat, then cast a final look about the
office.

"Go home, relax completely for a while, then go back
over the past week," North advised. "Try to remember
anything even the least bit out of the way that happened during that time. Say a clerk or a stenographer's
coming into your office unsummoned, an electrician
working where he wasn't supposed to . . . Along other
lines too. Suppose one of your staff asked questions
they'd no business to or was very late to work." He gave
the other an encouraging little smile. "You see what I
mean? Small things like that sometimes tie into an interesting chain of evidence."

"I'll do my best," earnestly declared the bent figure
beyond the desk.

"Oh, by the way, do you know where Lebov went
after you left the office this afternoon?"

"Yes. We had a drink at the club; he lives there, you
know. And if you've listed Lebov as a suspect you'd better cross him off because I called him at the club around
eight o'clock and spoke with him. He reached my house
just a few minutes later."

North expressed thanks, stored away the information
and then buttoned his coat. Tipton followed, his hat set
any which-way on his head.

"Think I'll make a couple of calls," North announced. "Some coincidences have taken place, and I
never did like coincidences."

The other's eyes were fixed in such a hopeless expression that North was moved to pity despite the over-whelming task with which this man's carelessness—or *was* it carelessness?—had confronted him!

"Try not to worry too much, Commander. There's always a chance we can get it back. By the bye, where does Miss Sinclair live?"

"At the Pinnacle, I believe. Some of their rooms are very inexpensive."

When Tipton hesitantly offered his hand North shook its damp and quivering fingers then, nodding, turned away in the direction of Battery Path and the cable tram terminal. Though the Metropole was temptingly convenient, he felt a strong desire to reach the mildewed magnificence of the Pinnacle Hotel with all speed.

Habit, however, caused him to pause at the corner of Ice House Road and glance down that dim, deserted avenue. Was it imagination, or was there a faint move-ment at the mouth to an alley just ahead? Experiencing no urge to settle the question, he stifled a snort of im-patience and turned back in the direction of the Bund.

Um. What a grim appearance the business district presented at ten o'clock of the evening. Queen Street's mist-haloed lamps revealed only a few incredibly ragged beggars foraging hopefully along the gutters; nothing else animate was in sight but somewhere a *pi-bao* player was drawing cacophonous wails from his three-stringed instrument.

He had progressed less than half a block ere a patter of bare feet and a thin hail of "Ricksha, wanchee, marster?" prompted him to halt and signal a glossy equipage belonging to the Do Be Careful Company.

It sped towards him, lamp wicks redly a-waver, and

Hugh North was reaching out to unhook its waterproof rain apron when perceptions sharpened by a precarious profession noted that the vehicle's body springs were supporting a weight. Barely in time he ducked under a stabbing streak of gold-red fire which sprang from the ricksha's depths. Though partially blinded and deafened, he nevertheless snatched at the ricksha's spidery wheel but slipped on the wet pavement and fell so heavily as to knock his wind out.

In helpless and breathless agony he watched the yellow-and-black vehicle whirl out of sight around a corner and tried to decide whether a bit of woman's skirt was not fluttering from under the apron's edge.

CHAPTER V

Cogs beneath the cable tram clucked an oily rhythm, and though its windows presented an ever-widening vista of the harbor, Captain North only ruefully regarded the ominous singed hole in the crown of a topper which on Fifth Avenue had cost a pretty penny.

"No doubt now that the local gentry mean business," he reflected. "Now who the devil felt it necessary to take a pot shot at me?" Deliberately he considered Commander Tipton's guests. Mr Tashima? Mr Martin, who spoke to his wife in French? The genial M. Lebov? Swazey, who gave the impression of keeping carbon copies of everything he said? What about the women? Valerie, the rabbity girl, he instantly discarded, but Mrs Martin, that lady of energetic eyebrows who had been so anxious to be friendly, was another matter. What about Consuelo Holden, who so loved to cartoon her emotions? A headstrong, irresponsible type, she would be capable of anything. Trina? No. For the moment she seemed his only sure ally.

Too experienced to waste time on conjectures which at this stage must be futile, he turned his attention to less ephemeral considerations and, settling back on

the cable tram's hard wooden seat, considered a succession of blackly dripping branches while reviewing the
past two days.

Good Lord. Could less than forty-eight hours have
elapsed since in Peking he had received a cable cancel-
ing his transfer to Manila? Now he could fathom both
the War Department's motives and the solemnity with
which Creighton, military attaché at the embassy, had
outlined T.P.A.'s troubles. . . .

Damned good ship that, Air Oriental job—a solid
G-38 Junker. The pilots, a pair of young Germans who
strutted about like cadets in a military academy, had
known their stuff too. . . .

In Canton he'd paid a good many dollars Mex. for
the privilege of a chat with a taciturn Scot who was
also Hongkong's inspector-general of police. From Sir
George Amberson, M.C., O.B.E., he learned not only
the facts concerning the tragic demise of Donaldson
but also the name of the "swell kid" and the fact that
T.P.A.'s Chief Engineering Officer was contemplating
a trip to the Portuguese colony of Macao. This move,
to North, had appeared a bit bizarre when one recalled
that Air Oriental was at that moment constructing a
terminal there for their projected Pacific run.

He looked up, for at Kennedy Road the tram paused
to take on a huge wash amah and a pair of parcel-
burdened urchins, undoubtedly "small pigeons" sent
out to replenish the liquor supply at some party on
the Peak.

Once the car had recommenced its climb North returned to reflections and tried to forget the headache
that pistol's report had given him.

On the run south he had struck up a friendship with the transport's pilot and, on arriving in Canton, ·fed that homesick young Prussian much beer and flawless German conversation. Later they had wandered, *sehr gemütlich*, along the Pearl River, drawing grave philosophical conclusions concerning the purpose of life aboard countless slipper boats and sampans lying moored on a stream of liquid garbage. Fast friends by now, the boon companions had boarded a "flower boat" and had talked at length with its fragile, painted inmates. Later there was beer and more beer, and they exchanged views on life, love and religion but left flying and aircraft severely alone.

North, bloated but patient, had concluded the binge at the New Hotel bar and, swinging wide of his objective, commented on the local flute pigeons which, because the Chinese lashed tiny silver tubes to their pinions, made a melody in the sky. Did Mannfred think such pipes would hamper a bird's flight? Yes? Wouldn't do for homers then—marvelous things, homing pigeons.

"Ja!" Mannfred had sighed, and suddenly his blue eyes grew moist. "Back in Güstrow a racing pigeon I once had. It six hundred kilometers flew the Grand Prix of Mecklenburg to win. Ach! Mecklenburg a beautiful place is—especially Güstrow."

With tears in his eyes Captain North had agreed. Marvelous, the homing instinct. Some species of plovers flew from Greenland to the Pacific isles, six thousand miles, and thought nothing of it, but a poor human couldn't do half so much with any certainty of arriving at his goal.

"Only three thousand miles? Nein, there you are

wrong, forgive me, *lieber Freund*," Mannfred belched
and placed an arm about his *lieber Freund's* shoulders.
"In another month we will be able to fly four thousand
miles without at a base stopping."

"Now you make fun of me." North's hurt had been
evident.

"Nein, *lieber Freund*. What I say is so." The other
had nodded owlishly and leaned far over his beer mug.
"Nein! A new fuel." He winked.

"Then you have this chemical?"

Smiling a bit foolishly, Mannfred had shaken his
close-cropped head. "Nein, but—but . . . You will tell
no one? Well, to prepare for test flights with it inside
of a week I am ordered. Now what do you say to that?"

Which little news item had prompted Hugh North to
board a smelly train for that human cesspool known
as Macao.

Just why should Mr Samuel Patterson, Trans-
Pacific Airways' chief engineering officer, be traveling
to Macao? He had a theory, but preconceived ideas,
he hastened to remind himself, more often than not were
erroneous. He was, therefore, lingering on the dock
when young Patterson, fresh and crisp in white linens,
stepped ashore, distinctive among the Chinese and
grubby Portuguese as the black tip of an ermine's tail.

He followed the C.E.O.'s lanky pole vaulter's figure
along an arcaded waterfront where old forts and ancient
churches threw their shadows across queer junks with
matting and khaki-colored sails. Patterson climbed a
long narrow street hemmed in by medieval European
houses painted blue, red and pink. Occasionally a Portuguese policeman or a gaudily uniformed black soldier

from Mozambique cast the T.P.A. man a glance. Finally a Goanese sergeant gave him directions which led the visitor up to the portals of a small office marked, "Directeur Compagnie Air-Orientale, S.A."

The Intelligence officer's Indianlike cheekbones became more sharply etched, and his interest achieved a new peak when before an open window paused a profile he would have known anywhere; such a terribly mangled ear, powerful jaw and brutal mouth could only belong to Staley—"Stag"—Melhorne.

Now what the devil would *he* be doing with Air Oriental? During the hour he awaited Patterson's reappearance he attempted to arrive at an explanation. As a rule the genial ex-colonel's services were only sought by gentlemen who needed an employee with an indurated conscience. . . .

To pick young Patterson's pockets on a deck so thronged as the SS Changte's was simplicity itself, but the haul yielded nothing of interest save a curt note from a "G. Travers." This, coupled with some fast driving after the bay steamer had docked, permitted him to reach that singular establishment on Shameen Street a few jumps ahead of the C.E.O. . . .

The cable tram halted at May Road Stop, whereupon he mechanically glanced up. Breathless from climbing up a very steep platform, yet rather dashing in her glittering evening wrap, Mrs Martin entered and advanced along the aisle, followed by the admiring eyes of a khaki-clad Sikh policeman and a turbaned Malay gentleman in ill-fitting evening dress.

Up flew her brows when she recognized the man from G-2, while a predatory gleam entered her look.

"Why, Captain North, this is simply too good to be true! Who *ever* would have imagined I'd find you here? Connie will be simply green with envy."

"This is a bit of luck, isn't it?" he murmured and quailed inwardly when, emitting an ecstatic little cry, the vivacious Mrs Martin settled on the seat beside him.

"Would you believe it, Captain, I was just thinking about you? And the trouble at the office. *Was* anything stolen? Poor dear Andrew looked so upset. I've been dying to know."

"Somebody had gotten into the safe," evaded her companion, "but nothing valuable was taken."

"Oh dear, how awful! How perfectly awful for poor Andrew!" Mrs Martin registered a crisis with her eyebrows. "You said nothing was taken?"

"Commander Tipton said nothing of importance was missing."

"Well, that *is* a relief! A great relief!" she sighed in obvious sincerity. "Poor Connie was all of a tizzy. Dear, dear, such a run of hard luck as they've been having at T.P.A., haven't they?"

Discreet inquiry on North's part elicited the information that Lebov had won the right to give a "consolation" supper party by compromising with Mr Tashima, who insisted upon buying the champagne and caviar.

"Mrs Martin, I'd like to know who suggested supper at such a dreary hole as the Pinnacle?" North donned his most winning manner. "If *I* had so charming a lady to take out nothing but the Hongkong's new grillroom would do."

"Oh, Captain, you do say the nicest things," Mrs

Martin fluttered, and she treated her companion to a glance intended to be ravishing. "Well, it was Connie who insisted on going up to that old barn; all on account of Sam Patterson, I suppose. You'll soon learn that if dear Connie makes up her mind to do something . . ." The eyebrows implied portentous consequences.

She saw him glance at her muddied slippers and giggled. "You wouldn't think it, but I'm headstrong too. I simply *wouldn't* let Louis leave the party. Joan—she's my little girl—was feverish when we went out, and her amah's a fool, a perfect fool, so I thought I'd better stop in and see how my little sweetheart was. Really, Captain, she'd love you—only three, and she's got an eye for a handsome man already."

A sigh of relief escaped North when the cable tram shuddered to a halt at Peak Terminal.

"Now we *are* going to see you again tonight, aren't we, Captain? Do join the party—we'll be in the café. I won't let Connie steal you this time. I simply adore Connie, don't you? She's such a sweet girl."

On entering the Pinnacle Hotel's faded old-fashioned lobby, the first person he beheld was Alexis Lebov who, eyeglass agleam, was jauntily descending from a mezzanine floor and casting restless glances at a large crowd of guests driven in by the inclement weather. At a distance, North perceived, the White Russian was more prepossessing. One could not see the puffy complexion, the pallid eyes and the flabbiness of the man; now he presented instead a rather well-proportioned figure, slow moving but still suggestive of sudden fierce activity —like a bear. He was deciding not to hail Lebov when someone smote him a jarring slap between the shoulder blades.

All his life Hugh North had entertained a sharp and ingrained distaste for back-slapping in any form; therefore he wheeled, angry color surging into his face —and was immeasurably startled to find ex-Colonel Melhorne beaming upon him.

"Well, damned if it isn't the old bloodhound himself!" The big fellow seized North's hand in a mangling grip and tried to pound him on the shoulder. "By God, *amigote*, I'm glad to see you!"

"Then prove it by not breaking my spine," gasped the Intelligence officer. "How are you, soldado? Still machine-gunning coolies at five hundred a week?"

"Hell no! Gave that up long ago." The big man's shiny, flat, red-brown features relaxed in high good humor, and, ignoring curious stares, he dropped an arm about North's wide shoulders. "No more rough stuff for me, Skipper. I'm in business. Don't I look it?"

Narrow-lipped slash of a mouth set in a grin, Melhorne stepped back, and even North was impressed. The ex-colonel's evening clothes were impeccable, his tie of the latest cut, and in his buttonhole glowed the ribbon of some colorful but unfamiliar decoration.

"What's come over you, Stag? Talk about your glasses of taste and mirrors of fashion . . ."

"Haven't been doing so bad lately. Say, are the girls still giving you a big tumble?"

"Not so's you'd notice it," grinned the detective, hoping that none of his lively conjectures concerning Melhorne's presence in Sam Patterson's hotel had leaked through his expression.

In the hotel's not-distant grill a dance orchestra began to blare as, radiating geniality, Melhorne slipped a muscular arm through North's.

"Come along, Skipper, and we'll throw a scare into a magnum of champagne." A gold tooth flashed as, grinning hugely, the ex-officer drove an elbow into North's side. "And say, I'll knock you down to the cutest little number who ever unbuttoned a step-in. What's the matter? All tied up?"

"No. Got to put in a phone call. Join you in a minute."

"Phone, eh? Two bucks it's a dame. Well, trot her out, and I'll match her with Eve, ankle for ankle, and fanny for fanny."

"No girl, worse luck," North grinned. "Where 'll you be?"

"Business?" Melhorne looked back at the stairs and elevators and for the first time seemed to attach a possible significance to his companion's presence, but he went on eagerly. "On that sort of glassed-in terrace. Eve, she likes to watch the harbor. Ever notice how nutty women are about a view? Make it snappy on the phone." He nodded and strode away.

Why, North asked himself, had Stag come over from Macao? Must have flown too. Was it to close that deal which had so upset Connie—otherwise G. Travers? More than ever sensing the necessity of earnest conversation with Patterson, he stepped into the phone booth and rang up the C.E.O.'s room. There was no answer, but the operator declared that a while back Mr Patterson had left a message saying he was stepping out for a few minutes but would be back soon. No. She didn't know Mr Patterson's voice; she was new on the job. Yes, she'd ring 423 every so often and have him phone the terrace when he came in. How long ago had Mr Patterson gone out? Half, three quarters of an hour ago. No, she didn't think he'd left the hotel. The doorman was sure he hadn't, so North possessed his soul in patience.

With increasing interest North found himself anticipating that moment when T.P.A.'s chief engineering officer and Air Oriental's *Directeur* should find themselves face to face, but he was momentarily distracted to glimpse M. Lebov's "consolation" party loitering at the grill's entrance. Um. They were nearly all there: Connie Holden, Mrs Martin, Tashima (white teeth flashing) and the rabbity girl. As far as he could see Mr Martin and Patterson were not in evidence.

"Hey, Skipper!" Melhorne hailed from halfway across the terrace. "This way. Lord, I'm hungry. Just flew over from Macao on business. Lousy night for flying. Only got in around ten. Usually do the trip in half an hour too."

While approaching a supper- and wine-laden table the Intelligence officer found himself deeply intrigued by Melhorne's companion; she was young and very lovely and was wearing an evening gown of jade green which fitted her figure with audacious fidelity. At first glance he guessed that somewhere in her ancestry the East had left its imprint, for ever so delicate was a little lift at the outer corners of her eyes, and the sheen of her skin was softly golden like the dust on a bee's wing. Her hair, of a lustrous black, she wore long and braided into an effective tiara among the strands of which a string of small pearls had been cleverly entwined.

North began an appraisal, as swift as it was covert, with her feet and noticed no stockings beneath her spike-heeled silver sandals. Her toenails as well as her fingernails, however, had not been tinted red but a metallic shade of green which harmonized with her evening gown in a most pleasing fashion. Whatever her Eastern blood had brought, it had not bestowed upon her the expressionless mask of the Oriental, and her facile features were rendered agreeable by an amusing little nose and a mouth reminiscent of Myrna Loy. Her voice was deep and rich like the ring of a golden coin dropped on a marble floor.

So this was the celebrated Eve Tanqueray—the "swell kid" for whom Dick Donaldson had gone off the deep end. Funny, she looked remarkably good natured and open.

"Evelyn," Stag said, "I want you to meet an old side-kick of mine, Hugh North. Miss Tanqueray——"

"I have often heard of you, and for a wonder you look as nice as I'd imagined," she murmured and held out a hand bearing a single ring set with a great glowing emerald.

"And you are even more beautiful than Stag described you," smiled North and, seating himself, was both interested and relieved to learn that this table commanded an excellent view of the lobby towards which Melhorne was glancing from time to time.

"Try that on your larnyx," Stag grinned, passing over a glass of champagne.

Ever cautious, North seasoned his generous portion

of caviar with a dash of grated onion and finished it to
the last morsel ere he thankfully turned to the wine.
How refreshing it was. Until this moment he hadn't
realized how really tired he was and how a knee bruised
in his fall ached with the dull, persistent pain of a
toothache. Thank God, that ringing in his ears had
almost disappeared.

Leathery features carefully devoid of expression,
Melhorne queried, "Well, Skipper, what brings you this
far south? Monkey business of some kind afoot?"

"On vacation," lied the Intelligence officer, then
forestalled further leading inquiries by turning to the
girl in green. "You wouldn't be having a twin, Miss
Tanqueray? I'm out of luck for a playmate."

"Be sure it's her sister you get," grunted Melhorne.

"I'm afraid I've none nearer than Penang, Captain,"
the girl laughed, her large dark eyes probing his quite
frankly. "But I know a few amusing people here in
Hongkong. What's your preference? A blonde?"

"We-l-l, I do have a weakness for blondes as a rule,"
North admitted with little crow's-feet at the corners
of his eyes. "But I don't think they stand the climate
very well out here. The only real qualification, though,
is that she has a slightly crazy sense of humor and
practically no dignity. You know—the kind who'd toss
an egg in an electric fan if she felt like it?"

A smile twitched at the corners of Eve Tanqueray's
bright, carefully designed lips. "Got it! There's just
one girl in Hongkong who'd fill the bill—she's pretty
as a hundred-pound note and crazy as a March hare.
Don't you think Connie Holden would just about suit?
Oh, Stag, what *are* you looking at?"

For a third time the big ex-soldier had turned to watch the elevators. North, on the lookout for Patterson, followed suit but saw nothing of the C.E.O.

"Connie?" Melhorne grinned absently. "Don't know her well, but they say she's all right, great stuff. Always ready for a foot race, a fight or a frolic. Likes the boys too." He glanced at a wrist watch. "Damn! I was supposed to call a guy at a quarter of eleven, and here it is five of. Excuse me, Skipper; be right back. Watch out, Eve. When it comes to pretty little gals Hugh North's the original big bad wolf."

So saying, he swung off towards the lobby and became lost among the bright, perpetually shifting pattern of evening gowns and uniforms.

CHAPTER VI

"DESERTED to a dreadful fate," Evelyn Tanqueray lightly complained and thrust out a vermilion underlip. "Even you, my gallant captain, seem to be distrait. Am I losing my justly famous charm?"

"Eh? Oh, not a bit." North, whose mind had been snapping at theories with the frenzied speed of a terrier killing rats in a pit, roused himself, was deeply apologetic. "I was just wondering if it were going to clear. The moon's out for a bit."

"And if it stays out"—Evelyn Tanqueray looked up at him through singularly long eyelashes—"wouldn't it be a grand night to do some flying? I adore flying in the moonlight. The world looks like a big silvered cake. It's a marvelous sensation."

"With a twin? By the way, Miss Tanqueray, do you know a chap name of Patterson—Samuel Patterson? He's an engineer with the Trans-Pacific people here."

"Why yes," she admitted readily. "I used to see quite a bit of him until that Holden kid I just spoke of made him fall for her. She's all he thinks of these days. Why?"

Eyes fixed on the intermittent blink of Green Island Light, North replied, "Have a letter to him."

In the perfect features across the table he read just a shade of tension ere she settled back in her chair. "Isn't that just like Stag? Go off and leave us *plantés là?*"

"No. He usually isn't so tactful," North laughed, then bending a little in her direction, demanded, "What can I do to amuse you till he comes back?"

"How about making some money for me? I never seem to have enough."

"Delighted." Reaching out suddenly, he produced a very substantial Yuan dollar from the vicinity of her small gold-tinted ear. "With my compliments, mademoiselle."

"Mon Dieu!" She laughed and, supporting chin on the heels of her hands, studied him with fresh interest. "Then you are a magician as well as a famous detective?"

"You flatter me."

"No, mon cher capitaine, the tribute is entirely genuine. I've always longed to meet you, to see what you really are like. You see, people have spoken of you so many times you've become a sort of legendary hero to me." In delicate enthusiasm she clasped slim fingers and almost mockingly surveyed him with head tilted to one side. At the same time he sensed himself undergoing a shrewd appraisal.

He made her a small bow. "And I'm charmed to have intrigued the most fascinating lady in South China. If only I weren't leaving in a day or so I'd——"

"You would what?" she demanded, a tiny catch of eagerness in her tone.

"Show you some more conjuring tricks. I've really much more amusing ones."

"Oh dear, is it fair to tantalize me? Tell me, Captain, have I been signally honored, or do you generally travel about taking silver dollars from the heads of girls?"

"It's an old hobby," he admitted while continuing to admire the perfection of her toilette. As svelte as an expensive car was Eve Tanqueray, the green-tinted fingernails constituting her sole break with convention. All in all she presented a singularly alluring vision.

"Which way are you traveling?" she demanded. "I'm leaving in a few days too. What fun if we happened to be shipmates."

"I more or less expect to catch a plane for Manila," North lied shamelessly. "Suppose I put a postcript to my prayers tonight?"

"That I'll be aboard?" Eve Tanqueray murmured.

"Ever hear that a wish won't come true if you make it aloud?"

Gently she clapped her hands. "Well done, mon capitaine. Even a Chinese couldn't have avoided the issue more gracefully. And for pity's sake, don't *you* begin looking at your watch!"

"I was just wondering what's happened to Stag. I wouldn't want him to come down and find me taking silver dollars out of your hair."

Eve Tanqueray was well pleased with him. There could be no doubt of it, for her laughter as the minutes slipped by was essentially genuine.

Perversely the man North had come to see put in no appearance, so despite Eve Tanqueray's amusing talk and decorative aspect he was casting about for an excuse to seek the phone booth when Melhorne's reappearance saved him the necessity. Though the big fellow's smile was still in place, a faint beading of perspiration was noticeable on the ex-colonel's red-brown forehead.

"Reach your man?" Eve Tanqueray queried.

"No, damn it," came the irritated reply. "He'd gone out, so I'll have to look for him. Sorry, party's over for a while." His speech was staccato and his manner that of one who is annoyed by an unexpected turn of events. "You'll excuse us, Skipper?"

"Guess I'll have to," North mourned. "Just my usual muddy luck not to get at least one dance with Miss Tanqueray."

"If you'll meet us here tomorrow night she'll give you two," Melhorne promised, then added, "Besides, there's a business matter I want to put up to you."

He turned aside to toss a couple of pound notes on the table while North picked up Eve's wrap and held it for her.

In slipping into it her sleek, faintly perfumed head brushed by his. "If you're passing through Upper Lascar Row," she murmured softly, "stop in at 507 tomorrow, and I'll give you a cup of tea."

"What's that?" Melhorne turned, his pale eyes alert, suspicious.

"Miss Tanqueray was telling me about a curio handler," came the easy reply. "Think I'll look in there and see if I can't pick up a print for my Chinese wild life collection. Good night, Stag, and thanks for the drink."

"See you later," the other nodded, and the last North

saw of that colorful couple was Stag bellowing for a
taxi.

Um. Why the abrupt departure? In view of the conversation in Shameen Street he felt convinced that Patterson had something to do with it. Hell! Suppose the
C.E.O. had gone out for good instead of merely leaving
his room a few minutes? Momentarily he debated shad-
owing the doughty ex-colonel, and he probably would
have, had he not himself searched Patterson's person.
Instead of getting stronger, his grasp on the situation
seemed to be growing increasingly tenuous. He tried
to stifle a growing uneasiness and, calling for the fourth
floor, hurried into one of the hotel's antiquated lifts.

A self-absorbed young couple getting off at the third
did not even glance into a descending car halting at
the same level, but North did and so noted Mr Tashima's
benign, blunt profile set in a singularly preoccupied
expression.

Before the door to Room 423 North paused, listened,
then rapped, and when no answer came he tested the
knob and called out.

"Anybody there?" On still receiving no reply, the
man from G-2 pushed open the door and found himself
in an unlit vestibule. Since the inner room was also
in an abysmal gloom, he flicked on the lights of what
seemed to be a sitting room and was greatly relieved
to find young Patterson drowsing placidly in an armchair.

To be accurate, he was not drowsing—his gentle
snores and slow respiration proclaimed him to be quite
sound asleep. From the doorway North seized this opportunity to make a rapid scrutiny of Patterson's

quarters and almost immediately encountered an incongruous note. As he looked several sheets of letter paper commenced to stir in the damp breeze beating in through a half-open window, and a few had even reached the floor, thus drawing his attention to an *ordinary hen's egg* lying in the pen tray of a writing desk!

"All right, Patterson, time to wake up and smell the coffee," North began, then, abruptly aware of a slowing in the other's breathing, hurried over and shook the Trans-Pacific's C.E.O.

"Hey! Wake up!" shouted North, but Patterson, instead of rousing, only slumped heavily sidewise in his chair and would have tumbled onto the floor had not the Intelligence officer checked him. His heart feeling like a clenched fist, North eased the C.E.O. back on his armchair and sharply called his name. Next he slapped the sleeper's freshly shaven cheeks, but the only reaction he got was a bronchial rattle in Patterson's throat. Eternities now seemed to elapse between each dreadfully deliberate inhalation.

Before ringing for the house doctor North hesitated, then, stooping, hurriedly pried open an eyelid and found the pupil contracted to a tiny dot. Just as he rushed for the phone Samuel Patterson emitted a weary little sigh, and his long-limbed body sagged still more. As if manipulated by invisible wires the C.E.O.'s eyelids then rolled slowly back to expose vacant blue eyes which stared blankly at the ceiling. Uglily the young fellow's mouth sagged open, and his tongue slipped out of one corner of it.

There being no need to call a doctor, Hugh North set down the phone. Just as well Connie Holden couldn't see her lover now: he was not handsome with all that saliva dribbling over his chin. The Intelligence officer had seen too much of death not to know it, but nevertheless he caught the boy's limp wrists and tested for a pulse and, of course, found none.

Thoughts rushing about his brain like autumn leaves on a forest floor held him motionless, seeking to reach some conclusion. Dead by poison; was that it? Self-administered? The faint, syncopated throb of the orchestra's drums became audible. Connie Holden was dancing down there. Out in the corridor voices and a loud burst of laughter marked the opening of someone's not-distant door.

Upon a table littered with various forms and diagrams pertaining to T.P.A. a half-empty bottle of Black & White stood beside two glasses, one nearly empty, one half full of whisky and water. Sniffing the latter told him nothing, but fingerprints were visible when he squinted sidewise at the table top.

Prints, eh? He hurried to the phone and demanded of an amazed headwaiter whether the table so recently quitted by Melhorne and himself had been cleared. No. Number 6 had not been. In that case the party was returning, North explained, and didn't want anything touched.

More prints were to be seen on a glass of water standing on the desk, but for the moment he disregarded them. From a lack of inscribed note paper and the fact that the desk's only penholder was equipped with a new, clean point one deduced that Patterson had not done any writing that evening. However, a scratch pad marked by someone's aimless scribbling—largely com-

posed of delicate circles and many interlocking triangles—testified that someone must seriously have
indulged in some hard thinking.

North went to the window and broke into a gentle
perspiration when he perceived that a person might, at
some slight risk, have swung over from an adjoining
balcony.

Turning, he lingered an indecisive moment, studying
those handsome if rather ineffectual features which had,
such a short time ago, responded to the warmth of a
charming girl's lips. What a devious chain of events
must have led up to young Patterson's death in this
faded Far Eastern hotel! Um. A big forfeit to pay for
wanting a girl above all other considerations.

Dreading interruption, the man from G-2 commenced an examination of the apartment almost as
swift as it was thorough.

"Now who in the devil's been up here?"

Following a long-proven routine, he surveyed the
meager contents of an ash tray, using a matchstick
to turn over the two stubs he found. One, only half
smoked, was dry, but the other was yet moist, and perhaps an inch from the unburned end its wrapper was
a trifle wrinkled, registering a roughly circular impression which was much too faint to permit accurate
identification.

The other was distinctly stale—perhaps two days
old and not suggestive of interesting possibilities. A
pipe, North gathered, was Patterson's favorite mode
of smoking; a rack of meerschaums, briers and even a
clay or two stood on the desk.

Stepping to the phone, he put in a call for the

Central Police Station, gave his name and briskly inquired for the inspector general's office.

"This is Sir George Amber-rson; good evening, Captain," cut in a precise Scottish voice. "I've been expecting ye to call before now. Can ye ar-range to drop in this evening——"

Succinctly North described his discovery in Room 423.

"Room 423? Young Patterson?" Sir George Amberson sounded greatly disturbed.

North was grimly amused. "How did you know?"

"Since the Donaldson lad's suicide we've made it a point to know what the T.P.A. employees are up to. Not to be nosey, ye know, Captain, only keeping a weather-r eye on them."

Long familiar with the aquiline quality of British officialdom's weather eye, North grinned. "What's he been up to?"

"Been playin' around with weemen," came the dour reply.

"Will you send over a good man right away?"

"I'll no' say just how good he is," came the sardonic reply, "since I'm coming myself."

Downstairs alto saxophones and clarinets were raising such a shrill throbbing clamor North was barely able to recognize the sound of footsteps in the hall. Breath bated, he heard them halt just outside, so, begging largesse from the goddess of chance, he flicked out the light and darted into the adjoining bathroom, then stifled heartfelt profanity, for the window here was open, and if the caller rapped he could not hear it above the music.

Who was there? Breathing as shallowly as he might, North recognized the click of a turning doorknob, and, easing the bathroom door open a trifle, he watched a dim form materialize in the vestibule.

In an instant he guessed the apparition's identity and saw the aspect of the work afoot grow foggier. Silently the silhouette closed the outer door, then called softly, experimentally, "Sam? Are you awake?"

Silence. A small rasping sound of finger tips testing a section of wall, then the lights blinked on. Trina Sinclair stood revealed, flushed and very lovely in the evening gown she had worn at Tipton's house. In her hand was a sheet or two of printed matter—looked like forms. The secretary, turning, checked herself in mid-motion.

She had seen Patterson's staring eyes, sagging jaw and utterly collapsed attitude. North watched the color ebb from her cheeks, read her startled, incredulous horror. "No!" she choked. "No. It—it can't be!" The papers she carried fluttered downwards as hands tipped by writhing fingers flew up to cover lips gone stiff and pallid. Motionless as any statue, Trina Sinclair remained in that attitude, staring, staring at the corpse. At last her hands fell, and Contempt came to fight with Pity on the battlefield of her expression.

"Oh, Sam," she whispered brokenly. "What couldn't we have accomplished if you'd only stuck. What a fool . . . Alone now . . . both of us."

After casting a fearful look about she stooped, snatched up her papers and had started for the door when North stepped out into the sitting room and said, "Just a minute, please."

Trina Sinclair gave a violent start, then halted and turned, a rigid figure etched against the wall's gray monotone.

"Why, Captain, w-what are you d-doing here?"

"Suppose I ask you that, Miss Sinclair," came the even reply. "I think you'd better answer first."

As if drawn by a sort of dreadful fascination the secretary's gaze sought the body, then flinched away.

"Why, why, I—I c-came to ask Mr P-Patterson to give me the Arm and Moment of an automatic pilot. Com-Commander Tipton w-wanted it in one of his letters."

North could not but wonder. Her explanation was so prompt, so plausible, he could not for the life of him decide on its validity.

CHAPTER VII

"Do you GENERALLY walk into gentlemen's rooms without knocking?" Captain North's manner offered encouragement, reassurance.

"B-But I did knock," Trina Sinclair protested. "You probably didn't hear—the m-music's so loud. I knew S-Sam k-keeps a set of Weight and Balance schedules here. . . ."

"You knew Patterson pretty well, didn't you?"

"Yes," she replied in a hushed voice.

"You loved him?"

"Yes. We were engaged once; but——"

"But what?" The Intelligence officer moved to face her, blocking out view of the corpse.

"But he broke it off. I've always thought his family made him do it," she said with a bitter look. "Probably the Pattersons of Orange County, being F.F.V.s, didn't consider a working girl fit to be mistress of Magnolia Lawns."

"Magnolia Lawns?"

Smoldering resentment broke into flames. "Don't say it! I hate to think of the place and the damned smug, cruel people who own it!"

So, proud, sensitive Trina had been jilted by the man whom Connie so intimately called Beanie?

"Why didn't you scream just now?" he demanded, not without admiration.

"I'm not the kind who does," came the steady reply.

"Commander Tipton said you live here in the hotel?"

"Yes, Room 733," she replied, giving him a curious look. "Why?"

The tall figure in evening clothes made no reply but instead went over to close the window lest more stationery be blown across the room.

"How . . . W-what do you suppose can have happened, Captain?" Trina demanded. "D-did he just die —or what?"

"Don't know yet. There's no wound, and there's no obvious evidence of suicide," said he and once more scrutinized the body so dreadfully pale in its neat double-breasted dinner coat.

Melhorne might have done it—the investigation would have a lot to say about that and also about the activities of the wooden-faced Mr Tashima. Why the devil should young Patterson have been killed? If only his search of the C.E.O.'s person had not been so thorough the answer would be clearer. Of course there *might* be some other explanation for the theft of the E.F., and Tipton, now cogitating at home, might give him the lead. What about Tipton? He and his stepdaughter made an odd combination.

Was Air Oriental somehow responsible for this tragedy? Certainly that organization was straining every resource to establish their bases and to begin flying. Um. Hard hombres like Stag Melhorne would be very useful if it came to discouraging a rival. More clearly than ever he perceived how entirely the whole cross-Pacific air trade hinged upon possession of the E.F. formula.

He'd give a lot to know too just why the polite Mr Tashima was in Hongkong. Certainly Japan would be no less delighted than any other power to gain the emergency fuel secret. The Pacific was such a wide ocean. Lebov? Of course the land near Canton might be his one and only consideration; just as Mr Martin might be wholly occupied with promoting his fog-piercing light beam.

As he stood there trying to fathom Trina Sinclair's role in the problem a consciousness of responsibility came home with terrifying vividness. If he, Hugh North, couldn't learn who had stolen the E.F. formula in short order T.P.A.'s hard-earned supremacy and American security were as the winds of a year gone by.

The sound of a hand trying the doorknob terminated his conjectures.

"In the bedroom," he whispered to the dazed girl at his side. Captain North applied to his face a pleasant expression, then, stepping into the foyer, turned the doorknob.

"Good evening," he greeted. "Sorry to have kept you waiting."

"*Bigre!* Again we meet by coincidence!" Possibly M. Lebov did not find the surprise entirely agreeable, but his manner gave no indication of it. "Imagine it!" he chuckled. "It is you who have been delaying our playmate, and I thought it mus' be one ver' charming lady."

Despite an earnest effort North could read nothing beneath the surface of Lebov's words, so he stepped back a pace.

"I make a poor substitute. Have we kept you waiting long?"

The Russian's features, suggestive of exposure to too much brandy and too little sunlight, relaxed into a wary smile. "But yes, over half an hour. You will join us, no? Mr Tashima has invit-ed us all to dance at Repulse Bay. We would feel so greatly honored."

"It's very kind of you to want me."

"Is Patterson ready?" Lebov queried, his pale and bloodshot eyes on the sitting-room door. "Or have you been too busy speaking of aviation?"

The Intelligence officer treated him to a deceptively indifferent look. "You know Mr Patterson well?"

"Well but not intimately," the Russian replied smoothly. "We 'ave met in connection with my property in Canton. But we must hurry, the De Sylvias' number goes on at midnight."

"Perhaps, M. Lebov, it would be easier for us to go in than for Mr Patterson to come out," was Hugh North's calm suggestion.

Never in his life had North observed a human face more intently than when, stepping aside, he opened the sitting-room door.

"*Bogu!*" Alexis Lebov ejaculated, giving a quick double blink to his pale-lashed lids. Then he recovered. He deliberately scanned the body ere he cast baleful look on his companion.

"One wonders, mon capitaine, if it was quite neces-

sary to shock one's sensibilities with such a tragic sight?
This is outrageous!"

"Don't take it that way," quickly pleaded North
as along his cheekbones crept a scarlet tinge. "I felt
it important to get a witness—a clever, competent witness—here as quickly as possible and before the police
arrived."

"Police? Police! Ah yes, but of course. Excuse, I
must go at once and find Miss Hol-den." Lebov's big
flabby figure moved towards the door, but, as if struck
by a secondary inspiration, he checked himself. "Is it
really necessary that I stay?"

"I'm afraid so," North replied, his manner a balm
to quivering nerves. "Now don't get alarmed, M. Lebov.
I'm not trying to embarrass you. Am I correct in as-
suming that this is your first visit to this room?"

"Mais oui. Before I telephoned. What? Who?"

Not far away the lift door rattled, and hurrying feet
preluded the arrival of a small plump Chinese and an
enormous khaki-clad constable of the Royal Victoria
Police.

The Chinese clasped his hands before him and jerked
a hurried bow. "Inspector Yu Shih reports ignoble
presence, sir. Two constables adorn corridor."

"Good. Please watch outside this door yourself, Inspector, and post one man near the lifts. The other
can go down to the terrace and collect all the silverware
and glasses from table number 6."

"Immediately, honorable sir," the Chinese replied
and after giving the necessary instructions drew near
again. "May this insignificant person inquire——"

An impatient cry sounded in the hall, then a patter

of running feet, and Connie Holden pushed past the startled Chinese.

"Beanie Patterson, you ought to be ashamed! If you think you can keep me waiting——"

Because Captain North and the inspector were blocking her view of the corpse her gaze settled upon Trina Sinclair, standing straight and pale as a caryatid in the bedroom doorway.

"You!" the Holden girl cried in her rich, slightly hoarse voice. "What the devil are you doing here? Why, what are you all staring at? What's happened to Beanie?"

"Maybe you can answer that question, Miss Holden," snapped the secretary, brown eyes beginning to sparkle. "Captain North would be glad to know."

"Why, Captain North—this *is* a surprise," Connie cried with a little click in her voice. "I didn't see you. . . . Where's Mr Patterson?"

"You 'ave only to look behind Captain North," was the Russian's bland suggestion.

Narrowly Connie evaded North's lightning clutch and slipped by him to halt, frozen into stark rigidity by what she saw.

"Oh, my God!" she gasped. "It—it can't be! I—I never thought——" Hands convulsively pressed to her face, finger tips dragging down her cheeks until her eyes shone red below, she sank upon a settee and commenced to sob.

The arrival of Sir George Amberson, a long-limbed Scot with very bright blue eyes and cheeks networked with tiny red veins, afforded North a badly needed chance to catch his breath. The inspector general cast a deliberate look about the crowded little sitting room, jerked a series of brief nods. "Evening, Miss Tipton, Miss Sinclair. How'd ye do, Monseer Lebov?"

He advanced with outheld hand. "Ye must be Captain Nor-rth."

"Yes. How do you do, Sir George?"

"Inspector Yu, phone for Dr Dixon. Rao Singh, watch the door," Sir George flung over his shoulder, then, utterly wooden of expression, surveyed the corpse at closer range.

"A cigarette, Con-nie?" Lebov produced a jewel-studded case and approached Commander Tipton's stepdaughter, whose slim figure yet shook with racking sobs. "Please. Tears make so red the eyes, ma chère, and they depress the rest of us."

"N-No th-thank you." It was to the dark-haired Intelligence officer she ran and, bending her head on his shoulder, continued to weep. "Oh, Captain, c-can't *you* discover who's done this horrible thing? B-Beanie was so alive, such a—vi-vital sort of person."

North, intrigued with her assumption, merely patted her shoulder.

"You *must* do something," Connie insisted, but when she looked up at him her piquant nose was not in the least red and her eyes only prettily overflowing. "Oh, I loved him, loved him so! I'd gladly have given my life for him."

Suddenly Trina Sinclair's voice flicked out. "Stop it, you selfish little liar! Quit telling those rotten lies! You d-didn't love Sam, you c-couldn't!"

The witnesses turned, amazed at the fury of Trina Sinclair's look; before it Tipton's stepdaughter winced a little ere she straightened with surprising dignity.

"The only thing in this world you l-love is yourself," Trina stormed on. "And the only thing you w-want is your own w-way!"

Sir George started to speak but thought better of it and remained looking on, brows furrowed.

"Such remarks, Miss Sinclair, are to be expected from one with your background." Then quite deliberately Connie turned to address North and Sir George. "It wasn't Sam she loved but his social position and his family's plantation!"

"That's a lie!"

Like wax figures in an exhibit the others remained quite still as Connie went on.

"I have thought many uncomplimentary things of you, Miss Sinclair, but until now I never took you for a poor loser. I presume you know I've asked Dad to discharge you, so you think you can talk like this and get away with it."

"A light, Miss Holden?" Smoothly North stepped into the breach, offering a flame, and used his wide shoulders to eclipse the other girl.

After perhaps twenty seconds, during which the two young women glared at each other, Sir George remarked, "Please, ladies, forget what seems to be a private matter with no bearing on the situation, and recall that Mr Patterson's death has not been explained."

He questioned rapidly, demanding an explanation for the presence in Room 423 of each person. Trina merely repeated the reason given to North. Lebov attributed his arrival to Patterson's continued absence from the party. Had he left the party on a previous occasion? Lebov admitted to having vainly attempted to telephone Room 423 perhaps half an hour earlier.

Captain North first caught Sir George's eye, then inquired as to the order of the arrival of Lebov's guests.

"We all left Mr Tipton's at the same time, around nine-thirty," the White Russian explained. "We agreed to meet here in an hour. Being host, I, of course, arrived first of all."

"You came alone from Commander Tipton's?"

Yes, he had. So had Mr Tashima.

Why? People usually enjoyed company on a trip?

M. Lebov smiled, said he liked to arrange parties by himself. Next to appear had been Valerie of the rabbit face with Mr Martin as escort. Mrs Martin, it seemed, had insisted on stopping off at home to see a sick child. Connie, too, had come alone.

"Since reaching the hotel did Mr Martin leave the party at any time?" North inquired.

Connie answered him, saying that the inventor had sighted a business acquaintance with whom he wished to make an appointment. He had only left the table a few moments.

"And you, Miss Holden? Why did you come up here?" Sir George murmured without taking his eyes from the body, the face of which had been concealed under a hand towel from the adjoining bathroom.

"To see what had happened to Alex—er, M. Lebov. We couldn't understand what was keeping him," Connie said. She hesitated. "Do—do we have to stay here much longer?"

"Only a moment. Excuse me please." Sir George disappeared through the bedroom door.

Lebov heaved a sigh and, closing his cigarette case with a snap, said, "But why, mon capitaine, should anybody wish to murder so charming a young fellow?"

North, however, made no reply, only crossed to a window and stood moodily regarding the lights of a cable tram creeping up from Hongkong.

Lebov tried again. "One wonders if we are not all jumping at conclusions? Is it not possible our poor young friend has committed suicide?"

"I don't believe it," Trina announced in a low, bitter voice. "Sam was in perfect health; he had every reason for wanting to live."

At that moment the bedroom door reopened, and Sir George Amberson reappeared.

"I propose, Captain, we allow these good people to retire. They are merely witnesses after-r the fact. To the ladies this scene must have been a verra unpleasant shock."

Beneath the surface of his words North read a carefully subdued excitement.

Sir George beckoned in the Sikh on guard outside. "Rao will take down your addresses, and I trust you will keep yourselves available. It may be necessary for Captain Nor-rth or myself to ask further-r questions." Ever so lightly he underscored the word "trust."

"I'm looking forward to a call," Consuelo announced, looking firmly into Hugh North's bronzed features. "I might tell you a thing or two of interest."

"I'll come if I can." Pleasantly North bowed her and Lebov to the door, then summoned an engaging smile.

"I'm so sorry, Miss Sinclair, that the evening has turned out this way. I'd been looking forward to a little tête-à-tête."

"Really? How nice of you!" She flushed prettily on adding, "This isn't the only evening you'll be in Hongkong, is it?"

"No. I'll get in touch with you," he promised. "Perhaps sooner than you think."

Her eyes, which looked tired and very strained, swung over to Sir George, busy examining the scribbling on the scratch pad, then again sought the Intelligence officer's face.

"Won't you let me help you? I'm not frightfully clever, but I do know a lot about the city. Kowloon too."

Gravely his gray-blue eyes surveyed her, trying to probe thoughts locked away behind the opaque screen of personality. "Tell me, do you think this man died a natural death?"

"No. At first I did, but the more I think of it the more I wonder."

Impulsively she laid a hand on his wrist. "You *will* let me help?"

"Maybe. You see, Miss Sinclair, Intelligence work isn't an exciting semimelodrama such as you read about. It's ninety-nine per cent wretched, ugly and sordid. You might be asked to do things you'd be ashamed of. If you want to go ahead on that basis I'll think about it."

"Oh, I do! Thank you!" Her whole being seemed to rush into those tragic eyes in passionate acquiescence. "You see, Captain, T.P.A. means a great deal to me. I—I haven't any family. Nor anyone to c-care for

—now. Besides, I was fond of Sam even after what happened. If he's been m-murdered I—I want to see the guilty persons caught."

Fresh respect entered North's glance. She was smart, smarter than he thought. Smart and so very lovely. All his life he had liked women who thought logically, who reacted sensibly to a given situation.

"All right," he smiled, "we'll work together. But remember, for anyone to get a hint of the idea would be fatal, you understand?"

She brushed by the stolid Chinese inspector so silently that Sir George did not realize she had gone until North came over to find him still frowning over the scratch pad.

"Suppose he made yon scribbles? There's no pencil here."

"In that case we might look in his pockets," suggested the Intelligence officer and, followed by Inspector Yu Shih's alert little blue-black eyes, he crossed, to stand looking down on the body.

"Wonder what the poor beggar took or was given?" Sir George commented.

" 'Was given' is the right verb, I think, Sir George." North spoke slowly with precision and a certain amount of deference. God knew he was going to need a lot of help inside the next few hours. "Because I couldn't find a container for the dose. Suicides aren't generally fussy about disposing of such trifles."

"Aye, that's a point. I see no acid burns, and there's no convulsion, so it canna ha'e been arsenic, strychnine or hydrocyanic acid. Any ideas, Captain?"

"The symptoms suggested a hypnotic poison—his

pupils were tightly contracted, which suggests a drug of the barbituric acid group. Any competent doctor should be able to tell."

"So? Well, nae doot Dr Dixon will tell us what's what. He's a clever mon. What's amiss?"

Captain North was standing, chin gripped between fingers of one hand, elbow resting on the wrist of the other. His gaze was thoughtful, fixed on the dead man's chest.

"Notice anything odd about that dinner coat, Sir George?"

A careful inspection of the body ended with a shake of the inspector general's iron-gray head. "Can't say as I do. What about you, Inspector?"

The Chinese shuffled forward, then said almost at once, "Contrary to custom, Excellency, this deceased has inexplicably buttoned coat on left side."

"Eh? Well, what of that?" demanded Sir George. "Chap was probably left-handed."

"Sorry, but I don't think he was," the man from G-2 pointed out. "If you look carefully you'll notice that buttonholes on the coat's right side—as we look at it—are stiff, unused; whereas"—while talking he stooped and undid the buttons in question—"it is obvious that the buttonholes on the left are stretched and worn with use. To my mind it's a pretty important point."

Sir George made impatient noises. "Perhaps, perhaps, but that's beside the question. If you'll recall, we were looking for a lead pencil in Patterson's pockets."

In the inner breast pocket a fountain pen was discovered but no pencil. A fat checkbook had slipped sidewise into a rip in the lining so new that broken threads waved like tentacles and two or three ends had fallen on the starched perfection of Sam Patterson's shirt front. Yu Shih noticed it, too, but his round little face changed its expression not at all.

CHAPTER VIII

W̲ḤEN A CAREFUL SEARCH of the sitting room revealed neither a pencil nor any other object of interest Sir George Amberson cast his wiry colleague a curious glance and observed, "Since we must look in the bedroom now, I'll tell ye that in there's one of the weirdest pieces of evidence ye'll have seen in many a year."

North's brows rose with his curiosity. Unusual indeed must be evidence which would evoke such a comment from the inspector general. Though prepared for a surprise, he was definitely nonplussed once Sir George had pushed back the door and pointed to a chiffonier across the bedroom. Standing upon it and revealed with almost dramatic intensity by a light directly above stood a plain glass water pitcher. About a third full of water, it contained *a woman's flesh-tinted stocking!*—or were there two?

"Well, I'm damned!" North muttered, striding over to stoop and peer into the container.

Closer inspection revealed that there was indeed but a single stocking and that of the sheerest possible weight. *Why* should it lie in a water pitcher, of all places, and on a bachelor's chiffonier? Had it reached

its rather grotesque position by accident or intent?
After sniffing the pitcher and smelling nothing odd
North stepped back and, while groping for an even
faintly plausible reason, surmised that the true explanation would come neither quickly nor easily.

Hopefully his look stole over to Inspector Yu Shih,
but that chubby individual's face seemed impervious
to either hope or despair, to satisfaction or disappointment.

Unblinkingly the Chinese inspector's bright black
eyes regarded the evidence, then stole questioningly
over to Hugh North's high-cheekboned countenance,
so brown above its white collar and tie.

"Suppose you give us your guess, Inspector," Sir
George directed. With a taut smile he added, "Yu Shih
is a great lady's man—nine children—but he's one of
my best C.I.D.s."

Yu Shih batted his eyes and bowed a little. *"Tajên**
will observe His Honor is fond of humor!"

"No need to be overmodest, Inspector," the American
said. "I've heard of you as far north as Peking; Major
Kilgour often spoke of your work."

Then indeed did the little detective's expressive dark
eyes glisten. "I am as little star, tajên, in presence of
moon. Worthless opinion is that silken garment once
bore stain, presence of which was unwanted. Alas, usual
washing place is too near by."

"Well, Captain, offhand what would you say?"

"Possibly it's a relic or an adjunct to a pretty festive
tête-à-tête—though just what the amusement would be
I can't quite imagine."

*Illustrious official.

"Aye, it would have to have been a verra queer party."

"And you?" North would not let the inspector general escape his turn.

"Ou-aye." Dubiously Sir George fingered his chin. "Well, it might have been used to make a compress—or-r . . . Losh, mon! The thing defeats me for fair!"

Gloomily Sir George regarded that enigmatic stocking in its pitcher, which so resembled a specimen in an alcohol jar. "Suppose we have it out?"

Watched by the two white men, Inspector Yu Shih gingerly fished the limp object from the pitcher and flattened it upon a towel stretched across the dresser. To a cursory examination it yielded no trace of spots or stains, no undue stress, though faint garter marks were visible in the reinforced band near its top.

North shook his head when the Chinese caught up the pitcher as if to empty it in the adjoining bathroom. "May need to keep the stocking wet."

" 'Tis an intriguing, wispy affair, and was no doubt expensive," Sir George pointed out. "Where's its mate?"

Though for over half an hour all three men conducted a search of Sam Patterson's rooms and effects, no other stocking rewarded their efforts.

Briefly the man from G-2 debated a disclosure of the catastrophic loss of the E.F. formula, but, Yu Shih being an unknown quantity, he decided to postpone the announcement and went back to the sitting room.

"Here's another facer," said he, pointing to the egg.

In frank perplexity Sir George rubbed his chin,

making bristles on it crackle softly, then, crossing to the desk, he picked up the egg and shook it gently. "Why, it's hard boiled!"

An expression of sharp irritation crossed North's face. Patterson had had a bag of lunch on the Macao boat. Was this merely a relic of an unfinished meal?

"Anything else? I must be getting back to my office. Got an opium raid on at three. Informer's chit came in just as I was leaving for here."

"These cigarettes might be of interest," North remarked.

Using a match, Sir George stirred the stubs. "Deceased smoked, I see. What's this?" He picked up the half-smoked cigarette and held it slantwise to the light. "Impression on this one—see it, Captain?"

"Yes. It's unusual too. A flat circle pressed into the wrapper. How would you explain it?" North flung the Chinese an interrogative look.

"Possibly cigarette holder?"

"Nonsense," grunted the inspector general. "The impression is easily an inch from the end. But, hold on, ye may be right at that. The mark might be caused by a cigarette holder of the ring type, which clamps a small pair of tongs about the cigarette. Ye see them pictured all the time in *Tatler* and such magazines."

The inspector general commenced to button his raincoat. "Weel, Captain, we'd better wait till we get the evidence to a laboratory." He hesitated in the center of the room's cheerful green carpet, then with a sudden rush of generosity said, "Ye'll have the run of our laboratories, Captain." He gulped a little, as if at his own rashness.

"That's very handsome of you, Sir George. I'll try not to be a nuisance."

"Ha-hrrumph! We'll welcome an opportunity to study yer methods." Sir George lingered, on catching an unvoiced appeal from North. "Inspector, ye'll go downstairs and phone C.I.D. to arrange for pictures and fingerprint tests. After the cadaver's been removed ye'll seal this suite."

Once Inspector Yu Shih's plump figure had disappeared Hugh North waved the wondering inspector general to a chair and in curt, precise sentences described all that had happened since Sir George had, over the telephone, warned him of Sam Patterson's projected trip to Macao.

By the time Hugh North's narrative had reached the scene in the T.P.A. office Sir George was sitting on the edge of his chair, lips compressed, bright blue eyes intent and riveted on the speaker's face. Like a man bracing himself for a shattering blow he seemed to anticipate news of the formula's theft, and once the worst was out he got up and strode nervously back and forth, bushy eyebrows merged into a single anxious line.

"This is frightful news, Captain," he growled. "Nothing worse could have happened. God knows where this all will end. There 'll be some terrific explosions at the Foreign Office. They'll be every bit as worried as yer State Department." He halted, gravely regarding the seated man in evening clothes. "Great God, mon, can ye understand what's possible if yon secret falls into the hands of—Germany or certain other governments we can think of?"

"Who can't?" came the somber reply. "The effect would be ruinous. I've been having cold chills ever since a quarter past nine tonight."

"Have ye any idea where the formula might be?"

A slow deep breath lifted North's shirt bosom. "I'm fairly sure one of two things has happened. Either Tipton is crooked and never put that formula into the safe, or else young Patterson stole it."

"But you said you searched him."

"I did and I know he couldn't have had it on him then," admitted the man from G-2. "But the robbery took place around eight-thirty, don't forget, and Patterson didn't phone until nine, which would have given a confederate plenty of time to clear out with it."

"You think Patterson had one?"

"Yes."

"The Holden girl?"

"I don't know. So far I can't make her out."

Mechanically Sir George's gray head inclined, and the next words fell from his lips with the methodical drip of medicine from a dropper. "If Patterson gave the secret to a confederate why was *he* and not the confederate murdered?"

"Probably the killer thought he still had it."

"One person might have thought so, Captain, but Lebov, Melhorne, Martin, the secretary and Miss Holden we know for sure have been in the vicinity of this room. Some of them didn't think so; I don't for a moment believe Lebov came up just to rout out young Patterson."

"Neither do I," North agreed. "It would have been more like him to send up a chit coolie or a bellboy.

Perhaps you're right, Sir George, and there was no accomplice present when the safe was robbed—if it was robbed by Patterson. Remember that tear in Patterson's coat needs explanation."

"I'm not sae sure it means anything," the Scot said slowly.

"Because of the way that coat was buttoned I differ with you. I'm firmly convinced somebody snatched something out of Patterson's dinner jacket, then rebuttoned the coat to conceal the tear."

"Who seems most likely to have done it?"

"Melhorne," was his prompt reply, and on his fingers he enumerated a number of points. "We know that Patterson and the Holden girl had dealings with Melhorne. We know that Melhorne's the Macao manager for Air Oriental. We know that that company can't operate without the E.F. formula. We know Melhorne was in the hotel for dinner tonight."

"And," Sir George interpolated, "we ken that Mr Tashima was once a lieutenant in the Japanese navy. At present in the postal service."

"But is he really here on postal matters?"

"We don't know. Mr Tashima's only been here a few days, and he's behaved himself. The Japanese are so confounded touchy we've made no inquiries as yet."

"And Louis Martin?"

"He's different. Give the name a French pronunciation, and ye have yer answer. Three days back I cabled for reports on that gentleman."

North made a little grimace and yielded to envy. If only American Intelligence officers could, by means of a simple cablegram, thus find at their disposal accurate information gathered by a well-paid, carefully trained and far-reaching organization!

"Mrs Martin, too, is worth watching," Sir George was saying. "She's Irish, and for all her East End accent she hates everything English like poison."

"Now Lebov—what about him?"

For the first time the craggy-featured Scot deliberated his response. "Alexis Lebov has lived in Canton and Shanghai ever since '23. He's supposed to be very anti-Red, and for a' that, he may be. But the fellow always has plenty of money which he can't possibly get from White Russian sources or dabblings in real estate. In fact, Captain, we're no' so sure he isn't a member of the NKVD, formerly the OGPU. That's pure speculation, mind you, and may be entirely false."

Hugh North nodded. "So then we seem to have Japan, France and possibly the Soviets accounted for. What about Germany? Does it seem likely the Gestapo would be asleep at the switch?"

"No. More than any other Power-r they'd want that emergency fuel. They've no petroleum in Germany, you'll recall. Well, we'll keep our eyes open for such a mon. Ye wanted to say something?"

"Yes, Sir George. Will you please tell no one about the theft—at least until dawn? I've a theory I'd like to work on."

"Verra good," Sir George said and reached for a bowler of conservative design. "I'll keep quiet, but the F.O. will have to be warned by seven. Is there anything I can do to help ye?"

Gratitude warmed North's being; never more welcome was such a steady, friendly voice.

"Yes. Will you try to learn just as quickly as possible what killed Patterson and the approximate time the dose was given?"

"We will. Anything else?"

"Yes. Melhorne mentioned he'd flown over from Macao. If you'd check his landing time with Kai Tak Field I'd be greatly obliged."

"Right. If ye'll be so good as to wait until Yu Shih comes back I'll take this scratch pad and be off." He offered his hand. "It's a terrible responsibility that's' been given you, Captain. Call on me for any help ye want. Good night."

Moving with that springy stride which so many Britons retain well into middle age, Sir George Amberson put on the bowler hat and disappeared.

Captain North was so lost in thought that Inspector Yu Shih had rapped and turned the knob before he could so much as rise from his chair. It was not the diminutive Chinese who stood in the threshold, however, but Mr Paul Swazey, wearing a very agitated look on his sharp features.

"What's this I hear?" the operations manager burst out. "There's a rumor downstairs that a man named Patterson has killed himself! Don't tell me it's true!"

"I'm afraid it is," returned the detective.

"This is bad for T.P.A.—ghastly! What won't the newspapers say? Do you think this has anything to do with——"

"Please!" North warned, blue pencils in his glare. In the background, restrained by a sturdy Sikh policeman, milled a group of Chinese houseboys, morbidly curious guests and distracted hotel employees. "Step in, won't you?"

"Yes."

"Come, we'd better get downstairs," North said. He didn't want Swazey or anybody else to go poking around Room 423.

"But, but can't I see the—er, the remains, Captain?" The operations manager seemed disappointed. "After all, I'm his boss. How do we know the"—he lowered his voice to an excited stage whisper which would have been audible ten feet away—"missing formula isn't somewhere in here?"

"The rooms have been thoroughly searched," cut in the detective and reached for his top hat but, recalling the bullet hole through its crown, ended by leaving the headpiece on its hook. "Sorry, Mr Swazey; even I must abide by police instructions. Come along. I'll gladly tell you anything I know."

Firmly he led the operations manager through gawking, murmuring crowds of guests clad in everything from dressing gowns to full dress suits, down to the lobby and over to the tram terminal.

CHAPTER IX

THE CABLE TRAM was, at this late hour, deserted save
for a couple of fat mandarins wearing rather coy peli-
cans embroidered on the breasts of their gowns. These,
as became Mandarins of the Fourth Button were belch-
ing in noisy reminiscence of what must have been a
really Gargantuan repast.

"Of all the confounded luck!" Angrily the operations manager donned shiny rimless eyeglasses. "This
murder will just about kill what's left of public confidence in Trans-Pacific. Wish to God the Hongkong
Clipper weren't scheduled to take off day after tomorrow." Momentarily he exposed a neat gold wrist watch.
"Guess it's 'tomorrow' now. Spencer, Tipton's assistant,
tells me he's booked solid for passengers and there's a
Condition D load of mail."

"I've spoken to Sir George and will do everything
else possible to keep Patterson's death out of the
papers," North reassured this acid individual. "You
and Tipton will have to keep T.P.A. personnel from
talking out of turn."

"I'll try to make them keep their mouths shut,"

Swazey promised as at last the car shuddered and started its downward course.

North, inside his pocket, flicked from his case the last cigarette before pulling out the silver container and inspecting it with a rueful smile.

"Never mind—I've got some." Mr Swazey pulled out a cigarette case.

His tobacco-stained forefinger flipped back an arm, the linked rings of which held the cigarettes in place. Strong, capable hands were Paul Swazey's, decorated with a single plain gold ring bearing a crest composed of three bull's heads and an elaborate helmet.

"Thanks." North accepted a light from the O.M.'s lighter. "I was wondering, Mr Swazey, what inspired you to come up to the Pinnacle at this late hour?"

Swazey stiffened a little, and two parallel scars, barely visible beneath strong gray-blond hair, reddened above his left ear.

"Patterson. Figured I'd learn something from a talk with him. Don't know how you feel, Captain, but I think there's something very fishy about the way that safe was rifled. Am I right?"

"Very likely."

"Obviously the job was done by someone who was familiar with the office. First he——"

"Or she," interpolated the man in evening dress and seemed unaware that his cigarette had gone out.

"What?" By the flickering car lights Swazey looked definitely startled. "Who do you mean, 'she'?"

"Aren't women also employed by T.P.A.?"

"You're right at that, but still . . . Well, anyhow, the thief would have to know the combination and how to disconnect the safe alarm. Who do you think knew those two things?"

"Tipton and Patterson, I presume. You really know more about it than I, Mr Swazey." After the hum of the cable had continued unbroken for a space North said, "You must find Hongkong quite a letdown from Valparaiso. June isn't the best month here—too damp."

"Yes," Swazey grumbled. "Wouldn't it be just my blasted luck to leave South America with spring coming on? Peru's fine then. Flying's easier too."

North's brows climbed a fraction of an inch. "Ah yes, I imagine hopping over the Cordilleras is scarcely a picnic in the wintertime."

"It isn't. Though the Whirlwinds on our old Hispanos were reliable, I like the Wasps on the clipper class even better." He turned on the seat, his mouth thinned to a colorless slash. "Listen, Captain, since that business at the office I've been making some inquiries. Do you know Patterson's been playing around with some expensive girls? Do you suppose he got hard up and stole the formula to sell it?"

"He might have, Mr Swazey. Go on."

"Well, then he guessed that you would catch him, lost his nerve and committed suicide?"

Gently North flicked the ash from his dead cigarette. "A very plausible explanation, Mr Swazey, but in that case why didn't the police find the E.F. formula either on his person or in the room?"

Swazey sighed and through shiny eyeglasses narrowly studied his companion. "Then he must have got rid of them first."

"To whom?" Very naïve was Captain North's manner.

"Hanged if I know unless—what about that Lebov fellow? He's an odd-looking duck. D' you suppose he might have been in cahoots?" Slowly he beat his knee.

The car having clanked to a halt, North arose. "Come along and have a drink?"

"It's after twelve; the bars will be shut."

"I've a spot in my luggage."

"No," grated the other. "I'm going back to my room and write a report on this business. Hanged if I want to be blamed for Tipton's dumbness!"

North wondered whether Commander Tipton was not also preparing to break the fatal news. Poor devil, he'd be out of a job very soon. After all, it *was* strange that the worthy commander on this of all afternoons should have permitted the bank to close, Lebov or no Lebov, without the E.F. formula in its vaults. He sighed. What murky depths were not yawning before him?

He bade the operations manager good night and with the wind stirring his crisp dark hair hurried down Garden Road towards the Hongkong Club.

Waiting in the lobby were two figures which arose promptly when the desk clerk said, "Good evening, Captain North." They paused, however, when the man reached into a pigeonhole and pulled out a pair of envelopes bearing the Australasia & China Cable Co.'s name. "These came about half an hour ago, sir. They were marked 'Urgent', and I'd have phoned you if I had known where you were."

North smiled his thanks and tucked the envelopes into his pocket because the two gentlemen had resumed their approach. The foremost was a big, confident man whose energetic stride suggested boundless vitality. The other, obviously an Englishman, had apparently been dragged away from a party—if his evening clothes meant anything.

From the larger man's anxious expression and apprehensive manner Hugh North immediately guessed that someone at the T.P.A. office had spoken out of turn. Carleton, most probably—he'd looked like a talker.

"Evening, Captain," he began briskly. "I'm Brundage, the American consul. This is the assistant colonial secretary, Mr Vickers. He phoned forty minutes ago——"

Captain North inquired how Mr Vickers did and, silently damning the talkative Mr Carleton, awaited the consul's next move, which was to bustle into a small sitting room designed for the convenience of guests waiting the arrival of members.

Fixing the Intelligence officer with an efficient steel pin of a look, he lost no time in coming to the point. "We're here, Captain, to learn whether a certain rumor which is spreading over town is true. Can you guess what that rumor is?"

North's answer was a shake of the head and a brilliant flash of silence.

"Mr Vickers heard—er—through sources, that a certain very important document had been stolen tonight from the Trans-Pacific Airways' safe. I trust this isn't so?"

He with the Indianlike features spread his hands in a little gesture expressive of helplessness. "Mr Vickers, I'm afraid, is very well informed."

"You don't mean it!" Brundage broke out, and his eyes flew wide open. "This is terrible, a calamity! State Department will be furious, raging. Cabled warning to-day—fact. Well, we've got to do something; move right away, eh, Captain?"

Suggested Mr Vickers mildly, "I say, Captain, you've no idea who might have taken it?"

"No," North lied. "Have you?"

"I have," came the astonishing reply. "Living in town is a certain gilded coaster with whom both Donaldson and Patterson were—er—familiar."

Onto a mental screen North flashed a photograph of Eve Tanqueray, leaning elbows on the table, looking very glamorous over the top of her glass.

"You surprise me, Mr Vickers. I'd been given to understand that Miss Tanqueray had become *vieux jeu* with Patterson. In other words that she'd been supplanted in his affections."

Vickers gave him a look sharpened with respect. "Doesn't take you long to learn things, does it, Captain? But perhaps you haven't yet learned that Miss Tanqueray was once given a key to Mr Patterson's room? The management told us so."

North looked his gratitude. "No, I didn't know that, and it quite changes certain opinions I'd formed."

Apparently neither man had yet heard of Patterson's death, a fact for which Hugh North was unfeignedly thankful and the meeting terminated in arranging for a conference early next morning. A capital idea, thought

Vickers; by that time His Excellency the Governor must have received instructions from London.

In the elevator an additional stratum of gloom settled over Hugh North's spirit. So Eve Tanqueray had a key to Sam Patterson's room? That was going Connie Holden and Trina Sinclair one better. Busy lad, Patterson!

Stuck into a clip on his door were a pair of telephone messages. To his surprise they were from Trina Sinclair, requesting him to call her at once. He had unlocked the door and was reaching for the telephone before he realized that the operator had received them much earlier, at ten and ten-fifteen respectively; at that time he'd probably been on the cable car, chatting with the handsome Mrs Martin of the muddied evening slippers.

Why had Tipton's secretary tried so hard to communicate, only to forget to mention her object when she saw him? No doubt in the stress of the moments in Patterson's room she had forgotten to state her purpose, but nonetheless he tucked the paradox away in the recesses of his mind.

Referring briefly but earnestly to a wicker-covered flask reserved for dread occasions when bars and similar oases were closed, he then stripped off his coat and thankfully removed collar and tie before pulling out the two cablegrams. Calling on Beelzebub, his favorite of the Seven Devils, to witness that cablegrams were a damned nuisance, he ripped open the topmost. It was from the War Department, the M.I.* Division of G-2. Decoded, it read:

*Military Intelligence.

EXERCISE EVERY PRECAUTION PROTECT E.F. 371 STOP
REPORTS ORIGINATING CANTON INDICATE SERIOUS AT-
TEMPTS UNDER WAY STOP CO-OPERATE STATE DEPART-
MENT STOP KELLER AND SOUCEK PROCEEDING FROM
SHANGHAI BARTON FROM MANILA STOP DRAW ON CON-
SULATE TO TWENTY THOUSAND STOP CABLE REPORTS
TWICE DAILY

FOX-CONROY

MAJ. GEN.

The other message originated in the office of no less a
person than the assistant secretary of state. It read:

OFFICIAL

INVESTIGATE CONDITIONS T.P.A. HONGKONG STOP AD-
VISING CONSUL CO-OPERATE ONE HUNDRED PER CENT
STOP LOSS OF E.F. 371 IRREMEDIABLE STOP TAKE NO
CHANCES STOP HIGHLY CONFIDENTIAL HUSTON T.P.A.
MANILA DIVISION SUPERINTENDENT ON WAY SUPERSEDE
TIPTON STOP WILL REQUEST COLONIAL AUTHORITIES DE-
TAIL GUARD AT BASE IF ADVISABLE STOP REPORT IMMEDI-
ATELY BY CABLE CODE

FITZHUGH

On finishing the second transcription, a budding
doubt ripened into full flower. Just what was the true
situation in T.P.A.?

He was stripping off that bane of masculine attire
known as the dress shirt when the phone began to ring,
and over the wire came Tipton's agitated accents.

"I've just heard the terrible news," he cried, "and I
don't know what to think. Patterson's always been so

reliable. I can't understand why he'd do such a thing."

"Who told you?"

"Connie rang up a while ago."

"Then she isn't with you?"

The other sighed, sounded very nervous. "No, she's spending the night with a friend."

"What friend?"

"A girl. Dorothy Wellington. Lives at Treguntha Flats, I think. Wish she'd come home, though. I—I guess I'm kind of upset. I tried to reach her but—well, sometimes she's a little selfish about doing as she pleases."

So? Before the receiver North's lips formed a little circle. Why should Miss Holden avoid her home when every natural reaction would be to seek it? The question, he felt, was worthy of further consideration.

"Had any cables?"

"No," snapped the other. "Haven't cabled San Diego yet. I—I was hoping you might have made some headway."

"Inside of three hours? Be reasonable, man, be reasonable."

"Sorry, Captain, but can't you imagine how I feel? Isn't there any hope?"

"Some. Haven't had any inspirations, have you?"

"Why no, except that Tashima's excuse for coming into the office so often was pretty thin."

"I see." Curious to learn if Tipton was aware of his impending supersession, he asked, "Heard anything from your home office?"

"No. I'm wiring for instructions in the morning. Don't like sending out the Hongkong Clipper under these conditions, but I suppose it 'd be fatal not to. You —you'll phone me if anything breaks?"

North promised to and, ringing off, concentrated on coding and dispatching the requested cables to Washington.

While unlacing his muddied patent leathers he reviewed Connie's conversation with the C.E.O. in her apartment. Logically she ought to know more about Patterson's movements than anyone else. Um. Possibly she'd be able to explain why that silk stocking had fallen into a water pitcher. In his desperation the badgered Intelligence officer even considered the possibility of someone's having planned to pack ice into the stocking with the intention of employing it as a weapon.

"You're going nuts, my lad," he muttered and, chuckling, stripped off his damp and badly wrinkled trousers. All at once he remembered Eve's feet; they had been bare beneath their silver sandals!

Changing into a dark sport suit, he exposed a torso no less limber and muscular than a college athlete's. No undergraduate's body, however, would show so many white cicatrices and dull red scars. The rain was making these reminders ache, and gingerly he tested a collarbone smashed by the bullet of a certain Spanish gentleman.

In his dresser drawer he placed the cigarette he had carried unlit from the train. Plain, acid chap, the new operations manager; sharp as steel, and if the new man coming from Manila wasn't a scrapper Paul Swazey would soon be running T.P.A. in South China.

Casting a yearning look at his bed, the man from G-2 instead strapped on a light shoulder holster of wash leather and into it slipped a .32-caliber automatic which had been so cut down as to cause hardly a wrinkle beneath his left armpit. Heartily he disliked the necessity of such a precaution, but that shot from the ricksha hadn't missed by any comfortable margin.

Belting a trench coat about him, he pulled on a dark felt hat and quit the club in the teeth of a gale which had risen again to lash the palms in the Public Gardens across the street.

"Two to one it's a wild-goose chase, my boy," he grunted, and, conscious of wind-driven drops patting his face like small wet hands, he solemnly placed a Hongkong half dollar in his watch pocket.

Ducking under the long and madly swaying signboards of Wing Lok Street, he turned into Morrison Street where he had some difficulty in ridding himself of a seedy individual who said he knew where dwelt a "very clean, very proper" number one girl.

In accordance with long-established practice he dismissed all thoughts of the case and for a while found a childish divertissement in trying to avoid stepping on cracks in the streaming sidewalk.

A cat, encouraged by a lull in the rain, ventured out and paused undecidedly in the center of the street.

"If that perambulating mousetrap goes left," North assured himself in all solemnity, "it means I'll bust this case high, wide and handsome; if he goes right I'm in for a licking."

Moving with stately tread the cat elevated its tail and set a course to starboard, whereupon North shamelessly attempted to stack the cards of Fate by detouring out on the dirty cobbles. Alas, the gaunt creature merely flung him a look of unspeakable contempt and stepped on the gas and skimmed triumphantly out of sight.

"An evil omen, my lad," panted the man from G-2. "That's what you get for taking liberties with Lady Luck."

Sooner than he expected the now familiar entrance to Shameen Street loomed through a rain squall, but he devoted a long ten minutes to a scrutiny of the environs of Number 12. All seemed well, so he again attempted the operations which had previously gained him admittance to G. Travers' pied-à-terre and, as he had half expected, found a shutter locked across his former means of entrance.

A leaky gutter played streams of chilly water on his neck, but, using the longest blade of his pocket knife, he groped for the shutter's catch. He succeeded in raising the shutter hook from its eye but an instant later shrank back among the shadows. Someone had entered the alley below, and to make matters still worse the loosened shutter was wrenched from his grip by a gust of wind and closed with a bang.

CHAPTER X

CAPTAIN NORTH moved just enough to avoid that glacial spout and then scanned the alley with patience worthy of an Eskimo at a seal's blowhole. Had he been wrong? Nothing moved down there except a strip of poster ripped by the wind from the greasy brick wall opposite. Yung-chen Tea. Still he waited, and the rain scampered up and down the roof beside him. He had to be sure. Too damned much depended on what might happen.

When at the end of half an hour he had detected nothing more formidable in the alley than a rat or two he raised the sash and, shedding water from his hat brim, stepped into an atmosphere of Nuit de Noël and stale cigarette smoke. He reclosed the window with care. At first glance the room seemed just as he had left it in the late afternoon. That afternoon! What a furious course events were running! A man had perished, and perhaps other lives were whirling on towards eclipse.

Captain North suppressed a small sigh of relief on glimpsing by the faint light of a street lamp a pair of round black satin garters bearing a monogram of brilliants. These, together with a pair of high-heeled slippers, lay before an easy chair over the back of which cascaded a bright blue evening gown.

"And now, my porch-climbing Lochinvar," he thought, "we'd better rouse our sleeping beauty from her dewy repose."

"Move, and I'll blow you in two!" a voice declared with deadly earnestness.

"Wouldn't dream of it," North avowed, gingerly raising his hands.

A flashlight flickered uncertainly, revealing a *k'ang* loaded with zebra-skin cushions, a fearsome gold dragon rampaging across a hanging of scarlet silk, a bottle of Enos and a glass standing on a copy of the Hongkong *Telegraph.*

"Turn around."

Though nearly blinded, the detective nonetheless perceived the menace of what looked like a .20-gauge shotgun.

"You!" cried Connie's husky voice. Did she sound frightened as well as startled? He thought so. "W-Why did you come here—like this?"

"One liked it here this afternoon. Possibly mam'selle recalls?"

"Oh-h!"

Without asking permission North lowered his hands and, reaching out, switched on a low, amber-shaded table lamp. Grinning, he solemnly put the Hongkong half dollar back in his trousers pocket. No wild-goose chase, this! Alert but desperately ill at ease, Connie remained beside the familiar spirit screen and made an unforgettable picture, clad as she was in a pair of mules and the fetching inadequacy of a rather sheer night-gown.

"Another reason I dropped in," the intruder explained more seriously, "was because I'd an idea you might be in for a bad night, Miss Holden. Sometimes it helps to just talk *at* someone."

A fugitive smile relaxed her rather sullen-looking mouth. "You sound as if you might mean that, Captain. I—I hope so because I *am* upset, horribly upset."

"You might put away the fieldpiece," he suggested when she lowered her weapon. "It's bad for pin springs to leave them compressed."

When unconcernedly she obeyed he was interested to observe that the gun really was loaded.

"A bit chilly, isn't it?"

Vigorously Connie's tousled head inclined. "Yes. Especially in a damn thin nightie like this. Wait a sec. while I find a wrap."

When she reappeared he struck a match for her cigarette and was interested to note that her eyes were swollen, though she had attempted repairs with powder and lipstick. Like a deadening veneer sadness restrained the normal vivacity of her features.

"Why did you come in by the window?" she demanded, picking a bit of tobacco from her lip.

He shrugged. "People might be watching your door."

"Why, what do you mean?"

"Don't you know that intriguing with an hombre like Stag Melhorne isn't the safest diversion in the world?"

Under cover of lighting a cigarette he in the dripping trench coat observed her far more closely than she imagined, found her bronze-hued hair distractingly

lovely when tumbling about the shoulders of a turquoise
negligee. Lovely, but wary— And, yes, she did seem a
bit frightened.

"Stag wouldn't bother me; we get along famously."

"Possibly he mightn't, Miss Holden," said North
with no conviction in his voice, then added, "but there
are some others who wouldn't hesitate at doing some
very unpleasant things to you."

"Others?" The look in Connie's eyes was like that of
a student nurse at her first operation.

"If you imagine Air Oriental's the only outfit out to
grab the E.F. formula you're badly in error. Stag's
ethics are lower than an eel's chin, but they're moun-
tainous compared to those of a couple of people I've
seen around."

She made no reply, so he tried to read what was going
on behind the suspicious, slightly sardonic mask which
was her face. He decided on a change of tactics—tried
direct methods.

"What's your game, Miss Holden? Why did you ask
Patterson to go to Macao?"

"It's this way. Donaldson fell for Eve Tanqueray.
Donaldson tried to betray the formula, failed . . .
killed himself. Eve started in on Beanie—took him away
from that Sinclair fool. I took him away from Eve.
Melhorne saw I could make Beanie jump through
hoops, and, as I'd figured he would, he looked me up.
Follow?"

Standing before her and listening for all he was
worth, North said he did.

"Well, he offered me—plenty if I'd get Beanie to
first show them how to adjust their motors to use the

E.F. and then to get Air Oriental a copy of the formula." She was talking rapidly now in her soft deep voice, looking steadily at him to see how he was taking it. "Well, I thought I was pretty smart and could trap Melhorne—fix his clock for good."

"You took a very dangerous way of trying to do it," he pointed out.

She bit her lip and nervously commenced to swing a long leg, around the ankle of which she wore a "dog tag" secured by a chain of platinum links.

"Thanks for those few kind words, Captain, but I— I had it figured out like this. I knew Stag would be very wary, so, to make him come into the trap, I planned for Beanie to really steal the E.F. and give it to me. Then I'd phone Melhorne to meet me, but at our appointment I'd have police ready to grab him with the secret on him. That would 'tend to him and remove T.P.A.'s greatest danger, don't, you see?"

"I do. Tell me," he demanded curiously, "didn't you realize lots of people get killed for less important things? Do you realize that you're in danger, grave danger of being murdered?"

She paled, but her look engaged his, held it. "Of course I'm not a complete fool. But I happen to be, well, old-fashioned. I may play round with foreigners, but it doesn't mean anything, not a damn thing! I like our country a whole lot, and I'd like to see us keep what's rightfully ours." She got up amid a flurry of thin silk. "You needn't believe me unless you want to, but it's true."

"All right, then it's true, Miss Holden." He suddenly became friendly as a basket of puppies. "And now if you'll give me the formula I'll guarantee to scupper Melhorne."

She halted her restless parade and treated him to a strained look ere she dropped her gaze. "But—but I haven't got it, Captain. Everything went wrong."

He could see her slim form droop beneath its turquoise negligee, and she gave him a pathetic little smile. "You do believe me?"

"Of course, my dear. Go on, please."

"Well, Beanie was supposed to meet me at Alex Lebov's party and pass me the secret. But, but—well, you know what happened instead."

"I know part of what happened. But don't worry." His voice was the essence of sympathy, his manner a balm to raw and quivering nerves. "We'll work this thing out somehow. You knew Stag was at the hotel tonight?"

"*Stag!*" Connie stared at him wild eyed. "But he couldn't have been; he promised he'd stay out of Hongkong till I phoned."

"Anyone in North China could have told you Stag's word isn't worth a last year's bird's nest with a hole in its middle. He came over here to beat you out of the money he promised you. He may have killed Patterson: his sort wouldn't hesitate a second if your friend wouldn't come across when asked. But, well, I've a hunch he *didn't* get what he was after. So, young lady, if you haven't got that formula you'd better watch out. Tell him you haven't got it, and he'll figure you're fixing to sell to a higher bidder."

"Well, I haven't got it, and he can't scare me, and that's that," she cried and changed her manner as definitely as a garment. "Now please let's talk about something pleasant. That act you put on this afternoon, for instance." Involuntarily a hand crept up, brushed her bright lips.

Out over Hugh North's gaunt cheeks crept a slight flush. "That's my big trouble: every now and then I just don't resist that impulse."

Connie flung herself into an armchair, turned sidewise and, hooking a shapely leg over its arm, commenced to swing a foot shod in a scarlet mule boasting a neat bow of gilded leather.

"That makes two of us. Ever since you went out this afternoon I've been wondering who you were. Tell me, do you often commit two—no, it's three—crimes on the same day?"

"Three?"

Her small coppery head inclined; very tense, she was merely manufacturing conversation.

"Yes. Pickpocketing, breaking-and-entering and stealing."

More good-natured lines came to hover about his wide mouth. "Stealing? I don't recall taking anything——"

"What about that kiss?" she challenged lightly.

"My error! I was thinking along less delightful lines."

"Then you're forgiven. Please take off that wet thing and sit down. I suppose even detectives get tired sometimes. You'll be nice to me?"

"Easiest thing in the world." Thankfully Hugh North flung his wet raincoat onto the floor before the door, dried his face with a handkerchief, then, inexplicably restless, he glanced over his shoulder at the window.

"Suppose I refasten the shutters?"

"Good idea. Meantime I'll twirl us a couple of high-balls, and if you don't think I could stand one right now you're nuts. Incidentally, I was right," Connie remarked, slipping over to investigate a small portable bar.

"About what?"

"Oh, the Harvard accent," Connie drawled. "And by the way, where did you collect that perfectly swell French? It had me rocked back on my heels."

"No credit of mine," he confessed. "It's merely the result of restless parents, a misguided youth and a couple of years in making the war for the beautiful France."

On considering the tactics best calculated to gain this astonishing young creature's good will and possibly a bit more, he decided to eliminate Star Chamber methods and substitute those of the L'Œil-de-bœuf. Certainly such a campaign was unlikely to end in an inconsequential skirmish; Connie, for all her languid, flippant pose, was thinking hard.

"Be a good boy and light the fire, will you?" her softly hoarse voice pleaded. "There's some tobacco in that silly Japanese plaster jar."

"What makes you say that?"

"You look as if you'd use a pipe," she smiled. "Here's your drink and there's no Mickey Finn in it, in case you're unduly suspicious."

"The temptations you present, my dear Connie, are irresistible." Because he was tamping tobacco into a short-stemmed briar he did not take the glass at once but towered above her, looking down into her lovely face. "Particularly with the water works turned on outside."

Fixing his gaze on the infant blaze, he dropped into a chair and all at once debated whether he was not rushing in where Gabriel and the rest of the lads might well have hung back. Anybody so young as Connie could not have come by such sang-froid in any casual fashion.

Tucking her feet up under her, Connie coiled in a big armchair and did a Narcissus into her highball glass.

"So you picked poor Beanie's pocket?"

"Yes, but it wasn't even fun; he was pathetically unwary."

"Wasn't he?" the girl sighed, and a catch in her voice was so ready that North wondered whether it was entirely genuine.

"Anybody so naïve should never swap Virginia for China."

By the firelight her eyes filled, grew luminous. "Poor Beanie! Other Southerners have told me what it means to be a Patterson of Magnolia Lawns. They're F.F.V. from the year one. Oh dear, that soft drawl of his always did things to me. I was terribly fond of him. Really I was."

"It seemed so this afternoon."

"Yes. Well—Beanie was always a gentleman, even up here."

"It seemed so. Will you tell me why you risked sending him over to Macao?"

"Why, to show Air Oriental's mechanics how to use the E.F. That was part of the understanding. Melhorne insisted on it."

"Um. Stag must have been pretty sure of getting the formula to put the cart before the horse like that."

"It would have been safer for Beanie to demonstrate *before* the secret got out rather than after," she pointed out.

"I still insist, Connie, you adopted some very peculiar methods," North commented. "Few people would credit your motives."

"The methods amused me, Hugh, and anyhow Beanie was much too sweet to end up like Dick Donaldson, via the Tanqueray route."

"Tanqueray? What do you mean?" North demanded, ignoring her evident approval of his profile.

"Evelyn Tanqueray's from the Dutch East Indies, and, mister, if you think little Eve can't open the pores of nine hundred and ninety-nine of you dominant males out of a thousand you're all wet!" Connie was talking at the fire, perilously balancing a mule on her big toe. "Anywhere she goes she's what's known as a sexation, and Lord knows how many men have cheerfully squandered their last farthing on her. But don't misunderstand me, there's nothing obvious or gold-brick about Eve. 'Value given for value received and no coy nonsense,' is her motto. Her English husband must have taught her that."

"Husband?" North had to rouse himself. Damn, but it was comfortable here; almost cozy.

"The Honorable Hugh got himself killed in a seaplane crash. Funny, isn't it? He'd the same name as you. Left her stoney." Veiled by long lashes, her eyes sought his. "A rich rice broker over in Canton came to the rescue, and since then—well, Evelyn's gone from bed to better. Must be pretty clever, though; her ex's stay crazy about her."

"Who's the lucky gent at this point?"

Connie smiled a private little smile. "You know perfectly well. We'll skip it. Like Stag, Eve's only God is money, and she admits it, so to my mind she's a sight more honest than a nasty-nice wench like Trina Sinclair!"

Replicas of the cheerful little fire shone in the Holden girl's narrowed eyes, and Hugh North took a sip from his highball glass ere he raised a quizzical eyebrow and observed, "Aren't you being a trifle severe? Miss Sinclair struck me as a singularly charming, efficient and well-bred young woman."

The turquoise negligee gleamed as she tilted her head back and uttered a peal of single-note laughter. "Do you know who Trina is?"

"No, Connie. Suppose you tell me."

"Well, she's Foxy Sinclair's daughter. Remember Foxy? He was that bucket-shop operator who deliberately swiped the life savings of I don't know how many poor people back in 1921. Got twenty years for it, though."

"Why blame Trina? She'd nothing to do with it. Must have been a child."

"Like a devoted little daughter she's trying to get Foxy pardoned. Of course she swears the old crook's innocent."

"Is it so unnatural for a daughter to want to clear her father's name?" North's sympathies for his hostess began to yawn.

"It would be if she really was sorry for him, but she

isn't. She hates her father like poison because, being a convict, he's made life socially impossible for her."

Extending a wet shoe to the fire, he watched a feather of steam rise from its sole before he asked, "Is it true Trina was engaged to Sam Patterson?"

"She was until he saw through her and broke it off."

"You didn't help lift that veil of ignorance by telling Patterson about her father?"

"Yes, of course. She was furious, simply livid. And did she put on an act? Got some poison and threatened to take it—but she didn't."

"Really?" North's manner became a little vague. "Well, maybe when she cooled down she decided a weak character like Patterson wasn't worth it. Personally, I'd agree with her."

A particularly vicious gust of wind tore at the shutters, rattling them, then scurried off in a wet smother to beat on some other window.

North raised his eyes, met those of the trim, vital young woman opposite. She was appealing like that, with the firelight drawing bronze tints from her hair and long legs gleaming beneath the nightgown's transparency. As if mesmerized, they sat for a long time. She smiled faintly at this leanly adequate man with the practical mouth and smiling, kindly eyes. He was desperately aware of her nearness, of the gracious contours of her body and aloneness. Suddenly he wanted to kiss her again; her lips looked so soft in the firelight. She was beginning to like him—or he thought she was.

At length he asked, "Do you think the Sinclair girl might have poisoned Patterson out of jealousy?"

"Why—I—I'd rather not say."

"Connie, will you tell me the honest truth?" his voice demanded from amid a miasma of pipe smoke. "Were you ever really head over heels in love with Sam Patterson?"

Deliberately Consuelo Holden ground out her cigarette, keeping her gaze on its crumpled stub. "I don't see just why I should answer that question. It's my affair."

"It is for the moment, but tomorrow it will be a police inspector's business. I suppose you realize some unpleasant interpretations might be put upon your meeting Patterson in this place?"

Connie selected a fresh cigarette and ruthlessly marred its symmetry by jamming it into a short jade holder. "I don't give a damn what the local felines think. I've been trying to help Dad."

North shifted conversational gears. "I am rather a nuisance, aren't I?"

"No, Hugh, I find you most diverting."

"Merci, mademoiselle," he grinned and tried a shot at random. "Do I stand any chance of competing with Lebov?"

Her eyes narrowed. "Why mention him?"

"Because I'm thinking yonder Russian gent intrigues you a good bit. Why not admit you're playing what the little theater movement would term a 'part' and that if you've done anything for your father it's incidental to the big thrill you're after?"

Her leg ceased its rhythmic swaying with such a jerk that her mule dropped off and exposed a narrow foot devoid of blemishes and tipped with skillfully tinted dark red nails.

"You may be aces up as a detective, Hugh, but as a psychologist you're a big washout!"

"Even so, my dear, I really do like your courage and independence. It occurs to me that since we're after the same objective we might co-operate as pleasantly as possible."

The girl's long body relaxed. "For that sensible observation, Captain, you may pour yourself a dividend and sit beside me. No, don't go getting ideas; I like your profile—distinguished and sophisticated, I calls it."

Once he had refilled their glasses he seated himself on the zebra-skin couch, wishing he could free himself of a nagging uneasiness.

"The gods were kind to bring you here tonight," she murmured, the appeal in her wide eyes very effective. "I—I was feeling so awfully sunk. Every time I think of poor Sam . . ." Quite deliberately her hand sought refuge in his. "Oh, I do so want T.P.A. to go on! It's Dad's whole life; with him, everything's flying boats, air bases or personnel, which makes it a rather lonely existence for me," she explained quietly as gradually the warmth of her body beat through his coat sleeve, for without a trace of coquetry she had begun to rest her weight against him. "Especially because I've yet to strike a man I could stay interested in. Don't you think a mutual respect and interest is much better than love?"

A thoughtful smoke ring burst from the detective's lips. "Yes, I think I'd rather marry somebody I respect a lot and love a little than someone I was crazy about and couldn't respect."

She snuggled closer, kittenlike, until her head came

to rest against his shoulder, bringing with it a faint suggestion of Nuit de Noël. Hair, fine as a baby's, brushed his cheek, and a curl, catching the firelight, glowed like molten copper. Quite naturally his arm went about her.

"Connie, you remember the story of David and Bathsheba?"

Her body quivered to a silent chuckle. "Good Lord, you aren't turning preacher?"

"Hardly. But wasn't your taking Patterson away from Trina Sinclair a bit like the malefactor of great wealth taking the poor man's one lamb? After all, you'd the pick of Hongkong—all South China, for that matter, while poor Trina——"

"I haven't any sympathy for her." Connie's deep voice hardened. "But that, my dear, wasn't the reason I butted in. Eve Tanqueray took him away from Trina, like that!" A coal snapping in the fire saved her the effort. "You see, Sam never loved Trina at all, except that she made him feel a big, wonderful man and oh, *so* important!"

"We all fall for that," objected the detective softly.

"Well, I flattered myself that the Tanqueray woman would have a much harder job getting Sam away from me."

"I see. And Sam was very necessary to your purpose?"

"Purpose? I don't understand."

The hiss of his slowly drawn breath was all the answer she got for a moment. Then he said evenly, "You knew Sam had access to the safe. Now, just suppose that you were simply crazy about someone, Lebov, for instance, and he wanted to get the formula——"

As if a live wire had touched her Connie sprang up, face afire.

"Get out of here! Get out!"

"Velly solly," cut in a third voice. "That umpossible! Pleass keep still or I kill."

CHAPTER XI

SOMETIME EARLIER North had, by force of habit, noted a picture, the glass of which cast a rough image of the door. Thus he was able to discern a thick-framed individual in a cheap tan-colored raincoat framed in the entrance. Behind him loomed the blurred outlines of two heads.

Sulphurously, wholeheartedly, he cursed his negligence at having surrendered his view of the door. He knew better than to move now, even when the foremost intruder stumbled over the raincoat he had flung before the door as a precaution. Had he been on the qui vive he must have detected some subtle sound when the door lock was being picked.

A sidewise glance at Connie Holden revealed her to be standing stiff as a stone image, but angry rather than concerned. Whether her attitude was due to courage or to ignorance he could not tell.

"No makee bobbery, Cappen. Makee hands velly higher," crisply directed the man in the tan raincoat. "Wong, look-see, maybe big fella pistol have got."

"You not b'long here," Connie objected indignantly, for all that her nostrils were pinched and her hands nervously clenched. "Better you go quick. What you want?"

"*You*, missy," grunted the leader, and eyes black and hard as bits of coal bored out from under his golf cap's sodden visor.

Prompt and very matter of fact was the removal of North's .32 and the application of handcuffs. North was hard put to stifle a groan when the cold metal imprisoned his wrists; cords or thongs an ingenious prisoner might hope to loosen, but the only treatment for case-hardened steel was an acetylene flame.

Shedding dark raindrops on the rug were a tall Manchu who gave the impression of being both powerful and tireless, a small Cantonese and a hard-faced blond European clad in a black leather aviator's jacket. With a complete omission of brandished pistols, melodramatic gestures and threatening looks the invaders set to work. First they searched North from top to toe, then devoted their attention to Connie. Apologetically the Manchu pulled off her mules and then tested her hair.

North, standing with Connie in front of the *k'ang* which had been his undoing, morosely watched the two Chinese commence a very thorough search of the apartment. The big European stood guard and seldom took his eyes off the prisoners for so much as an instant. First Connie's desk and the portable bar were minutely ransacked, then the Manchu riffled through every book and magazine in the place while his diminutive helper pulled pillows from the couch and chairs and tested the upholstery. Next all the pictures and hangings came down to undergo a detailed inspection. Conversing in low-pitched Cantonese, the searchers united to roll back the rug, and when this maneuver gave no satisfaction the Manchu angrily groped in the tobacco jar and even held the whisky bottle to the light.

In stony silence Connie first inspected the bright rings of nickeled steel about her wrists, then, not without interest, watched the skillful looting of her possessions. Only when the searchers descended upon the bedroom, turned her bureau drawers inside out, made a riot of her lingerie and ripped out the linings of slippers and shoes did she venture an impatient but quite ineffective protest.

Once the big Manchu, whose name, it seemed, was Hsing, paused, handed two sheets of paper to the man in the aviator's jacket. North was able to see that these were a rough diagram of an engine part, probably sketched by the late Mr Patterson in explanation of some point, and a mimeographed form of some T.P.A. office report.

At the end of half an hour the searchers admitted defeat and, perspiring heavily, tramped back into the living room and addressed the prisoners. Mr Hsing informed them that they were to accompany him, left no room for doubt that any attempt at outcry or escape would be punished by instant death. On the other hand, he would endeavor to make their captivity as easy as possible.

"Missy go like this, Honorable Hsing?"

"No, ancestor of crawling things," the Manchu rasped. "Catchum coat for lady—allee samee fur collar have got."

"If you really insist on our going places and doing

things, Mr Hsing, please let me put on shoes and stockings," Connie pleaded with a valiant attempt at carelessness. "As Bea Lillie says, 'It's better with your shoes on.'"

"Catchum shoes plenty quick but no makee bobbery!" he in the tan raincoat directed with a head-waiter smile.

"I b'long," Connie muttered. Then she bent to tie the lace of her shoes, and her hair fell over forehead like a bright gonfalon. Looking up, she stared intently into the Manchu's impassive flat features and warned, "You makee plenty big mistake catch Captain fella. Soon number one piecee Air Oriental man plenty mad."

"No talk, please," the Manchu warned, still good natured.

"Not Captain fella," Connie insisted, "and I talk all I please!"

The resounding smack made by the Manchu's hand on her cheek cracked like a pistol shot and tumbled her onto the floor. Semidazed and utterly outraged, Connie remained as she had fallen, weight resting on one elbow, her legs outthrust and seeming incredibly long and white in their thin rolled stockings.

Only by an effort could the man from G-2 restrain himself; but, sensing the futility of intervention, he said nothing, did nothing. Nor was the European taking any chances; he pressed the barrel of his pistol into the small of Hugh North's back.

"Velly solly." Grinning as if all this were a huge joke, the Manchu crooked a yellowish forefinger. "Get up, missy."

Connie, however, remained at the Manchu's feet, dark

blue eyes filled with angry tears. Tenderly she tested the four red streaks barring her cheek and glowered up into Mr Hsing's impassive bronze features.

"My mean what say. Get up!" hissed Mr Hsing and, bending, dealt her rear a resounding smack.

Scarlet with outrage, Connie sprang up, whereupon the Cantonese quickly pinioned her, but she struggled wildly, endangering the fragile protection of her negligee.

"Don't be a fool," came North's cold advice. "Do as they say."

Consuelo flung him a bewildered but undaunted look, then obediently held out her arms and was helped into the coat the Cantonese had brought. A sibilant gasp escaped her when handcuffs were resnapped about her wrists.

The Manchu abandoned his pidgin, bowed to North and remarked in suddenly perfect English, "One perceives reports concerning North tajên's intelligence do not err. As Li Tai Po observes, 'He who resists the whirlwind is indeed a fool.' I regret, most distinguished Captain, that my orders are to blindfold you, but if you promise silence I will not apply gag."

Just before a thick hood dropped over his head the Intelligence officer glimpsed the little Cantonese methodically bandaging his companion's eyes. Rigid with revolt, Connie seemed frightened at last but resolutely endeavored to conceal it by biting her lips. North felt a sudden glow of admiration for her.

The prisoners were led stumbling down to the street, where they waited bareheaded in the drizzle until some rickshas rolled up. A low command was given in Manchu, then the moldy-smelling vehicles were whirled off over the cobbles. From the rickshas' steadily downhill progress Hugh North guessed they were going towards Connaught Road and the Bund—Hongkong's teeming, ever-restless water front.

His elementary deductions proved correct, for at length the rickshas rolled out of the wind and rain into a building. Once the rain ceased drumming on the ricksha's hood he could catch the gurgle and splash of water and a hollow bump of a craft nosing into a wharf.

What the devil was going to happen? A trickle of ice water flowed down his spine when low-pitched voices cackled and hissed in the unintelligible Hakka dialect. Forewarned, even the average person can stand a surprising lot of grief, but this was like having a dentist hurt one without warning.

What would be done with Connie? God help her if, in spite of her denial, she really had received the formula. Resolutely he switched his train of thought onto another track. Who, for instance, was responsible for this pleasant little junket? Melhorne? Louis Martin? Lebov? Possibly the punctilious Mr Tashima? Or was the nebulous German agent entering into the situation at last? He'd have to look sharp if he was going to learn the answer.

How in hell did Houdini, Thurston and the rest manage to get rid of handcuffs? Voluntary dislocation of the joints, probably.

At last he caught a familiar word, "boat", and his heart executed a sickening nose dive when he thought of that great chaotic fleet of bamboo-cabined sampans and slipper boats moored off the Bund. Unknown to the

Royal Victoria Police, much might go on out there.

Whether Connie also had been brought aboard the motorboat into which he was led Hugh North had no way of ascertaining, but as he clambered over the thwarts he dug his nails deep into the craft's painted rail.

"Please to lie down, most honorable Captain, and keep still," came Mr Hsing's guttural command.

Awkwardly the prisoner settled down on a couple of jacket-type life preservers and let his head come to rest upon a box of tools. Almost at once a smell of hot oily metal grew so strong he guessed he was reclining beside the motorboat's engine, and once the launch got under way he could tell it was a two-cylindered one. This he jotted down in his mental notes; also the fact that the southeast wind which had been blowing was striking the boat bow-on. So she was not heading either for Kowloon or Macao. Where then?

Rain fell on his face, and when the launch churned further out into the harbor chilly flirts of spray joined in wetting him. The wind steadily grew rawer, and the engine's heat felt so good on his shoulder blades he rolled over and pressed his chilled hands against the water jacket and found his forefinger in contact with a small smooth surface marred by certain cracks and crevices. Hooking a fingernail into one of the crevices, he patiently tried to follow its course and failed, due to a savage plunge of the little craft. Twice, thrice, he repeated the operation. Um, two small circles had been engraved in the smooth surface—something like an Arabic figure eight. What came next? A four, perhaps.

Gradually the launch's motion grew so violent she

began shipping water, but her skipper did not reduce speed—shrill voices and a rancid smell suggested the sampan fleet's proximity. Soon the motorboat's exhaust reverberated, and for some time her sides bumped sizable bits of flotsam. Then the engine was cut off, permitting the sad plaint of the wind to be heard again.

"Here is the ladder, Captain. Catch hold and climb." Mr Hsing's command was barely audible over the rushing wind.

"Put my hand on the rung," North pleaded, wondering whether he was about to be treated to a modern version of walking the plank. His hands, however, gripped wet wood, and he climbed twenty rungs up a swaying pilot's ladder.

"Now the woman," directed a gruff new voice. "Careful!"

This vessel, judging from the number of rungs he had climbed, must be a high-sided wooden vessel, in all probability a junk. A hand gripped the Intelligence officer's elbow and guided him out of the weather into an atmosphere tinctured with the odors of *bêche-de-mer*, creosote, pearl oyster slime and the inescapable pungent smell of raw ginger.

Everywhere sounded voices in sibilant, high-pitched Cantonese, and wind made a queer sighing as through bamboo matting awnings every time a squall boomed by. The creak and groan of cordage, the slow squeak of timbers filled his ear.

Soon he expected to recognize Stag Melhorne's voice; Mr Hsing, the Cantonese and the man in the leather jacket were of a pattern with the ex-colonel's direct, "knock-'em-cold" methods. Yet the C.E.O. had not been crudely or brutally disposed of; that deed had been performed to a different and subtler tempo. How come?

"This way. Remember, distinguished Captain, no talking. You also, Miss Holden."

Hugh North would have given much to read Connie's thoughts as they stumbled obediently along a passageway with dirt softly rasping underfoot.

Eight-four-three-seven-nine—was that it? He sighed, wondering whether those numbers might prove anything.

"Here he is, Excellency."

After a door had closed Mr Hsing observed, "We are pleased to make your acquaintance, Captain."

"Sorry I can't reciprocate," the prisoner replied. "When do we put to sea?"

"You leap to conclusions," the Manchu pointed out in precise English. "That, in a detective, is not clever."

Several people entered the cabin, the acoustics of which indicated a small-sized room. As nearly as North could determine he and Connie stood facing a table behind which two persons were sitting and conversing in such low tones that he could not even determine the language they spoke.

Without preamble or circumlocution Mr Hsing began, "Well, Captain, what have you done with that formula you took from Mr Patterson's room?"

Emphatically North denied the assumption that he had found anything.

"Suppose we put the question differently?" the spokesman suggested in that careful English employed by those to whom the language is not native. "What did you do with it after Miss Holden gave it to you—or you took it from her?"

"I tell you I know nothing about the formula's present whereabouts," crisply insisted North, thereby provoking a murmured conference beyond the table. Someone coughed and spat behind the prisoners.

"Then, Miss Holden, we are to believe that you did not give the document to Captain North?"

"I haven't seen it." The girl's words were bravely spoken, but a tremor in her tone suggested a growing fright at seeing Hugh North's predictions fulfilled with such uncanny promptness and accuracy.

"Do you deny that the late Mr Patterson—er— took the secret because you desired him to?"

"Absolutely!" There was a complete lack of expression in her tone. "Neither he nor I knew anything about it."

Somewhere far above the deck a yard creaked eerily ere the unknown said, "It will do you no good to lie like this, Miss Holden. We know Mr Patterson was in Macao this morning, that he came directly from the boat to your apartment."

"You're making this up!"

"Are we?" Hsing's voice was insultingly patient. "A chair coolie now on board followed your gentleman friend to Macao and back. So, dear Miss Holden, we are certain you lie. Come now, you must know what has become of the secret."

"But I don't, really I don't!"

In the depths of North's imagination necessity was forging a plan. Once ashore he could accomplish—well, in any case he could accomplish more than he could as a manacled and blindfolded prisoner. A solution to the situation, however, like mercury still escaped through his mental fingers.

"Did you not plan to meet Mr Patterson this evening?" the Manchu was demanding.

"Why yes," Connie admitted in a flat voice. "We were going on a dancing party together."

"Does it not strike you as odd, Miss Holden, that Mr Patterson would even consider going on a party when a secret of such enormous value had just been stolen from his company?"

Silence.

"Of course it does. Therefore, we are forced to conclude from your previous intimacy with Colonel Melhorne that you do know where this secret is, so we really must insist you tell us, even at the cost of our earning your ill will."

Somehow, without specifying anything the Manchu's voice conveyed the threat of ghastly, quite unnameable alternatives.

North held out manacled hands indicative of helplessness and, staring into the baffling dark of his blindfold, felt his breath beating against his eyelids. "Very well, Mr Hsing, have it that way if you want to, but has it occurred to you that Mr Patterson wasn't the only one who had access to that safe?"

There ensued a small pause, a muttered conversation beyond the table.

"Thank you for the suggestion, distinguished Captain," came the precise voice. "Then you imply that it was not Mr Patterson who stole the formula?"

"I imply nothing, gentlemen," the man from G-2

insisted with grim exactitude. "I only suggest that the
C.E.O. is not certain to be guilty."

"You are most careful of your words, Captain; I
wonder why?"

"Do you recall the Chinese saying, 'To guess is cheap
—to guess wrong is expensive'?" queried the Intelligence officer.

A foot scraped restlessly, a chair creaked under the
weight of someone settling back, and the smells of ginger and creosote battled for supremacy of the atmosphere.

"Your adroitly put alternative is interesting, Captain. Commander Tipton just might have stolen his
own secret."

Like fuming acid Connie's voice bit into the situation.
"No! No! That's a lie, a damned rotten lie! Dad
wouldn't do such a thing! He'd cut off his hand first.
This stupid detective is only guessing! Really he is!"

"Mr Hsing, you aren't by any chance a student of
Shakespeare?" North wanted to know.

An amused chuckle and the sound of breath drawn
quickly through the second man's teeth reached North's
straining ears, then a whispering ere Hsing said, "You
refer to the Play Queen's speech from *Hamlet?* How
does it go? 'The lady doth protest too much, me-
thinks'?"

How utterly exasperating was this inability to read
reactions, to learn who was sitting just a few short feet
distant. Was he Melhorne, Martin, Tashima or Lebov?
North would have given a finger to be sure.

Eight-four-three-seven-nine? Would those numbers
afford a solution to all this?

Feet tramped, and a door closed but did not shut off the sound of voices in heated debate. Nearer at hand a guard coughed as only a Chinese can and spat resoundingly.

"Why did you say that, Hugh?" Connie's husky accents impinged on North's furious calculations. "You ought to be ashamed!"

Recalling visions of the three Rs, he racked his memory and blandly replied, "Ad-hay o-tay. Eems-say our-yay est-bay ance-chay. Et-gay it?"

"Es-yay, ou-yay ig-bay ut-nay," came the instant retort. "Ut-whay ill-way ey-thay o-day o-tay us?"

"Enty-play! Etend-pray our-yay ather-fay as-hay it." And he smiled beneath the sweaty hood. A far cry, this, from St Peter's Episcopal School! Visions of varnished desks, chalky hands and exotic pets swam by his eyes. Then the door reopened, whereupon the guard rendered a report in some excited Hakka.

"What were you two talking about?" Trenchant suspicion dominated Mr Hsing's tone.

"I was trying in her own language to persuade her to talk," North explained in all seriousness. "There's a lot of gipsy in her."

"Gipsy? I had thought all gipsies were dark skinned. Well, no matter."

Connie emitted a strangled noise and ended it in a cough.

Mr Hsing said, "There may be something in your suggestion, Captain. Logically either Miss Holden or her stepfather *must* know what has happened to that formula; if not one, then the other. Therefore we have decided to detain Miss Holden. If her stepfather has not produced what we want by eight o'clock this morning we will know he has not got it. By simple subtraction, then, we turn to this so-charming young woman as the person to deal with."

A stillness, electric, ominous, descended upon the cabin, and the junk, again swinging to her anchor, shifted uneasily.

Connie uttered a little cry supremely eloquent of terror. "Please, Mr Hsing, you *must* believe me! I don't know what's become of it, really I don't. Tear me to shreds, but it won't change that fact."

"Possibly, possibly," returned the Manchu's voice. "Conduct the lady to my cabin, Wang."

"Hugh! Hugh! Don't let them hurt me," pleaded the distracted crescendo of her voice. "Let me alone! No! No! Hugh! Where are you? Don't let them——"

A hand must have descended upon Connie's mouth, so abruptly did her voice die. Feet thudded and scraped, a door opened, and presently the sound of footsteps died away.

The man calling himself Hsing said, "Well, Captain, inside of four hours you're going to bring me the formula."

"So you've taken up clairvoyance? Well, you're wrong. I'll do nothing to help you."

"You are not yet old, most illustrious Captain."

"No, I'm not exactly creaking at the joints as yet; but you're not scaring me."

During a long instant Mr Hsing held his silence, then said, "I assured my colleague that threat of personal injury would accomplish nothing."

Another murmured colloquy ensued, during which

the man addressed as Excellency several times drew his breath in sharply.

"Might one inquire whether 300,000 in first touch sycee* would affect your decision?"

"You're at liberty to inquire, but the answer is no."

"We feared it would be."

"Why?"

"It is known that you once declined a $200,000 bribe offered to you in Shanghai. Ah yes, we have looked you up since you got that cable in Shanghai, and we have learned that when it comes to the ladies, Captain, you are quite chivalrous."

"Thanks. What are you driving at?" North queried sharply.

"If something—er—unpleasant happened to your dear friend Miss Holden, you would feel very unhappy?"

Though his wrists were aching with a dull, nagging ache and the vicissitudes of the day were beginning to crisp his nerves, Hugh North could have smiled. Things weren't going so badly.

Eight-four-three-seven-nine. Again and again he silently repeated the number.

"I said, you would feel pretty bad?" insisted the ominously dispassionate voice.

"Who wouldn't? Miss Holden's a very charming person."

"So you are going to listen to reason. That is good. We do not like violence—not in the least. But, business is business. You will persuade Commander Tipton to surrender the formula *to you!* You will say nothing

*Best quality silver.

concerning this little interview, or Miss Holden will not be seen again in any recognizable condition."

The Intelligence captain nodded. After all, the numbers 84379 might save the situation. If, in spite of everything, he failed, well, it might be some consolation to remember that Connie had brought this grim situation on herself.

"On your way ashore, Captain, you will be told what to do," announced the Manchu. "Carry out your instructions, and whether you want it or not money will be deposited for you in the bank." A faint chuckle sounded. "Twenty thousand dollars deposited to the credit of an army Intelligence officer by persons unknown would call for much explaining, would it not?"

And this, North realized with a small sigh, was no less than the truth.

CHAPTER XII

CAPTAIN NORTH was too old a hand not to follow instructions, so he remained on what seemed to be a pier, counted to a hundred and rubbed wrists recently freed of their manacles. Finally he removed the blindfold and discovered himself standing in the lee of a tall pile of freight. The proximity of sundry huge godowns and the Western Market told him that Mr Hsing's boat had landed him on Pasig Wharf. A patient scrutiny of the harbor revealed only the riding lights of steamers and the dim black outlines of the sampan fleet.

Um. The wind was still from the southeast. This determined, he started up the Bund at a fast jog, subconsciously noting that the city's clocks were disagreeing by some seconds as to the exact moment of three o'clock.

While his heels echoed on the damp asphalt he sifted his recent observations. For example, Mr Hsing's comment about knowing that he, North, had received a cable ordering him to Hongkong was not without weight. Further he deduced that although Mr Hsing & Co. had been following the T.P.A. situation with great care, they certainly did not have the

144

formula. Nor were they even certain who had stolen it.

Poor Connie! Her thirst for thrills should be sated once and for all. Plucky kid, though. Being long familiar with the Orient, he felt sick when he pictured what might happen to her should he bungle his part.

That Patterson's death and the theft of the E.F. formula had thrown the Royal Victoria Police into a turmoil he guessed by a blaze of light in the C.I.D. Division's windows. A courier ran down the central station's wide steps and jumped into a car bearing the Government House crest even as the hatless and dishevelled Intelligence officer ran up to the wide front steps and a pair of plain-clothes men stopped him just inside the entrance; but only momentarily.

The instant they learned his name they hurried him into Sir George's office. The inspector general was not affable, and many badly chewed cheroot butts littered a tray before him.

"Where have ye been?" he rasped. "Good God, ye've had us fair scouring the city."

Ever louder drummed Sir George's blunt fingers as in brief sentences the man from G-2 described his visit to Shameen Street and its aftermath.

"I feared for ye when Yu Shih found that flat in Shameen Street turned upside down," the Scot admitted and joined his shaggy gray brows ere he added, "By the bye, the night steward phoned to say some kerl got into yer room at the club and made a hell's delight of it."

To North this news was interesting if not pleasing; it seemed unlikely that Mr Hsing & Co. would so divide his attention as to conduct a kidnaping and the invasion of a gentleman's club at the same time. Ergo, somebody else must still be hunting the formula. Who the great leaping Croesus *had it?*

"Of course our first consideration is to rescue Miss Holden," North observed. "So we'd better try tracing that motorboat as quick as we can. Incidentally, we'll not be wasting time from the main problem either; if we can grab Mr Hsing we'll eliminate a suspect for the theft and make things a little simpler."

"He'll wish he'd stuck to larceny," grunted the inspector general. "Kidnaping is no' safe a diversion on British soil. Now, gi'e me the best descr-ription ye can of the launch."

"She's cabinless, has a linoleum flooring bound in metal, is painted green outside—along the rail at least —and white inside. She's driven by a well-tended two-cylinder engine bearing the serial number 84379."

Behind the document-littered desk the inspector general's spare figure straightened. "And how did ye learn all this wi' a hood over yer head and yer hands mana-cled?"

Grinning, North held up a forefinger. "When I climbed over the side it was easy to scratch off a bit of paint—it's this shade. Inboard I repeated the job with my middle finger. Then came a lucky break. They made me lie alongside the engine, so I felt for its serial number plate and found it."

"One sees how yer reputation was made," Sir George commented and, picking up a phone, gave a rapid description of the launch in fluent Hindustani. He hesi-tated, hand over mouthpiece. "I don't presume ye ken what course she took?"

"Southeast for about twelve minutes from the wharf. Hsing's junk is lying near the edge of the fleet; I counted only seven exhaust echoes." Tilting back his narrow dark head, Hugh North searched his mental notes. "The junk had a pilot ladder of twenty rungs; it was new, too, because the edges of the treads were sharp." He held out his left middle finger, exposing a bit of color beneath its nail. "She's got a yellow rail."

He got up, cheekbones highlighted by the inspector general's desk lamp. "Incidentally, it would be distinctly dangerous at this stage to do more than to send a couple of Chinese detectives out to look around, dressed as fishermen. That fellow aboard wasn't fooling about what he'd do."

"Verra well, I'll get you a report on the launch soon as may be. But the serial number-r may take some time. 'Twould be entered in the harbor-r master's register-r, and that office is shut tight. However, I'll have it opened at once." He passed a hand over anxious, bloodshot eyes. "Losh, Captain! The wind's up for fair-r. Every department i' the government is competing to make life miserable for us. What is it?"

The man from G-2 had risen. "How long before there's any chance of getting a report on the launch?"

"Say an hour and a half to two hours if we're lucky."

"I see. By the way, has an autopsy been made on Patterson?"

"Aye. You'd better go in and get Dr Dixon to explain it. He's in the laboratory the now, wor-rking on the evidence. Ha'e ye any suggestions?"

"Only one, Sir George. Send out a general alarm for

our friend Melhorne. He knows plenty about Patterson. By the way, when did he land last night?"

"Oh, I forgot to tell ye. It was nine fifty-five of last night. Had trouble, too, in a' that wind."

"I see. He wasn't in evening clothes?"

Sir George shook his head. "No. He wore a gray tweed suit, the airways man said."

"Well, I want him arrested in any case. The Holden girl admitted she'd dickered with him to steal the formula."

"What about yon Holden lass?"

For a moment Captain North fell prey to indecision. "Hanged if I know what to think. She puzzles me more than anybody I've come across in years: may be crooked as a ram's horn, and on the other hand, she might be a singularly fine and patriotic young woman."

"Just a minute," Sir George said when someone knocked. "Here's somewhat to eat."

"Thank you, Sir George."

"Don't gi'e me the credit, Captain. 'Tis the department's expenditure."

In caustic humor the Scot watched North wolf a couple of sandwiches and drink greedily the hot coffee brought in by a felt-slippered Chinese orderly. Beyond a sketchy snack aboard the Macao boat he could not recall having eaten in nearly twenty-four hours. The food did him good—no end of it.

North was working on an apple when the phone rang and Sir George's craggy features contracted. He answered, then a little sigh of relief escaped him.

"For ye, Captain," stated the inspector general, then, quite blank faced, added, "It's Tipton."

"That you, North?" Tipton's voice sounded miserable to the verge of hysteria. "Been trying to reach you
everywhere."

"What's wrong, Commander?" he demanded, wondering if news of the raid on 12 Shameen Street had
reached him.

"Any progress yet?"

"Nothing definite. Have you anything you want to
tell me?"

"Why no, nothing specific, that is."

"Then why call me?" North was moved to no great
sympathy; bunglers always irritated him.

The man on the other phone hesitated. "Can't you
stop round? I—I'd like to talk with you. I'm worried
about Connie: she didn't go to Miss Wellington's."

And well might he worry, was the Intelligence officer's
grim reflection, but all he said was, "I wouldn't get all
upset. She may have gone to a hotel. I'll try to stop
in later."

He replaced the phone on its hook and turned to
Sir George.

"Tipton's having the jitters—bad. Wonder if——"
He broke off, frowning. The superintendent was neither
young nor well off—nor would he ever grow rich in the
employ of Trans-Pacific Airways.

"What do you think about Tipton?"

Sir George frowned and spread his hands to indicate
helplessness. "It wouldn't do to overlook even a sma'
possibility. Do ye need help?"

Hugh North hesitated, inquired for Inspector Yu
Shih.

Silver hairs glistened at the inspector general's nod,

and he summoned the little Chinese and ordered him to carry out Captain North's orders.

"This lowly worm is most humble in the face of too great an honor." Yu Shih clasped hands over a stomach which promised ere long to assume a Buddhistic rotundity.

"It is this person of no consequence," North countered politely, "who will be privileged to sun himself in the greater knowledge of Inspector Yu Shih."

Yu Shih beamed.

"And now one last thing. Can you lend me an automatic? I don't like to use them as a rule, but I think I'd better take one along."

North felt especially bitter over the loss of his precious .32 when he tested the ungainliness of a police Webley Sir George pulled from a drawer.

"She's no' so handsome," admitted the inspector general while jotting down the serial number, "but she hits har-rd, and by the bye, she's worth nine pound' sterling." A handful of cartridges rattled onto the desk top and were carefully counted by Sir George. "Here's an even dozen, Captain. Each of which costs saxpence, so don't go banging away out of sheer lightness of spirrit."

"If I break this case I will, and hang the expense!" he promised, making no attempt to conceal a grin, which faded as he proceeded down the corridor with Yu Shih.

"Better get a bite to eat, Inspector; I won't be needing you for about fifteen or twenty minutes."

As the Intelligence officer's fingers closed over the cold brass knob of a door marked "Chemist" he drew a deep breath and, entering, saw an adequately, if not an elaborately, equipped research laboratory, quite empty save for a round-shouldered, sparrowlike individual hard at work over a three-stage microscope.

Gravely Captain North made himself known and was heartily welcomed by an obviously awed Dr Charles Dixon.

Dr Dixon, it appeared, had just arrived from the morgue and an examination of the deceased's stomach.

"Tell me, Doctor, did you find traces of hard-boiled egg in the stomach?"

"Why yes. How in the world did you guess?" The doctor's bright little shoe-button eyes widened, and he cocked his head to one side, for all the world like a robin considering a promising worm cast.

"A bit of eggshell was found on the scene of the robbery, and I was just wondering."

Um. There could be no doubt now who had dropped the bit of eggshell. The question of *why* Patterson should have elected to eat an egg at such a place and at such a moment, however, remained a problem to gnaw, ratlike, at his peace of mind as his eyes flickered over to a work bench upon which the evidence had been ranged in sedate review.

Tallest of all was the water pitcher with its silken enigma lying limp on the bottom.

"What in hell happened to the water?" sharply demanded the man from G-2.

Dr Dixon stared. "Why, I don't know; the Sikh who brought it here must have emptied it on the way down from the hotel. Why?"

"He shouldn't have done that. Please pour a little

distilled water in there. Just enough to keep the stocking damp."

While the police doctor hurried to comply North considered the champagne bottle and glasses from Stag Melhorne's table. Next, like the younger children in a photograph of a large family, were arranged the whisky and water glasses from Room 423. Forming the lower phase of an arc were the egg, the scratch pad, the cigarette butts; flattest of all, samples of note paper from the floor of Patterson's room brought up the rear.

His blue-gray eyes steady and penetrating, the American inquired, "Were you able to learn what killed Sam Patterson?"

The alert little doctor produced a spectacle case, donned a pair of gold-rimmed glasses and after batting his eyes once or twice to get them in focus selected a sheet of paper from a clip board.

"Case #73144, C.I.D. Division, dated June 29," he droned in the manner of a professor addressing a class. "Death resulted from administration of dipropyl-barbituric acid, 7/10th grams. This drug, Captain, is known to commercial chemists as 'proponal' and belongs to the same group of hypnotics as veronal. Though not generally in favor with physicians because of its dangerously powerful action, it is sometimes prescribed as a soporific."

North made no comment, merely wrote the information down on his mental slate.

Inquired Dr Dixon, "Did you happen to notice, Captain, whether the deceased's pupils were contracted or dilated?"

"Contracted," came the pleasant reply. "Was there any other food in the stomach?"

"No. Deceased apparently had not eaten in a good time; there was a fair amount of alcohol, however. By the way"—shyly Dr Dixon looked over the top of his glasses—"I suppose you know it would affect the action of the drug?"

"Yes, I was coming to that." He pulled out and commenced stuffing his pipe to hide an anxiety over the answer to his next question. "How long, Doctor—this is very important, so please weigh your answer—how much time would you say elapsed between Patterson's swallowing the proponal and his death?"

Eyes fixed on the exhibits, Dr Dixon slowly washed his hands with invisible soap and imperceptible water, then, speaking slowly, said, "In this case the drug was unusually effective because of the stomach's empty condition. Seven-tenths of a gram is a heavy overdose and should—mind you, this is as close as I can come—have killed the patient in not less than an hour. You see, Captain, it's very hard to gauge these things. The patient's resistance, his nervous condition, his degree of fatigue, all enter into it."

"Then it's safe to say," North queried impressively, "that the drug was administered not much over an hour before I found him."

"I think you could, Captain. Proponal is very powerful stuff. It probably had him unconscious in less than five minutes. Then his breathing would grow heavier and heavier, accompanied by snoring and deep sighs. As the end approached his respiration would grow shallower and his pupils contract."

"The deceased felt no pain?"

"It's unlikely. Is that important?"

"It might be," moodily returned the Intelligence officer.

After a brief silence Dr Dixon looked up inquiringly. "Do you remember whether you or Sir George tampered with the dead man's clothing?"

"Why do you ask?"

"Because when I first saw the cadaver it's double-breasted coat was buttoned on the wrong side!"

Satisfaction warmed North's heart. Here was the kind of an assistant a man might long pray for and seldom get.

"Yes, Doctor, I unbuttoned Patterson's coat and rebuttoned it the way I found it. What do you make of the fact?"

"Almost all men button a double-breasted coat on their right side," the doctor observed, then added with an unexpectedly impish little grin, "and when I was a lad a girl buttoned her coat on her left side—and her panties too."

Beneath North's close-clipped mustache appeared a vast grin. "They still do, Doctor, just in case you're interested." Then, mercurially, his amusement vanished. "It seems likely that Patterson's body was searched by a woman. She was careless and buttoned Patterson's coat the way she would her own."

Modestly the doctor pointed out that a person, even a man, facing another person and doing buttons, easily might become confused and secure a coat as one would before a mirror.

A measure of the Intelligence officer's elation faded.

"That's very true," he admitted sadly. "Guess I am taking too much for granted. Had time to look at any of the other evidence?"

"The Bertillon man developed these." Dr Dixon, through a rag, caught up one of the champagne glasses and indicated fingerprints skillfully brought out with mercury and chalk. "These look like a man's, Captain."

"Yes." North grinned and held out his hand. "They're mine. See. Recognize the scar on the third finger?"

"Right-o. But what about these? Look like a woman's to me."

"Get your Bertillon man to check them against possible records of a woman called Eve or Evelyn Tanqueray, and label this set that way; the same goes for the other glass. You can label it as Colonel Melhorne's."

"Here's a set of the deceased's," Dr Dixon ventured, his rosy apple of a face quite serious. "His prints and only his prints are on these glasses from his room." He pointed to the two whisky glasses and the lone water glass which had stood on the desk.

Gloom fell over North like an advancing shadow as he beheld the props knocked from under a fond hope. "You're *sure* nobody else's prints are on that half-full highball glass?"

"Never a one, and what's more, we can find no traces of lip marks around its rim."

So? Who, North asked himself, would Patterson have known sufficiently well to have entertained in his room, trusted enough to make it possible for that person to drop proponal into his highball? A number of people suggested themselves, and though he tried hard to arrive at some conclusion, the thought of Con-nie kept digging distracting spurs into his conscious-ness. Nor could he forget that odd quaver in Tipton's voice which argued that the superintendent, innocent or guilty, was nearing a crisis.

"Got to be going along, Doctor," he explained, glancing at his watch.

"Oh, I say, Captain, can't you delay a bit?" The other looked distinctly crestfallen. "I've been looking forward to analyzing that egg which, barring that silk stocking, is the damnedest clue I've ever seen."

"Sorry." The Intelligence officer's smile offered sin-cere regrets. "There are some things I ought to look up, pronto. In the meantime you might see what you can learn about that cigarette with the impression in its middle."

Beneath the strong daylight bulbs Dixon's head inclined. "I'll get a micrometer to work, and I'll have a report of some sort by the time you're back. You are coming back, aren't you?"

"Yes, as soon as I can, and thank you, Doctor. I couldn't ask for more efficient help than you've given me."

He left the little man beaming and found his Chinese assistant awaiting him in the hall.

CHAPTER XIII

FOLLOWED at a discreet distance by Inspector Yu Shih, North sought the Pinnacle Hotel, where he left the moon-faced little man in amiable conversation with an elderly night watchman in a palm-leaf raincoat, who was patroling the establishment's grounds.

Thanks to a call from the Central Police Station, a distinctly unhappy assistant manager gave Hugh North such information as he required and a passkey which enabled that astute gentleman to arrive before the door to Room 733 unobserved by anyone more important than a Chinese houseboy who shuffled by, bearing an armload of shoes needing polish.

He listened but could hear nothing nor, stooping, could he distinguish anything inside. Idiotically he recalled the simile, "Mad as a bellhop at a plugged keyhole," as he gently tried the passkey. To his satisfaction neither it nor the door hinges made a sound when he quietly swung open the door.

Trina Sinclair was dressed, but her pale hair was cascading in a shimmering torrent over a sweater of light blue. Commander Tipton's secretary sat at her desk, working at a portable typewriter. Beside her a

157

neglected cigarette was raising a twisting blue smoke pillar. If one were to judge by the presence of several sealed and addressed letters Miss Sinclair presented indeed the picture of a conscientious secretary intent on carrying out an assignment.

North hesitated and was debating how to address her when a draft caused by the open door stirred her hair, prompting her to turn and notice him standing quietly in the doorway. She sprang up, eyes wide with fright, but she did not cry out, he noticed.

"Why, Mr——" Trina broke off, flushing into an astonishing loveliness. "Do you g-generally enter a-a lady's room without knocking, C-Captain North?"

The moment was Molnaresque, poised on wings of drama; beneath North's neat mustache his teeth gleamed. "When I don't want to advertise the fact I'm calling." Without further explanation the man from G-2 stepped inside, closed the door and appealed to her with a reassuring look. "Please don't be frightened, and remember, you told me I could call on you for help."

"Help? Why yes, of course. What do you want me to do?"

Because she wore moccasin bedroom slippers trimmed with a soft white fur of some sort Trina looked smaller than his memory had sketched her. As she took a step towards him, he guessed the depths of her agitation from the quick lifting of firm breasts faintly outlined by the thin blue cashmere.

Without invitation he unbelted his trench coat, seated himself on the edge of a chair and looked her in the eyes. "Answer some questions, please, about Commander Tipton and the personnel as a whole."

Straight as a candle's flame, she paused by the foot of a bed which had already been turned back to reveal the hem of a blue nightgown peeping out from beneath the pillow.

"Whatever outside forces are at work, I feel more and more there's something smelly about the stealing of that formula."

"Do you, Captain?"

"Yes." Idly his eyes wandered over to the envelopes lying beside her typewriter. One, in ignorance of Mr Huston's rapid approach, was addressed to T.P.A.'s divisional superintendent in Manila; the second was sent to Pratt & Whitney; the third was intended for the oil company supplying T.P.A.'s fuel.

Also on the desk was a diary, one of the kind which can be locked but which never is, and he would have given much for an immediate glimpse at the entries against June twenty-ninth—that day. Again he marveled at the willingness of some people to transcribe thoughts which, by any one of countless accidents, might become exposed for the whole world's inspection.

"Miss Sinclair, when did you last see Patterson—alive, that is?"

"Why, at the office," she said simply. "Don't you remember? Carleton got me a ricksha."

"I see." Entirely agreeable was Captain North's assent. "And where did you go after you left the office?"

She had, Trina stated, gone straight to her room. She'd been badly upset and needed time to think, to pull herself together. After a while she had succeeded.

The Intelligence officer leaned forward, a smile hovering beneath his close-clipped mustache. "And that was when you phoned me?"

It was not difficult to tell that Miss Sinclair had forgotten all about those phone messages to the club, but she said yes and sat on the chair by the typewriter.

"What did you want to reach me about?"

"Why—what was it?" Her look was apologetic. "So much has happened I . . . Oh yes! I remembered that M. Lebov was very late for his appointment with A.W. It was for two-thirty and he didn't show up before three-fifteen."

North settled back on his chair and prepared to listen.

"Well, I was in the next office; there's only a glass partition in between. I could hear everything they said." She paused, restlessly drawing one moccasined foot up under her.

"They talked about Lebov's land, I know. Was there anything else?"

No, Trina said, there wasn't, but Lebov kept beating around the bush, wouldn't come to the point. North pointed out that that was a Russian characteristic. Trina said he seemed to be deliberately wasting time. Did Captain North think such news important? Captain North said he did; also the fact that Tipton hadn't told his visitor to put up or shut up when he had the E.F. 371 in the office and knew the bank would shut at three o'clock.

Trina frowned, looked most unhappy, so North veered to another tack.

"I wonder, Miss Sinclair, if you could give me any logical reason why Patterson should have taken a hard-boiled egg up to his room and placed it on his desk?"

"Egg?" Trina's brown eyes looked her amazement. "If there was an egg in his room, Captain, there's something queer about it because Sam simply hates—hated hard-boiled eggs! He wouldn't even look at some perfectly lovely stuffed ones I t-took on a picnic to Green Island. After that I never brought any along. He doesn't—didn't like anchovies either."

"May I remark that you are observant as well as charming, Miss Sinclair?"

"In the East you've got to keep your eyes open or you don't get far," came her bitter observation. "You've no idea how t-tense things have been, still are for the Airways. But"—she drew herself up, the golden splinters in her dark eyes agleam—"Commander Tipton and some others of us intend to keep the T.P.A.'s s-secrets where they belong."

"To keep them there is the reason I came to Hong-kong," he reminded.

To his surprise the girl came over to him and when he rose stood close, very close, and raised an eager face, haloed in glistening hair.

"Oh, Captain, you don't, you *can't*, know how much it means to have someone come along we can trust. You're like the U.S. Marines in the melodrama; you're like the——"

"Aren't you infringing on Cole Porter's territory?" He relieved her vibrant self-consciousness by humming a bar or two of "You're the Top."

"You *are*," she cried. "And I hope you get to like

Hongkong." She glanced at the mosquito bar gathered as if to pounce upon her bed. "It's so romantic and picturesque and mysterious. I love its contrasts; age-old China on Wing Lok Street and the newest American cars on the Bund, Swatow junks in the harbor and our great clippers in the air."

"You make it sound fascinating," North murmured. "And now, before we go along, I wish you'd tell me what you think was the real situation between Sam and Tipton's stepdaughter."

He sensed rather than saw the fluid mask of animosity which descended, hardening Trina Sinclair's expression.

"A number three singsong girl down on Tung Street has more real decency in her little t-toe than Connie Holden has in her whole body," stated Trina in the monotone of deadly hatred.

"You paint a graphic picture," murmured the Intelligence officer and stole a look at his watch. Damn! He should be getting on, yet Trina's promised to be an illuminating dissertation. "Could you give me *facts* about her, not personal reactions?"

"I'll try to, though I 'hate her to pieces' as Popeye says," came the flashing answer. "Back home she got into so many scrapes, did so many crazy things, she got thrown out of one smart f-finishing school after another."

"Please go on."

"She's been more or less engaged four times since she reached Hongkong; once it was to a young Englishman who was fool enough to try to shoot himself when she gave him the air. Last year she skipped from F-Florida

just in time to avoid being supoenaed as witness in a
raid on a gambling joint. She keeps her father perpetually broke, and she's dramatized herself so much she's
f-forgotten the cue for truth!"

Trina Sinclair paused by the foot of her bed, slim
shoulders vibrant with indignation, and faced him.

"Watch out, C-Captain. I saw her looking at you
with bedrooms in those damned b-beautiful eyes of hers.
Clever as you are, she'll fool you, given half a chance."

"Oh, come now," skillfully North scattered fresh bait
on the water. "Miss Holden may be careless, but I
doubt if she's ever gone off the deep end."

"Look, Captain." She paused before him. "I've told
you you can call on me. I mean it. I'll go anywhere,
do anything you tell me—if you won't credit that
dreadful little harpy."

"You *do* hate her, don't you?"

"Yes," blazed the secretary. "She deliberately stole
the only man I've ever loved." Fiercely she stared at
the desk and its empty chair. "You'll never know how
I worshipped S-Sam. I adored him and wanted to die
when she stole Sam from me."

Carefully considered was North's procedure at this
point. "Somewhere I heard Sam—er—fell for someone
else first."

"You must mean Eve." Trina shrugged away the
suggestion. "Oh, that was nothing serious. Any good-
looking man is bound to have girls making eyes at him.
Besides, Eve plays fair; that's the way she gets on so
well with men. She soon found Sam hadn't any big
money and was losing interest when that Connie butted
in—vamped him shamelessly." .

"Stole him, as you say . . ."

"She did worse than that, though."

"Yes?"

"She killed him!"

It was as if a knife had severed a cord, so complete became the silence in the room, and the whine of myriad insects dashing themselves in fury against the window screens sounded loud out of all proportion.

"Have you any proof of that?" Captain North queried almost casually.

Trina gave him a miserable look and reached for a cigarette. "Oh, I don't mean Connie actually murdered him, but she killed everything that was fine and good in him, which amounts to the same thing, doesn't it? She knew as well as I that the Pattersons of Virginia are proud, idealistic and *very* jealous of their personal honor. Yet she deliberately cut the roots of his personal honor beneath the ground and let them die." Much sadness entered the shadows about her eyes. "Later I found out he borrowed money from me to take her dancing at Repulse Bay. A man has to sink pretty low before he'll do a thing like that."

"Or be pretty much in love."

"What do you know about love?"

"Not a great deal," Hugh North admitted with a small smile. "It's as silly as thinking you understand women."

"Which shows," Trina flashed over her shoulder, "that you know a great deal. But seriously, won't you let me help you? I can, you know."

"I'm going to, Miss Sinclair, and probably sooner than you think. What size stockings do you wear?"

"Nines," she replied automatically. Then her laugh rang out. "Surely you're not going to compromise an assistant to the extent of buying her stockings?"

"As the Chinese say, Miss Sinclair, 'Life is a succession of surprises, some of which, by the law of averages, are bound to be pleasant.' And now if you'll put on some shoes and fix up that perfectly elegant head of hair, we'll be going."

"Going?" Trina looked disappointed, surprised. "At this hour? Do you know it's nearly four-thirty?"

"Yes, I do indeed. Allee samee, 'men must work and women must weep.'"

"I'm all wept out—have been for nearly a month." She smiled and, seating herself before her dressing table, began to plait her hair with the infinite grace women possess at such moments. "At that, it's lucky we split up before this happened. Guess I'd have gone out of my head."

"It's too nice a head to leave—especially when you hold it like that."

"Bet you've sat in on this operation plenty of times?" Trina was securing the braid, halolike, about her brow.

"Witness declines to answer on grounds it might incriminate," grinned North. "While you're making yourself dangerously beautiful I think I'll wash a little rich, rare and racy Chinese mud from my mittens," he announced and, arising, strode over to a half-open door beyond which white tiling suggested the existence of a bathroom.

"Oh, don't, there's—there's some washing," she pleaded. "It's simply a mess in there."

"You forget I'm used to travel," he laughed and,

flicking on the light, viewed sundry stockings drying on the edge of the tub. He was surveying a medicine chest well filled with cosmetics when soap stung suddenly, appraising him of a scratch on his wrist. It was small, but North, being familiar with Chinese microbes, sought a disinfectant behind a row of nail-polish bottles. In groping for it, one fell with a crash into the wash basin.

"Goodness, you m-made me jump!" Trina cried from the doorway. "What were you l-looking for?"

He showed her the scratch.

"Why didn't you tell me, silly? The iodine's over there."

He could see, however, that she was thinking of something else and felt her eyes come to rest upon him in a speculative half smile.

When he reappeared she was bending above a dresser to adjust the set of a jaunty dark blue felt with an orange quill.

"Contact?" he called.

"Contact! Let 'er go! What's the course, Pilot?"

"A call on your boss to ask him a question or two."

Apparently this was the last place Trina Sinclair had imagined to be their destination, but she said nothing, only pulled on a hooded raincoat of transparent blue silk.

Out in the hall she bent to lock the door, then hesitated. "Oh, just a minute," she pleaded. "I might as well stamp my letters and put them in the post."

She stepped inside and must have found some difficulty in locating stamps, because he waited in the hall a good minute ere she reappeared, the letters neatly stamped. There were four of them, three typewritten and one addressed in longhand. At the first pillar box they saw she dropped them in.

At this hour it was not surprising that neither chairs nor rickshas were available, so, quite resigned to a long walk, the two bent their heads into a light drizzle and struck off along Upper Albert Road past Government House, standing dim and dark to their right.

"Mercy, you are in a rush." Trina was almost trotting to keep up with his springy stride.

"I am," he admitted. "I'm worried—meant to get to Tipton's much earlier. He sounded plenty jittery over the phone."

They swung along for some minutes quite companionably, though neither spoke—a fact which endeared Trina to him.

At last he said, "You mentioned Lebov earlier. What do you think of him?"

"I can't quite make him out," the girl admitted, slipping her arm through his to slow his gait. "He acts like a worn-out playboy and looks like one. And yet, every now and then I think he's putting on an act. You know, he *must* be clever to play us against Air Oriental as well as he does."

"How long has Lebov been in Hongkong?"

"Around a couple of months."

"Did T.P.A.'s trouble begin when he arrived?"

"No. Dick Donaldson had been making a fool of himself over Eve Tanqueray before that," demurely replied Miss Sinclair.

Down the street the ungreased axles of a market-bound hay cart screeched like a pig under a gate. The

Intelligence officer said, "What do you know about Swazey?"

It appeared that Miss Sinclair knew little beyond the fact that because of his outstanding record in South America Trans-Pacific had made a dicker for him with Pan-American. Yes, Mr Swazey had been sent out in a hurry. A base couldn't function properly without a competent operations manager.

Frowning a little, North leaned forward. "Could I see some typical transfer orders and credentials— say, Donaldson's, Swazey's and Patterson's? Also a list of your personnel?"

"All you have to do is to stop at the office, though A.W. may have some in his study. He does a lot of work there. Look, isn't it getting light in the east?" demanded the secretary. "I hope so; maybe a new day will bring us all better luck. Yesterday was awful."

With emphasis Hugh North agreed, then continued his conversational research.

T.P.A.'s administration at the moment was complicated, he learned, being divided between the nearly completed base in Kowloon and the temporary offices on Zetland Street, which were to be given up on completion of an administration building in Kowloon. Eventually nothing but a booking office would remain in Hongkong proper.

"Can't wait to show you over the base," Trina cried. "Our pilots and mechanicians are such perfectly swell hombres. Lost my heart to Bill Bentley—he's the San Diego's god of gadgets—until the hound confessed to a wife and three kids back in Oakland."

"God of gadgets?"

"All first engineering officers are gods of gadgets. To watch Bill Bentley make those SIA4G Wasps sit up and beg is an education." Enthusiasm swept color into Trina's damp cheeks. "You'll like Cupid Vidarek, who navigated the 'Flying Gas Tank' out here a lot. She's our survey ship."

While Trina talked about such esoteric matters as minimum pay loads, trim tabs and condition scale settings, North listened to her with flattering attention.

"I don't wonder you're proud of Trans-Pacific. You people have pulled off a great, inspiring job."

"A.W. has worn himself out. All of us have worked like niggers, and some of us have died to establish it," she murmured. "You can hardly blame us for wanting to keep our E.F. 371."

"No, can't say as I do blame you," North admitted. "Well, we'll be there in another minute."

Several shuttered windows of Tipton's now familiar house were yielding golden rays of light, so in response to some inordinate urge the man from G-2 lengthened his stride up Robinson Road. Trina had run up the steps and was reaching for the knocker when the portal fell back before her and Tuck Fat appeared, panting, his bare feet showing beneath the hem of a nightshirt and his slightly popeyes agoggle.

"Makee quick, Cappen!" he babbled, grabbing at North's hand.

"How fashion?"

"Makee walkee chop chop! No savvy Marster talkee he!" And, nightshirt aflutter, he darted back in the house with North and the girl at his heels.

CHAPTER XIV

CROUCHED ON A CHAIR in the library and swaying slowly from side to side, Andrew Tipton sat staring emptily into space. His iron-gray hair was wildly disheveled, and his twitching scarlet face had been raked by several scratches that shed blood upon his collarless shirt.

"Sorry, Spencer, it's no use; Department Commerce won't pass it," he called. "A letter, Miss Sinclair . . . Seven, twelve, back to six. Damn dial's slippery, Lebov. Seven, twelve, back to six . . . That 'll fix them! No, Donaldson, you forgot to figure it at the extreme pitch. Quick, Vidarek, for God's sake, tune in the beam. . . . I . . ."

Now rising, now sinking to an indistinct mumble, the superintendent's voice rambled on, and the three figures standing aghast in the doorway might have been shadows for all the attention he paid them. With a catch in his throat Hugh North took in details; Tipton's torn sleeve, his shoeless feet, dirt on his shoulders and three deep gouges along his powerful forearm.

"Commander," he demanded in a low, compelling voice. "What's wrong? What's happened?"

"Why nothing," giggled the specter. "Nothing."

Leaving Tuck Fat to goggle in the entrance, North and Trina darted across the room. Tipton heard them coming, flinched, then got up, gathered himself, frowning.

"Commander. Please—it's I." Hesitantly Trina approached, one hand outheld. "Let me help you."

Tipton stared, straightened mechanically, tucked his shirt into his trousers top more neatly, then beamed.

"Why, hello, Laura. It's so good to see you, darling. You've been away a long while. Oh, Laura, dearest girl, I've missed you dreadfully; been so lonely."

In answer to North's sharp look Trina whispered, "His first wife."

"It's all right, Commander. That's it, settle back in your chair," she urged in a soothing voice, each accent of which was like a caress. "We're here to help you—there, there."

"Who's that? Tell me, Laura!" Terror-stricken, he flinched away from North and began to whine. "Please, please leave me alone. No, no, I won't! Won't listen—no! I know I'm broke but . . . Laura!" His voice dropped. "Send him away, dear. I—I'm too tired. Oh, my head hurts so!" And, shuddering violently, Tipton buried his face between his palms and began to sob, the deep, racking sob peculiar to men.

Trina put an arm about his shoulder and patted him gently before throwing North a look of ineffable horror. Clearly she had no idea what course to follow.

Because the scratches were very fresh, Hugh North risked placing a hand on Tipton's shoulder. "If you'll

tell us what's happened, old man, maybe we can fix
everything up—straighten things out for you."

It was all North could do to keep his own nerves in
harness when the superintendent raised a dreadful,
quivering face. "I didn't take it, Captain. Before God,
I didn't!" he cried, and his lips writhed like those of
a man suffering an exquisite pang. "I didn't mean to
kill him. Make him stop staring. . . . Laura! Laura!
I didn't mean to do it!"

At once North went into action. "Stay with him,
Laura. You understand him. You'll excuse me, old
man, I think I'd better look around." Eyes busy, every
sense attuned to its greatest efficiency, he beckoned
Tuck Fat after him and sought the depths of the house,
trying to shake off a heavy sense of impending doom.

"What ting have got before time my b'long?"

"No savvy, tajên," babbled the number one boy,
waving agitated disclaimers. "Makee shut-eye. Catchum
bobbery down side. Makee look-see. Catchum Marster
talkee no fashion."

Venting an exasperated curse at the fellow's stupidity, North switched on the light and thrust his head
into the living room, only to find everything in order.

With the number one boy's bare feet pattering after
him he hurried down the carpetless corridor, his own
tread echoing—sounded as if his shoes were empty.
Every shadow he subjected to careful scrutiny, every
door he tested ere he passed, until a great, glistening
drop of blood on the study's threshold gave him warning. Tuck Fat uttered a little squeak of fear and shrank
back when North reluctantly took out the Webley and
slipped off its safety catch. Standing clear of the door,

the man from G-2 turned the knob and pushed the panels open.

"Anybody in there?" he called, conscious of stale, smoke-laden air drifting past him. Though no answer came, he *felt* someone's presence.

His finger tips began to tingle, and he was aware of a mad desire to yawn when, reaching inside, he groped for the switch and flooded the study in a sudden glare. Behind him Trina called out something, her voice shrill, urgent, but he could not move. There before him Paul Swazey lay on his back amid a litter of papers, face purple and tongue protruding between large irregular teeth. An overturned chair, a smashed lamp and the contents of an ash tray scattered far and wide were a graphic explanation for Tipton's scratches.

"Ai-e-e-e!" Out in the corridor Tuck Fat commenced to blubber and to wring his hands.

Shaking off the paralysis of complete astonishment, Hugh North eyed the body an instant, then sprang forward and sent the operations manager's shirt buttons flying. Ear pressed to Swazey's chest, he listened and thought he caught the faintest possible of heartbeats. Though Trina was calling imperatively, he wasted not a second in heaving the limp, blue-faced body over onto its face and, squatting astride of it, commenced artificial respiration.

"Hugh! Hugh! *Come quick!* I c-can't control him!"

"Can't come!" he shouted back and cursed the whole Chinese race because Tuck Fat chose that moment to scuttle off towards the kitchen in a frenzy of fear.

Counting, North kept up his measured strokes, not even interrupting them when he caught a flying patter of Trina's slippers down the hall. Breathless, she ran to his side and commenced tugging at his shoulder.

"Quick! You've got to c-come!" she pleaded, pushing loose strands of hair out of her eyes. "He's got a g-gun! He's crazy—clean c-crazy!"

"Let go of me," he snapped. "Shut the door. Lock it!"

Though her bare shoulder and a strap gleamed through her badly ripped sweater, Trina rushed to comply. "No key! And he's coming. I—I hear him," she quavered.

"Prop a chair under the doorknob. I can't stop. Swazey's almost gone."

Body taut with effort, Trina slipped a chair back into position a split second before the door handle was tried, then rattled furiously. Outside arose a puzzled, incoherent muttering, a dull thumping of stockinged feet.

Trina turned, eyes enormous, questioning.

"Phone the police!" he panted between strokes.

"Phone's n-not in here," she wailed. "It's d-down the hall."

"Get to the window, yell, make all the noise you can. Yu Shih's out there."

She had no time to obey before the lights went out, plunging the study into an abysmal, heart-chilling gloom. How absurd, North thought, to have to go on pumping like this.

"C-Can't work the damn bolts," Trina cried after hurriedly stumbling over to the window. "Got a m-match? I think——"

Tipton's voice, thick and furious, drowned out the

rest of the sentence. "Going to kill you—shoot you dead, you damned thieves . . . Break into my house, will you?" Mutter. Mutter. The door rattled under a hard shove. "Kill you . . . Seven, twelve, back to six . . . Wasn't a good safe, Mr Sensu. You in there, North?"

Silence.

"Don't lie—I *know* you're in there! Think you're clever, don't you? Well, you won't pin anything on me."

Again the door rattled under a heaving impact; the propped chair groaned a little.

"Oh dear, what can we do?" Trina sobbed. "I can't keep the chair from slipping."

"Let it be," North hissed and groped for his Webley. "Lie flat."

"I'll get you! You blasted devils."

For a third time the madman battered at the entrance, hurling his heavy body in a frenzy until the panels groaned and the whole room shook. Next time the door would give, North felt sure, and he prepared for a wing shot while maintaining his efforts at resuscitation with his left hand. Unaccountably the assault ceased, and the breathless couple could hear Tipton go padding off up the corridor.

Ha! A measure of encouragement reached North when Swazey's lungs began to function a little of their own accord.

"Isn't it terrible?" Out of the almost tangible darkness came Trina's shaking voice. "What d-do you suppose A.W.'s doing? Where's he g-gone?"

"God only knows, but—— Quiet! Here he comes again!"

By now the superintendent's mutterings had grown crafty in pitch, utterly incoherent and interspaced with occasional sibilant sighs. They heard him pause in the corridor, listening. His labored breathing was perfectly audible. At last a furious rustling sound reached their ears, and the sound of retreating footsteps.

"What the devil?" North began but fell silent, having already got an answer. Smoke! On the back of Hugh North's neck little hairs prickled and writhed. Damn! There could be no more temporizing. He'd have to do something!

Thank God, Swazey was breathing normally, so, stung to action by a small red glare beating under the door, he sprang up and wrenched aside the propped chair. A perceptible tightening of his abdominal muscles accompanied the jerking off of his trench coat; to open the door would be the riskiest part of what he had to do. Very likely Tipton was crouching just outside, drawing a bead on the door. Nothing remained but to find out, so, standing beside the door frame, he wrenched it open, and in rolled the ball of flaming newspapers which had been propped against it. Nothing was to be seen but the flame-lit wall of the corridor. In a dextrous gesture he flung his trench coat onto the flames, smothering them into clouds of choking smoke. No one spoke, no shot rang out.

"Take care of the fire," he flung over his shoulder, then, coughing, he bent well over and entered the hall. There he waited, allowing his eyes to become readjusted, but the precaution, beyond warning him of

Tipton's presence towards the front of the house, helped not at all because it was utterly lightless in the corridor.

Bemoaning his unfamiliarity with the ground plan, he pressed himself flat to the wall and commenced edging down the hall. Would it be possible for Tipton to circle, gain his rear and possibly re-enter the study? Fervently he prayed Trina would have presence of mind enough to re-secure the door.

Out of the rushing turmoil in his brain crept the decision to try to reach a window and yell for Yu Shih. Should he risk firing a warning shot? Surely the Chinese would be astute enough to take swift action. Yet to shoot was to betray his whereabouts, and Tipton in his murderous frenzy might be anywhere.

Damn! He was quite lost. Doors and chairs appeared where he least expected them. Which way was the front door? Bloody nuisance the ground floor was protected by solid shutters! He halted, thinking to detect a small clicking sound somewhere off to his left.

North, crawling on hands and knees, became aware of an aura of danger so definite he could almost smell it. In the dark the other man, in retreating, brushed something, made a little rustling noise. Hugh North checked his crawling long enough to wipe away the great drops of sweat stinging at his eyes.

All his life he had had a deep aversion for mental aberration in any form and fortunately had had few calls to deal with it, but those few examples of what horrors a diseased brain could perpetrate made it all he could do to keep his own mind functioning clearly, surely.

Thrice he barged into the furniture but kept on

gaining. Fervently he prayed that some crack of light
might relieve this baffling gloom, for just ahead a board
in the planking had creaked. The faint reek of burnt
paper stung the Intelligence officer's nose just before
a curious snuffling anticipated an abrupt cessation of
the other's retreat.

"Come on. I'm not afraid, Martin."

North sank flat to the floor, tried a soothing monotone. "It's all right, Commander. Nobody's going to
hurt you. Be a good fellow and put down the gun."

He was answered by a guttural snarl and a shot, the
bullet of which sang a good two feet over his head and
smashed some object on a table in the living room.
Heavily the report echoed throughout the house; in
the distance Trina Sinclair uttered a wailing cry.

Panting, dusty and clinging to his composure with
a tenuous grip, North raised himself on one elbow. He
had him now. The pistol's flash had shown Tipton
crouched under a grand piano, naked to the waist and
all hunched up. Unwillingly, sick at heart, the man from
G-2 drew a bead along the bearing of his left forefinger. An acid tide flooded his mouth. At such a range
he couldn't miss. Ghastly jobs he had had to perform
ere now, but none of them could compare with this;
a bloody executioner, that was what he was. It was
like shooting a bird sitting.

"Don't want to hurt you, Tipton, but I've got you
covered. Now be a good fellow and drop this foolish-
ness."

Again a discharge momentarily limned the living
room, but this time no bullet hissed over North's head.
Instead, as the roar of the report faded he heard a little

choking grunt, the clatter of a pistol striking a hard-
wood floor and the sound of a heavy fall.

Shaking, bathed in perspiration, Hugh North stayed
where he was, listening to the sound of the other's
breathing; a slow gasping it was, ending in a little
wet sound at each exhalation. Reassured, he delayed no
longer and struck a match, the flame of which showed
Tipton huddled on his side beneath a baby grand piano;
he had extended one dusty bare arm as if trying to
reach a big navy Colt lying just beyond the tips of
slowly working fingers.

Already a widening pool had crept out from beneath
the huddled outline to reflect the match flame. On the
mantelpiece North found a candle and by its dancing
light went over to examine the body. Tipton's eyes
were open, their insensate gleam gone. "Sorry," he
sighed. "Where are you, Laura?" Then he died.

North's first consideration was Trina. He could hear
her calling his name, not loudly but with an urgency
imperative of immediate attention. He found the door
to the study secure, and when, standing amid charred
newspapers, he tried its handle, the girl within uttered
a terrified sob.

"It's all right, Trina. It's I. Poor Tipton's killed
himself."

The door was unbarred, and in an instant Trina
all but knocked the candle out of his grip in running
out to fling herself into his arms.

"You were fine," he murmured, stroking the fragrant
disorder of her hair. "Simply fine! Kept your head.
Most girls would have been an infernal nuisance." In
admiration he kissed her gently, felt the violence of

her sobs diminish. Somewhere a whistle was blowing like the screech of an exasperated imp, but he forgot it when Trina drew his head down until the warmth of her lips could rest against the hard thinness of his cheek.

At length he said, "How's Swazey?"

"Getting along better. I kept on working over him after you'd gone. Who's that?" She started convulsively at a loud hammering on the front door.

"The police; late as usual." He set off down the hall, but heavy, official feet were already sounding in the vestibule.

It was Inspector Yu Shih with two big, red-bearded Sikh constables at his heels. In crisp sentences the man from G-2 told them what to do. Yu Shih was sent to telephone; the taller Sikh, a sergeant, he ordered to make sure no spark of life lingered in Tipton's body and sent the second constable in search of the master switch. Loudly snuffing the stale smoke, the Indian took his flash and went about his task with such intelligence that presently the lights came on, revealing Swazey propped up on one elbow. Slowly the operations manager was rubbing his throat and coughing a little.

"How are you feeling?" North asked and lent him a hand as the other gathered suède shoes under him in an effort to rise. Odd how the crepe soles made his feet seem so much larger than they really were. The operations manager, however, could only blink stupidly and emit a faint croaking sound.

The deadliness of his struggle with Tipton was written in his dusty face and badly torn tweed jacket. His ripped shirt still sagged open, exposing a spread eagle boasting long spikey pinions and some very jaunty, curling tail feathers tattooed across his chest. The bird's head, though nearly lost among the hair of Swazey's chest, seemed to be crowned with an ornament of some sort.

Yu Shih's dumpy figure remained just inside the door, his jet eyes, beneath their fatty lids, darted about the room like questing swallows, flitted from the Hongkong Clipper's silver-painted model to a number of clip boards and letter files which had showered their contents pell-mell across the office's cheerful blue Chinese rug. They lingered curiously on dim snaps portraying old navy shipmates and pictures of T.P.A.'s early flying boats hanging askew, then sought a brightly colored chart-poster explaining the seating arrangements of the Trans-Pacific clippers—it had been torn in half.

Yes. Swazey must have put up a game fight. Leaning against the door frame, North rubbed his head and strove to coax some practical deduction out of the chaos in his mind. First Donaldson, then Patterson and now Tipton. Damn it! The employees of a modern, well-established air line shouldn't die like characters in a Ruritanian novel. Such tragedies weren't reasonable or to be expected, for if ever a set of humans were hard-headed, practical and matter of fact it was men engaged in commercial aviation.

Inspector Yu Shih raised troubled, owl-like eyes. "Your orders, tajên?"

"Please ask the C.I.D. people if any progress has been made in tracing the motorboat. Sorry I forgot about it before."

Once the inspector had disappeared North methodically wiped his fingers, then freed his cheeks of dusty, sticky sweat.

"You'd better s-sit down, Hugh," Trina pleaded. "*Please.* You look s-simply dreadful."

"Glass houses . . ." he reminded, aware that within these last few minutes Trina's face had lost its fresh color, had aged five years.

She nodded, humbly sank into a chair and sat with her small head inclined as if forestalling a fainting spell.

"A.W. was always so w-wonderful to me," she choked. "It's horrible, too simply awful! I—I can't bear it. Treated me like one of the family. T.P.A. 'll go to hell out here now. S-Spencer's got no guts and Horton no s-sense."

From wretched eyes she watched North drop onto his knees and commence a search of Swazey's person so deft that a pickpocket might well have been moved to envy. He found nothing of interest in the operations manager's possession, not even a passport, that laisser-passer without which most travelers dread to stir.

"Water . . ." gurgled Swazey and, on being helped to his feet, sank heavily into a chair. He drank eagerly the water brought by Trina. Finally he rubbed his eyes, cleared his throat once or twice and for the first time seemed cognizant of what was going on.

"What's happened?" he mumbled, mechanically closing his shirt. "Thought . . . I . . . finished."

"You would have been," Trina informed him, "if C-Captain North hadn't k-kept his head."

At that moment Yu Shih and the Sikh sergeant

appeared, and before North could stop the latter he saluted and gravely announced, "Commander Tipton is dead, Captain Sahib. There can be no doubt of it."

"Dead? Tipton *dead?*" Swazey's battered gray head swung about, and his voice climbed.

"Oh, it's too awful!" The shock of her employer's death did not seem to have really come home until now. "Poor A.W. I——" She broke into a flood of tears, the first she had shed. "Oh, they shouldn't have worked him so hard! If only they'd paid him more he could have—could have——"

Trina swayed a little, earning a sharp glance from North.

"It's home for you, young lady, soon's I can see you to the cable tram. You'd better take a look-see upstairs. Maybe you can find a sedative of some kind."

"I *hate* those things," she choked. "They're d-dangerous. D-Don't you worry about me, Hugh. I'll go wait in the library—be all right."

More police and a number of reporters with eager anticipation written all over their manner came stamping in. Then an ambulance roared up to disgorge an interne and a pair of stretcher bearers.

"Be with you in a minute, Trina," he smiled. "You've been aces up!"

"Maybe I was until A.W.—died. I—I just can't get over that." Slowly she moved away, passing the disinfectant-spotted stretcher with a visible shudder.

Taut brain directing a merciless rally of his energies, Hugh North returned to the study and, banishing everyone save Yu Shih, examined it with great care. The window was tight, nor were there any marks on sill or shutters, but the desk drawers were in considerable disorder and documents fluttered half out of a portable filing cabinet.

Inspector Yu Shih was tactful about his approach.

"Does tajên recall adage that 'Unspoken word is slave. Spoken word is master'? Desire removal of men from newspapers?"

"Yes," North snapped in instinctive reaction. Then a sudden inspiration swept, meteorlike, into his scheme of things. "No. Give 'em the whole story. Play up Tipton's death. Tell 'em to splash it."

"Splash? Be patient with this one's incredible stupidity, tajên."

"Sorry, Yu Shih. I mean they're to give the story all the space they can."

"Your wish is my law, tajên." Yu Shih turned and went out.

Symbolically, perhaps, the Hongkong Clipper's silvered model had crashed to the floor, crumpling one wing beyond repair.

Then he turned to Swazey who, coughing every now and then, told a simple, direct story. A phone call from Tipton, he said, roused him from his bed at the Metropole. Tipton had begged him to come over, but naturally he had not wanted to get up at that hour of the night. So evident was the superintendent's agitation, however, that he agreed to go.

Had Mr Swazey, North wanted to know, gathered that Tipton had had any specific fact to discuss? Swazey thought so. At any rate the base superintendent seemed very grateful of his coming and had led directly into the study. There they had talked at length concerning the robbery. All the while Tipton had grown increasingly agitated.

"Poor ol' Tipton got terribl' work' up," Swazey said, rubbing his throat and keeping his bloodshot eyes fixed on North. "Finall' he 'ccused me of stealing—formula. 'S if I'd even had a chance to! That got me mad, Captain. After all, 'f I'd gotten up four o'clock 'n morning it wasn't t'be 'nsulted."

"What did you say?"

"I got pretty mad, I guess, and told him *he'd* had a damn sight more opportun'ty steal the formula than I."

"That was natural, I suppose," the Intelligence officer admitted, "but most unwise."

"I'll say it was!" agreed Paul Swazey with emphasis. "Then and there he flew off his trolley. He sprang at me, and though I fought back, I didn't stand a chance." Swazey gulped another mouthful of water. "At last he got me down and began to choke me. Well, that's all I remember until I heard that Indian cop say Tipton was dead."

To it all Hugh North listened, then, heaving a small sigh, queried, "Have I got this straight, Mr Swazey? You arrived here, went directly into the study and just talked with Tipton?"

"Yes."

"Then he went crazy and tried to kill you. Is that it?"

"That's it, Captain."

CHAPTER XV

A WATERY pink-and-gray dawn was sketching the Peak's bold mass in silhouette when Hugh North hailed an early double ricksha and rode away from the house on Robinson Road. Beside him the secretary, her reserve badly cracked at last, could not cease shivering.

Hugh North himself felt a thousand years old. The C.I.D. had said no reports concerning the engine serial numbers could be expected for another half or three quarters of an hour. The operations manager had had a close call; at that, Swazey didn't seem entirely collected, even when a constable escorted him back to his hotel. Um. The more he considered Swazey's story, the more thoughtful he became.

Once the ricksha had begun to roll noiselessly over Hongkong's rain-scoured streets Hugh North instructed the coolie to slow to a walk and wisely postponed further conversation. Trina, he felt, needed to regain her bearings. As if lost in heavy thinking, she sat quite still, her gaze only mechanically registering shop signs which, brave with scarlet and gilt, whirled by in endless succession and afforded North no end of amusement. Tavern of Harmonious Hearts, Hang-On

186

Buildment & Contraction Co., the Golden Ox, Glove & Fan Makers, Crystalized Prosperity Deparmen's Store.

Street hawkers vending hot water, tea, noodles and rice cakes began to appear, some of them blowing into miniature portable stoves, all of them scratching at the night's accumulation of bites. High above them a thousand chimneys sent thin spirals of smoke climbing towards flocks of pigeons gaily rioting about the sky.

After its drenching Hongkong presented a strangely refreshed aspect. Somebody's "small pigeon", dispatched on an early errand, whistled impudently at pole porters jogging by under heavy loads, but they only grinned and went on munching a breakfast of toasted melon seeds and shelled peanuts.

"Feel better?" North smilingly queried when at length they stood on the cable tram's empty platform.

"I do. The air's so fresh. I love the streets in early morning," she confessed with a sort of forlorn perkiness. "The city seems so intimate then. Ever notice it?"

North said he had—many times, and from a ragged Chinese moppet he purchased a bunch of dewy violets, offering them with a deep bow. "Permit me, mademoiselle, in appreciation of your invaluable assistance."

"Oh-h! All for little me-e-e?" she trilled, clasping ecstatic hands.

"Aye, my good wench, each and every little blossom is intended to remind you of me—and of the fact I'll be calling on you later."

Her slipper grated on the platform, and her light mood evaporated. "Oh, then you aren't c-coming up with m-me? I—I——"

"No," he explained quietly. "I'd like to, but, well—
you can imagine I've a few things to do. However, if
you're uneasy———"

"Of course I'm not afraid. I'm just silly, but . . ."
She buried her nose among the violets and sighed.

His eyes feeling as if their linings had been sanded,
he led her to a far corner of the deserted shed and sat
down.

"Hang onto your nerve, my dear. You're going fine,"
he pleaded. "Will you notify the right people at T.P.A.
of Tipton's death?"

"Yes. If you wish me to."

"And you'll be very careful what you say?"

"Of course."

"Who'll take over?"

"Hal Spencer, I guess—worse luck," Trina said
through her teeth. "He's one of those hotheaded go-
getters they ought to have kept at home. Maybe it'll
be Bill Horton, though. He's chief radio technician
over in Kowloon. Don't know . . ."

Briefly Captain North debated mention of Huston's
impending arrival, but decided against it. Perhaps the
new superintendent wanted the advantage of an unexpected appearance.

"Oh dear, I—I guess I'm all in," she murmured,
leaning a little heavily against him, and raised such a
drawn face he was prompted to place an encouraging
arm about her shoulders.

"Thanks," she said in a small voice. "It—it makes one
feel so—so sort of safe. I like it."

"Thought so. Wonder if you don't want security
more than almost anything?"

"How did you guess?" The golden splinters were quite visible when her eyes came to rest on his deep-set gray ones. "I'm tired of fending for myself. You see, Hugh, I've never had any security since I was a little g-girl." She hesitated, then rushed on. "My father is in——"

"I know about that. It was a great pity."

"You *know*—and it doesn't make any d-difference?" she demanded so fiercely he was astonished.

"You're not your father, Trina. And I—well, I've always had a hankering for people who won't let themselves be downed by circumstances."

"I haven't. I'm not going to," Trina stated as if it were a credo she dared not falter from. "S-Someday I'm going to be a great lady, a grande dame. That's what the French call them, isn't it?"

"Yes, Trina."

"Someday I'm going to have a social position, heaps of worthwhile friends, and I'll enjoy the g-good things of life." Her gaze rested on Kowloon, where a great white-painted liner, in getting up steam, sent triple smoke pillars climbing into the sky, blue as it only is after rain. "I wonder if you know how hellish it is to be lonely, a—a semioutcast? It wasn't fair for Father to . . ." She bit her lip, and her slim shoulder rose in a little shrug. "That's why it hurt so when Sam let me down. Of course he never knew how cruelly he hurt me, but Sam stood for everything in the world I admired and wanted. Sam was a gentleman, such good fun, and everything he did was in good taste. You should have heard him order a dinner. Headwaiters, porters, desk clerks—people like that who recognize breeding better than most of us—would turn themselves inside out for him."

"In the office he seemed a very pleasant person," North said.

"I'm not telling you this as a bid for sympathy, Hugh," she explained hurriedly. "It's only to make you understand a little better why I so need . . . must find security."

She looked at him, and he saw two great tears draw bright paths down her smooth cheeks. His arms tightened, and he bent his dark head as her mouth, blindly groping, was raised. A distant clicking of the cogs warned of the tram's approach, and he released her. Blushing, she set straight her hat, and they awaited its arrival in silence.

"Kipling *was* right," she murmured. "Hugh, you'll find me—look me up soon?" she pleaded, looking at the advancing tram. "I—I've got something I want to ask you. It's terribly important to me."

"Yes, my dear," he promised, "and when I do, I want to find a girl who's been resting. Just now you resemble something the cat brought in and wouldn't eat."

Trina's laugh rippled out over the screech of brakes, and she caught up her violets. "For them kind words I thanks you, sir." Her hand closed convulsively on his arm. "You won't take chances, will you, Hugh? I can't explain it, but I—well, I think it would k-kill me if anything happened to you."

Without a backward glance she hurried off and got into the cable tram.

Deliberately pouring the oil of philosophy upon the troubled sea of his thoughts, North glanced at his watch, yielded to the dictates of an outraged stomach and sought an establishment bearing the pleasing name of Floating Jasmine Blossom No. 1 Yellow Wine Tea House. Passing beneath the silver urn and blue banner, insignia of its guild, he penetrated radiantly painted doors to enter one of those miniature dreamlands into which the Chinese are able to metamorphose even a tiny patch of earth.

While sipping tea from a fragile little cup and awaiting the rest of his breakfast the Intelligence officer relaxed, absently followed the movements of a gray and white crane wading about a pond so small it suggested a frame for an enormous water lily glowing in its center.

Reluctantly he diverted his attention to a droning hum in the sky. A British naval plane roared by so low that its red, white and blue cocardes were momentarily reflected in the lily pool's surface, then droned on above a fleet of early morning kites, leaving in its wake a host of disquieting thoughts.

Comfortable, homely noises from the kitchens made it easy to wipe clean his mental slate, and he fell to sniffing the spray of jasmine bestowed upon him by the shy child of a waitress who wore a gleaming kingfisher's feather in her hair.

Pretty spot, the Floating Jasmine Blossom No. 1 Yellow Wine Tea House. Mustn't forget it, if the eggs are really fresh. Wonder how Connie's making out? Um. What would the amiable Mr Hsing do when the extras about Tipton's suicide came out? Probably Hsing would figure Tipton had been caught red-handed. The news might gain Connie and himself an hour or two of grace. *Oh, who the devil really had the formula?*

Sun feels good . . . Best tea I've had in a 'coon's age. . . . Funny, Hsing's talking pidgin, then Oxford English—wonder who his boss really was? . . . Um. So Swazey went calling in crepe-soled suède shoes on a wet morning. Damn that fool sergeant anyway!

An enormous tiger cat materialized from under a stone bench, advanced with lordly stride and, seating itself on the graveled walk, considered the detective with doubtful mien.

"Hell of a big night, wasn't it, my feline friend?"

The tiger cat blinked in agreement and directed a speculative glance at a pat of butter.

Frowning, North continued. "Well, Lo Foo, my little cat, do you think Commander Tipton and his romantic stepdaughter have been playing games?"

The cat merely opened a pink mouth and yawned in delicate ennui.

"Bored, eh? Wish I were. You're lucky, Lo Foo, to have your problems limited to the pursuit of mice and eligible tabbies."

The waitress pattered up, smiling, and placed a tray before him, whereupon Lo Foo, scenting the odor of fried fish, became extremely friendly.

Probably Connie would welcome a pot of hot tea too; her costume of nightgown, overcoat and shoes and stockings would scarcely be warm. The more he considered Connie's position, the more critical he deemed it. Um. Would she suspect that her extraordinary maneuvers in Shameen Street might have contributed to her stepfather's death? Probably not.

Consuelo and Trina Sinclair: what a pair to draw to! Damned attractive, both of them. What about Melhorne? Bet old Stag had grabbed that formula in spite of everything; otherwise he'd be butting in plenty. Or was he playing a waiting game? Once the matter of Connie was disposed of he'd consider that point.

The cat oozed up onto a vacant chair and from this point of vantage delivered a sudden assault upon a bit of fried fish; thwarted, however, by a flick of North's napkin, he retired, cursing. Nothing, Lo Foo's manner indicated, was less tempting than fish. Grinning, the man from G-2 detached a section of fillet as a peace offering, but Lo Foo nursed his injured dignity and would have none of it.

After finishing his third bowl of a tea delicate as the jasmine flower beside him Hugh North arose and had tossed a Hongkong dollar onto the table when a scrap of paper tucked under the sugar bowl drew his attention. Deeming it to be the bill, he unfolded it leisurely and read:

So Tipton did have it. Be at Pasig Wharf 8 sharp. You *be there!*

Well, there it was. "You be there!" In those three words he read more menace than in a whole page of threats.

CHAPTER XVI

CAPTAIN NORTH didn't get into the police station. Sir George Amberson himself was sitting in a private car outside, smoking a cheroot and talking quietly to a solid-looking Englishman whose cherubic countenance and guileless blue eyes did not deceive the man from G-2 a bit. He'd encountered guileless blue eyes like those before, generally to his education.

His fat-lidded eyes restless, Inspector Yu Shih stood by the running board, talking rapidly and waving his hands a little. When he saw North coming he stepped aside, Sir George leaned forward, said something to the chauffeur, who immediately started his motor and opened the tonneau door at the same time. Captain North got in without asking any questions, and Yu Shih seated himself beside the driver just as the sedan swung away from the curb.

"Boat's been found," Sir George remarked. "We're holding the Chinese who was in it. Oh, by the bye, this is Chief Inspector Duveen—Captain North. Duveen runs yon menagerie we call the C.I.D."

Quickly the car accelerated. "We're moving quickly,"

Sir George explained. "Ablins someone saw the boatman taken into custody."

North nodded, his lips compressed. It wouldn't be so good for Consuelo Holden if that had happened. "And to whom does the motorboat belong?"

"To a Manchurian," Captain Duveen succinctly informed him. "Name of Ting Tso-chang. He runs the Flaming Sun Line, a fleet of cargo junks plying between here and Yokohama—Manchukuoan registry."

With the white clubs of Indian traffic police clearing a path for it, the car sped on down Pottinger Street while Sir George questioned his companion concerning the events at Tipton's house. North, on the other hand, learned that no trace of Melhorne had been found; he returned to the problem at hand, wondering whether he'd ever be able to recognize that junk.

He hadn't much to go by, only that bit of ocher paint beneath his left middle finger and a few less positive clues. Once the car whirled off along the Bund his gaze sought the sampan fleet's disorderly tangle lying beneath a low-hanging haze of breakfast cooking. As if exhausted by the fury of the night before the harbor now lay slick and glassy as any woodland pool. He glanced at a clock on some distant building and saw it was six twenty. Good. The men on the junk mightn't be expecting anyone so early.

"Fancy you can find the proper junk?" Duveen queried.

"If the crew hasn't shifted anchorage I might. Tell me," North inquired, "what's likely to happen if the kidnapers take alarm?"

"They'll strangle her, most likely. Tie a brace of fire

bars to her heels and drop her over," replied the C.I.D. man, as matter of fact as if he had been describing a recipe. "We often find them like that."

On the jolting seat North felt a chill on the backs of his hands. They'd have to move very, very cautiously —overlook not even the minutest precaution. Strangled, Connie Holden wouldn't look so pretty. He wondered what she'd do when she learned of her stepfather's death. *If* she learned, rather.

Mr Ting Tso-chang's green-and-white motorboat was lying beside a government wharf opposite the Harbor Office, and, gathered at a little distance from it, stood a small group of Chinese. Three of their number were garbed in the inevitable blue cotton rags of dock laborers, but the other two wore ill-fitting European clothes. In their midst stood the boatman, a chunky little Cantonese with hideous pockmarks all over his face.

North inquired politely, "Do you want me to handle this, Sir George?"

The inspector general nodded. "Aye. You know the ground, Captain. I won't go cluttering up the scene, but suppose ye take Duveen here along; he's a handy man in a pinch."

With Yu Shih interpreting, Hugh North questioned the green launch's engineer but even when threatened with all manner of punishment he swore up and down he'd no idea of the junk's position. His business, he grunted, was to run the engine. B'long somebody else to do the steering. No, he'd no idea how many men were aboard the junk; his only interest was his engine. Had Mr Hsing and "Excellency" gone ashore? Maybe. He didn't know for sure, the Cantonese said, and spat before repeating his duties for a third time.

North felt like trying a few shrewd kicks on the boatman's shins; most Chinese couldn't stand that. Sir George, however, probably would not approve—"wasn't done." Besides, the fellow was in all probability far more frightened of his employers than of the police.

Half-past six was striking when North, Duveen, Yu Shih and three Chinese detectives—one of whom greatly resembled the enigmatic Mr Hsing—clambered down into the green-and-white motorboat.

To the boatman North gave firmly to understand that if he gave away the show by even so much as a wink he'd be bowing before his ancestors in no time. Once the whole party, with the exception of Yu Shih and himself, had concealed themselves under a tarpaulin in the motorboat's stern he noted the exact moment and calculated that twelve minutes later he should be nearing the vicinity of the junk. He himself steered the launch away from the pier, picking a devious course among myriad fishing boats on their way to market. Once the great coastline of the sampan fleet revealed itself his heart executed a barrel roll; it seemed as hopeless to pick the right vessel out of that hurrah's nest as a pole from the depths of a jackstraw heap.

"Not so fast," he flung at the engineer. Last night the boat had been bucking a sea and a strong wind to boot.

North swung the motorboat's prow southeast and, surrendering the wheel to Yu Shih, caught up a pair of marine glasses from the boat's chart locker. Through them he scanned the miscellany of vessels anchored on the fleet's outskirts. Yonder he recognized great high-sterned junks from Tientsin and from Amoy, *lorchas* claiming Canton, Shanghai and Formosa as their home ports. There were even a few rakish craft from the French colonies of Tonkin and Annam.

Yellow rails? Great eyes, invariably decorating the bows of the native craft, mocked his rising despair. At least one in every six junks had a yellow rail. Damn! He was rapidly approaching the fleet, so once the motorboat commenced to nose through refuse and garbage on the outskirts he turned his coat collar up and pulled down the brim of the hat Sir George's chauffeur had lent him.

"Our junk won't be on the very edge," he warned Yu Shih. "She'll be in a little."

"Yes, tajên, a big junk with red side."

"Red side? How do you know that?"

"This excellent motorboat's bow, tajên, indicates recent contact with redness. Scraping perhaps in dark."

That, North thought, gave him a little better chance. A red junk with a yellow railing would cut down the field a bit.

"Slower," he flung at the boatman who had begun to spit and sweat a good deal. "Duveen, please cover that fellow at the engine, and if Yu Shih takes his hand off the rail, *shoot him!* Yu Shih, you watch the boatman. If he says or does anything at all suspicious take your hand off the rail. Now tell the Cantonese what I've said."

Now and then scrawny watermen loafing on the rails of dilapidated sampans yelled at the passing motorboat, prompting their women to thrust curious Medusa heads from beneath the bamboo mats forming their cabins. Urchins, naked as angleworms save for ginger-ale-bottle floats lashed to their backs, cavorted back and forth, waving and shouting. Other motorboats chugged by, bearing heavy cargoes of fish and market produce from the mainland.

North cast them not a glance because dead ahead lay a big seagoing junk, yellow railed and painted a rusty red. A buzzing sensation numbed his finger tips.

"Cut the motor," he snapped, not wishing to attract unduly the attention of such men as might be on her decks.

Briefly the green motorboat hid herself in the lee of a big sampan loaded with timber, then slid out into plain sight once more, with North hoping that headway alone would carry them under the red junk's counter. Risking a backward glance, he saw Duveen's eyes, hard and bright, looking out from under the tarpaulin; just below them shone the metallic glint of his pistol barrel. The boatman was trembling and pretending to fuss with the engine.

The harbor's glassy waters were casting a perfect reflection of the junk from Yokohama, even reproducing the coop of chickens on her fo'c'sle, which were stretching and flapping their wings in the warm morning sun.

Contrary to all expectations, no one hailed, and when Hugh North hurriedly scanned the length of the rail he could not even see a head. A poignant fear stabbed his consciousness. Had the crew taken fright and cleared out? If so, they certainly would not have encumbered themselves with a prisoner. North swallowed hard once or twice. Certainly it was inexplicable that, with matters so tense, no one should be on deck. Was this the right junk? A doubt shook him until he scrutinized the rapidly nearing pilot ladder. Two, four, six, fourteen, eighteen, twenty steps. Yes, by God, and its treads were new.

Skillfully he maneuvered the launch to the ladder's foot, and Yu Shih whispered, "Boatman very frightened, no trouble."

Alertly Duveen came forward with his gun out, thereby earning some curious looks from a bare-breasted slattern busily washing clothes on the stern of a slipper boat some thirty yards away. Quite calmly the man who looked like Mr Hsing brought his automatic's butt down on the boatman's head, hard, and the pock-marked man slumped forward, his flat nose nuzzling the motionless flywheel.

North, as he started up the ladder, wondered; the Chinese are notoriously thin skulled. A sharp hail from another boat drew from Yu Shih a sibilant curse.

"Quick! tajên, that brother of thieves hails this craft in warning!"

Crossing the rail, North appreciated, would be his most ticklish job; if the junk's crew were merely biding their time they could pick him off at that moment with the ease of a boy taking an apple from a bough. The sunlight, however, wrought no furtive shadows on the deck; North's heart sank. Beyond a single set of footprints, the beading of dawn dew *had not been disturbed!*

"They've skipped," was his bitter diagnosis as he waved up Duveen and all but one of the detectives. Then all at once the subdued sound of a voice somewhere below forced a revision of his opinion. "Going to try to catch us below decks," he breathed to the diligent C.I.D. man. "Less risky than putting up a fight on deck."

"Fancy that's their idea," the Englishman said, and his cheek muscles tightened a little. "Now if you hear a whistle," he instructed his three beady-eyed but otherwise impassive followers, "come below and come fast."

North sent a man forward to guard the fo'c'sle companion, another one aft and posted Yu Shih at the main hatch, then, stooping, unlaced and removed his shoes.

"Better give 'em the least warning possible, Duveen."

"Right-o. They'll kill, given half a chance." Duveen's blue eyes were not so mild looking now.

A smell of scorched flesh was very faint at the entrance to the main companion, but it was enough to set sweat breaking out on North's palms. Damn the brutes, they hadn't even waited until eight! As, preceded by their shadows, he and Duveen tiptoed below he could see some of the ruddiness fading from Duveen's face. He, too, had guessed what must be taking place down there.

"Must be somewhere amidships," breathed the Intelligence officer, his eyes alone successfully piercing the semigloom. Faugh! The dreadful reek grew stronger, overpowering the familiar smells of pearl oyster slime and ginger.

Somewhere ahead down this passage could be heard a low mumble as of men in tense consultation, then a voice spoke in strident, cackling Chinese.

Breathing shallowly, eyes ranging along a series of doors, North put his head close to Duveen's, raised brows in inquiry.

"The bloody swine!" panted the chief inspector. "He said, 'This time she shall suffer greatly.'"

Again a number of people all spoke at once, filling the hull with their gabbling. If a white man was beyond that crude teak door he was speaking in the vernacular.

"They're going to work," Duveen panted, an ugly set to his wide mouth. "Fellow said something about lifting or raising her."

The scorched odor grew more noxious, and a steel band seemed to clamp about North's chest when he detected a soft hissing sound as a thumping and shuffling of feet in the cabin made it easy for the boarders to close in. Suddenly they halted.

Through a crescendo of Chinese voices filtered a woman's voice, apprehensive but disdainful. "Go ahead! Do your damnedest. I'm not quitting!"

Five feet short of the door Hugh North paused and, wetting his lips, sought Duveen's eyes; the other man nodded and visibly braced himself. Shifting his Webley to his left hand, the man from G-2 gripped the door's greasy wooden latch, lifted it and very, very slowly drew the panels towards him.

Save for a small slapping sound, breathless stillness ruled in the cabin, but the effluvia of many unwashed and perspiring men, of rank tobacco smoke and stale food came creeping out into the corridor. The first thing the boarders beheld was the sweaty, bronze-hued shoulder blades of a man standing bent far forward and braced against the shoulders of a seated figure in a sort of ragged turban. Then a tense semicircle of men, motionless as figures in a wax-work group, came into view, among them an individual who, judging from a soiled apron about his waist, must be the ship's cook.

Metal clattered, and as if controlled by a single in-

visible wire all the yellow and brown faces bent forward
a few inches. Suddenly he in front of the door pushed
further into the cabin and disclosed to North's thunder-
struck gaze a vision of Connie Holden, very small and
bright lipped, seated at a table and hemmed in by
wholly absorbed, lynx-eyed Chinese. In front of her lay
a small mound of silver, bills and trinkets. Apparently
still clad in no more than nightgown and coat, she
shoved aside hair tumbled in bright confusion over her
fur collar.

From where he stood, absolutely unnoticed in the
doorway, North counted nine players and three on-
lookers; most of them carried knives or pistols in their
belts and wore odd scraps of gray cotton clothing. An
insane desire to laugh all but conquered his self-control
when Connie shoved a grimy five-pound note out onto
the table ere she pulled a crumpled cigarette from her
coat pocket. Without taking his eyes off the game a
gap-toothed seaman hurriedly lit a match for her. Connie nodded her thanks and, pushing the hair out of her
eyes, sat back, studying the flat, utterly expressionless
faces around the board.

"So you will get tough? All right, I'll raise you," she
announced, whereupon the best dressed of the lot, a big
fellow talking the Yangtze dialect, translated for the
benefit of his men.

The scene in this smoky little cabin was outrageous,
absurd; yet North, well aware of the average Chinaman's insane love of gambling, understood the possibility of it. No other power on earth could have drawn
the watchmen from the deck and the cook from his
galley.

Daylight beating in through a port glanced on the naked shoulders of a Manchu who at some time had lost most of his left ear when, wooden faced, he drew a clasp knife, hacked four links from a heavy gold chain and threw them onto the five-pound note. All the other players save the well-dressed man dropped out.

North could feel Duveen staring at him, but for the life of him he couldn't interrupt that game.

"Raise you, Charlie." With a slim forefinger Connie pushed a pair of rings out onto the greasy board. The well-dressed man nodded, tossed in a small pearl and said, "Call."

The Manchu added two more links, and the circle of impassive faces grew tighter. Connie blew a great burst of smoke from her lips and faced her cards.

"There! Aces up on tens, you yellow heathen!" And a furious squalling broke out.

So intent were the players that not one of them turned his head, but Connie, collecting her winnings, saw North. She waved a friendly hand. "Hi, Captain, how's about sitting in and giving a gal some real competition?"

"Raise your hands!" Duveen ordered in sibilant Chinese. To him this was not funny, and in succinct accents he told the men in the cabin just what would happen if anyone made a move. Then in answer to his shrill whistle feet came pounding down from the deck.

"Say, what's the idea?" protested the seated girl as, under the influence of the pistols, the players arose and lined up against the wall. "I was going fine."

"So it seems," North said. "But every good time must end. Come along."

"All right. Lose your shoes in a game?" And she smiled as she very calmly pocketed her strange assortment of winnings.

The Chinese sighed; they knew better than to move. Only the cook looked restive.

"Pleass, tajên," he said, "my b'long galley. Meat she scorch."

Aquiver with relief, North invited him to go to hell.

CHAPTER XVII

THEY SEARCHED the red junk down to her bilges, but never a trace was found of either Mr Hsing or the blond gentleman in the black leather coat, a fact which caused North acute annoyance. Time was flowing stanchlessly away, and he was very little closer to answering the question raised by Patterson's murder than he had been six hours earlier. Nor did it cause him any anticipatory joy to dwell upon the cablegrams which undoubtedly were piling up on his desk; even less was he inclined to dwell on the progress his competitors might have made.

At Captain North's request Duveen questioned the crew and as he fully expected heard these moon-faced individuals deny any comprehension whatsoever of the business in hand. Outwardly bland, the junk's skipper insisted he had merely received instructions from his owners to obey orders given by a gentleman known as Mr Hsing. Until last night he had never before seen Mr Hsing.

What really bothered the Intelligence officer most of all was his absolute failure to identify Mr Hsing's companion. None of the crew would admit his existence, let alone describe him, so he was forced to draw on his own meager recollections. Chinese, Germans and Japanese, North knew, were more prone to use the title, Excellency, than other nationalities. Um. What about those two or three little sharp inhalations he'd heard? Did they indicate that a Japanese, say Mr Tashima, might know something of all this? Unfortunately three hissing sounds really weren't much to go by, and there were many Japanese in Hongkong. He was still debating the question when he helped the Holden girl into the launch and bade a stalwart detective steer for the Harbor Office's wharf.

For a little Connie merely clung, trembling, to his arm, watching the red junk drop astern. At last she gave a queer little shudder and said as if to herself, "I was so scared I had to do something or go nuts; thought I'd play solitaire. Asked my guard for a deck of cards, and he got so interested I remembered how crazy the Chinese are about poker. I figured if I let them win my rings maybe I could get them to let me go—you like somebody you can trim. Well, I started in to lose and" —she gave him a wan smile—"so help me, I couldn't lose! Ever tried to lose? Why, I filled inside straights, three-card flushes, and when I threw away two of four fours I drew a full house! The Charley boys couldn't understand it and began calling to each other to come and watch. And were they nuts about the game! I'll bet you could have stood there an hour without being noticed. Whew, what a game! You'll never know how glad I was to see you standing in the door."

This sounded more like it, North reflected; she'd have been an utter fool if she hadn't really been frightened. Tactfully he postponed the business of breaking Tipton's death until they found themselves alone in Sir George Amberson's office. The chief inspector, he learned, with a tinge of uneasiness, had been summoned posthaste to Government House.

When, as tactfully as possible, he told Connie, she sat rigid, stunned into immobility. Never had he beheld a person go so pale without fainting. Strange girl, this: she didn't cry, only looked empty eyed. Then jerkily words began to fall from her lips in slow, colorless sequence.

"Dad killed himself . . . Dead . . . Never figured . . . work out like that. He'd be alive now. I—I'm a fool."

He got up and looked out of the window. Out there in a deluge of morning sunshine trousered coolie women were scrubbing door stoops, and slant-eyed urchins were shrilly peddling morning newspapers.

Blazoned across the front of them was the Tipton affair. "ANOTHER T.P.A. MYSTERY!" "AMERICAN BUSINESSMAN SUICIDE!" A frail little coolie, bent under two enormous loads of firewood in his carry pole's basket, momentarily blocked Captain North's view, then a man stopped just under the window. Beneath pictures of the Hongkong Clipper and a rough snapshot of Tipton ran a staring black headline, "TRAGIC AFFAIR ON ROBINSON ROAD. THIRD AIR-LINE OFFICIAL DIES. ARE OUR POLICE EFFICIENT?"

"You mustn't blame yourself too much," North said experimentally and did not turn around. "What happened was partly his own fault."

"Oh no, it wasn't!" was her bitter retort. "If I hadn't messed in——"

"Someone else might have stolen it." He felt touched, yet allied wariness with his emotion.

An examination of a presentation cigarette box on Sir George's desk indicated that the inspector general was not one to leave cigarettes lying carelessly about. There was not even a crumb of tobacco in it. Connie pulled out her case and flipped back a little arm composed of interlocking circles designed to keep the cigarettes in place.

"Have one of mine."

Absently the man from G-2 smiled, accepted it but forgot to strike a match in demanding, "Tell me, what do you know about Lebov?"

Her reply was not very prompt, but she murmured, "Not a great deal. Do you think he's after the secret too?"

"I'm sure he is."

She looked up in dull surprise at that.

"Lebov went on his own initiative, or because someone sent him, to delay your stepfather until the bank had closed."

"But who would have sent him?"

"Melhorne, perhaps."

"Why?"

"Patterson, under Stag Melhorne's orders, went that same evening to take E.F. 371, so Lebov *must* have told Melhorne. I think that's fairly clear."

The girl in the gray coat nodded, and when she mechanically brushed the hair back from her face some coins clinked in her pocket. "You didn't really think Dad had embezzled the E.F.?"

"For a while, but I don't now. Crooks seldom go

crazy over worry. Reputation doesn't mean that much
to them."

"Well, won't the others figure it out that way too?"

All at once he focused his eyes, found them on the
cigarette between his fingers and started to tap it on his
thumbnail. He looked more closely, and when he saw
the shape of the faint impression upon it he suffered
from a minor mental crisis and regarded the girl in the
gray coat with a new caution.

"I doubt it," North continued, "so you, as a possible
confederate, will have to watch out!"

For the first time he began to appreciate the depth
of his fatigue, and so he dropped into an armchair.
Watching the gray-faced girl far more intently than she
suspected, he resumed his comments.

"Somehow Patterson took that formula out of the
office, and I'm pretty sure he managed to get it as far as
the hotel. Am I right?"

"Why—why, what makes you so sure?" Agitatedly
she caught up a pencil on the near-by desk and commenced to draw many little crosses.

"His dinner-coat pocket was torn as if something had
been snatched violently out of it. Come now, didn't you
go up to his room right after the dinner party broke
up?"

Uncertainly her eyes sought the floor. "No, I didn't."

His sympathy, as well as his patience, began to wear
thin. "Oh, Connie, for God's sake, tell the truth for a
change!"

Her head snapped up. "Are you calling me a liar?"

"Something damned close to it," he rasped. "You

went to Patterson's room right after the robbery, didn't you?"

She took refuge behind injured manner. "What's the use of my answering you, Hugh, if you won't believe a thing I tell you?"

"You were in his room."

"I wasn't!"

Rising in the jerky geometry of extreme fatigue, he stepped to the door, and, calling Yu Shih, he requested him to fetch Exhibit F, a magnifying glass and some pulverized red lead. Then idly he glanced at her scribbled crosses and went back to his seat.

Once the Chinese appeared, bearing the desired objects, Connie roused herself, apprehensive and increasingly ill at ease. "What are you going to do?"

"Wait and find out," he replied. For the moment Hugh North could cheerfully have beheld this handsome young woman's ashes on a shovel. "I know you have been through a lot, but weren't you in Patterson's room sometime around nine thirty?"

In spite of himself he felt a sneaking admiration for the way she said no with the force of a man driving a rivet. Frowning, he used a pair of tweezers to pick up the cigarette stump marked Exhibit F.

"This, my charming, truthful friend, was found in Patterson's room with its butt moist enough to tell us it had been smoked within a couple of hours!"

In a sort of breathless way Connie pushed the hair from her brow and watched him. "That doesn't prove a thing, maestro. There's nothing on it to identify it."

He disdained to reply, merely spread a sheet of clean white paper on the desk top, then shook the red-lead caster, gently dusting the cigarette which he held at an angle of 45°. Once it was well covered he blew the minute particles the cylinder's length, repeating the operation until two marks rather like thick parentheses became clearly visible about an inch from the end of Exhibit F.

"See those?" He glowered up at her from beneath straight black brows.

"What do they prove?"

For all her drawn appearance and hollowed eyes he could barely resist an impulse to shake her. Damn the little fool! Why couldn't she realize she was wasting precious, irreplaceable minutes?

"See this skag you just gave me?"

In less than a minute he was able to develop exactly similar parentheses marks and angrily showed them to her. "Measure them. I'll stake my reputation they're identical with the exhibit. Give me your cigarette case. Come on, come on!"

When she surrendered it he, without comment, slipped the half-smoked specimen beneath the retaining arm. One of the linked circles descended, fitted, perfectly obliterated all sight of the red mark.

"You win," she sighed in a dim ghost of a voice. "Go ahead and arrest me."

"I ought to," he snapped. "You've wasted valuable time."

With a little sigh, eloquent of despair, she flung herself onto the couch. "I'm sorry. I suppose I should have admitted being there but—but I was so afraid I'd be arrested if I admitted it." Quietly she went on, "I—I was hoping I could repair some of the damage myself,

But now"—she managed a stiff smile—"I suppose it's
a case of 'the condemned woman ate a hearty breakfast'?"

"Don't dramatize," said he, collecting his materials.
"When did you go to Room 423?"

"About nine-thirty, I guess. I went directly from the
dinner party to his room and waited till he came in. I—I
was worried about him."

Oh, why the devil did she have to be driven to this
admission? A sudden rush of returning suspicions had
swamped his confidence.

"Well?"

"He was very excited, admitted having taken the
secret but wouldn't give it to me. In fact he told me to
get out!"

"And did you get out?"

"No!" She made a grimace expressive of utter discouragement. "I must have stayed ten minutes, pleading with him to give me it, but he refused, saying it was
too dangerous for me to have it for the time being. Then
he said he'd been shadowed all the way from the office,
that Eve Tanqueray was downstairs and had given him
a very queer look."

"Yes?"

"I got mad and reminded him he was supposed to
give it to me."

"*And he didn't?*" His look pinned her as effectively
as a bayonet.

Her slim hands tightened spasmodically on her knees.
"No. I don't blame you for disbelieving me, but I did
so want to repair the damage I'd done, by myself." Suddenly she got up and ran over to him. "Please, Hugh,

believe me. Let me help you. I'll go crazy if I just sit around thinking about Dad. Hugh! I—I'm *so* miserable! Please trust me!"

She sped over tó the protection of his arms. He said nothing, merely held her close, steadying the quiver of her slender body. At length she looked up at him, forcing a tortured smile.

"If you don't arrest me, I'll do anything to help you. Poor Dad! Do you suppose any of the directors back in New York will realize he gave his life for T.P.A.?"

"Probably not," he replied softly, trying to make up his mind. "Businessmen don't think along those lines. And now, Connie, tell me one thing—did you notice an egg on Patterson's desk when you went there?"

"An egg? Did you say 'an egg'?"

North said that he had.

No. Connie had noticed no egg, but then, she had been flustered.

"Now you're to go home," he stated, "and get some rest." His manner was intimate, very serious. "I'll probably want your help later on a delicate and dangerous job. Think you can face it?"

Coppery glints shone in her hair as her chin, small and deliciously rounded, went up. "Hugh, I've an awful lot of mistakes to make up for. I'm going to stick like— like cocklebur until I find out who killed Sam and took that formula."

North saw her to a taxi and added a few comforting words before quietly assigning her a detective, both as shadow and guard. This done, he departed for the laboratory where Dr Dixon made him welcome.

Present also were an anxious trio of men he hadn't

seen before. He was hanging up his coat when they bore down on him in phalanx formation.

"The name's Kelly, Captain, Ted Kelly, Columbia News Syndicate," the foremost announced, holding out a press pass in a leather case. "This is Bum MacAllister of A.P. This big gorilla works for Hearst. What about old Tipton's suicide—is it on the level?"

"Sorry . . ."

The Hearst man worked on his gum a moment, then said, "Don't want to cramp your style, Captain, but we've all gotta live."

"Three Trans-Pacific deaths are a news natural," observed the A.P. man. "Who killed Patterson? And why?"

North cast the syndicate men a compassionate grin. "Want to swap jobs?"

"No," Kelly said, "I wouldn't."

"Well then, stay put and don't go ramming around this lab. I'll give you the dope as it comes along."

MacAllister flashed a grateful gold-toothed smile. "Thanks, Captain. We won't cramp your style."

North, having donned an acid-stained smock, slipped on rubber gloves, then picked up the egg, crossed to a window with Dr Dixon at his side. Keenly watched by Kelly and his confreres, the man from G-2 narrowly scrutinized the gleaming white oval through a magnifying glass, then invited Dr Dixon to do the same. When neither of them discovered anything of interest the Englishman suggested the evidence be tested before a fluoroscope. Beyond registering a yolk and an air sac at the egg's end, the X-ray revealed nothing at all.

North swore briefly, lit a cigarette and riffled through

his mental files. Why *should* this egg have found its way to the room of a man who did not like eggs, who, in fact, was allergic to them? Possibly the ovum constituted a symbol and signal of some sort? Finding this train of thought promising, he climbed aboard. A sign? Um. A message? That bit of shell found in the office would seem to further the supposition. How could a message be conveyed?

"Got a microscope handy, Doctor?"

"Yes."

They repaired to a small room where North adjusted sundry mirrors and lenses and critically examined every inch of the shell by daylight. Next he switched out the lights and exposed the evidence to beams of light shot from above, below and finally from all sides. Overruling a mounting impatience, he revolved the evidence, fiddled with the focus screws, then nodded a little.

On invitation Dr Dixon removed his spectacles and, squinting through the eyepiece, deftly manipulated the egg. In the distance firecrackers sputtered and popped in celebration of some Chinese festivity, and nearer at hand the screech of bus horns and hum of traffic was growing steadily louder.

"Looks to me," announced the Englishman, rubbing his eye, "as if the shell's been cut in several places."

"Yes. Can't you make anything of it?"

"No. They don't seem to follow any line or pattern; look more like some odd shorthand characters."

"Made by a sharp instrument."

"What makes you say that, Captain?"

"Look carefully and you'll see scratches that are too sharp, clean cut for a hen to have used her claws on it."

Perched like a buzzard on a stump, Kelly leaned forward on his laboratory stool. "Maybe those scratches were made by tableware in the picnic basket that hen fruit came from."

"Not a bad explanation," grunted North. "They don't seem to make any sense—just a few loops and a couple of scratches at right angles; but to be on the safe side let's try a few standard reagents. Hell of a joke if we developed writing of some kind."

"Who'd write on an egg, with all the paper there is in China?" The A.P. man grinned and somewhat skeptically watched Dr Dixon select an array of bottles filled with various brightly colored liquids.

"Thanks, Doctor," North said seriously. "Suppose we try chloride of tin?"

After rinsing an ordinary water-color brush in distilled water the Intelligence officer dipped it into the chemical, then drew a loose spiral about the egg and held it to the light, all the while blowing to dry it. Would a line of letters materialize?

CHAPTER XVIII

To SEE YOUNG PATTERSON and Tipton go had been bad
enough, but what assurance was there that Swazey,
Trina or any other T.P.A. employee was safe? A new
load of discouragement weighted his spirit when no
reaction was visible.

Despite sinking hopes he repeated the operation with
oxalic acid, potassium ferrocyanide. Then in swift succession he tried the various other reagents.

"No go, eh?" grunted Kelly, climbing down from his
perch. "Damned shame! Had a swell caption set—
'Death Lays an Egg!' "

"Hard lines, Captain," condoled the Hearst repre-
sentative. "What you've got there is a piece of some
misplaced picnic."

Still North hesitated. At the back of his mind an idea
was struggling to take shape.

MacAllister begged, "Why not take a whirl at that
silk stocking? That woof's a dud; bet you a dinner at
the Peninsula."

"Being as I'm stubborn, I'll take you." Brows
merged, North stalked over to a shelf in search of more
reagents and read: Chlorine, picric acid, ether, alum,

218

sodium hypochlorite, potassium, perma—— His eyes
checked their progress along the shelf, flicked back to
the bottle marked "alum." In an instant he had it down.

"Chase out and fetch me some sugar," he flung at
MacAllister, whereupon that skeptic hurried out with
the speed of a rabbit surprised while lunching.

"What's up, Cap?" Kelly and the Hearst man hurried over to the lead-topped workbench, and Dr Dixon,
over the tops of his glasses, watched his collaborator
tilt a tablespoon of alum into a beaker.

"Just remembered something—happened during the
war." Enthusiasm had re-entered the gaunt Intelligence
officer's manner. "Kelly! Beat it. Find me a hard-boiled
egg; bring it back dead or alive."

The C.N.S. man stared an instant, then pulled on a
shapeless felt hat, flung his chewing gum at the waste-
basket and missed. In leaving he almost collided with a
young man, very breathless in his dark blue uniform.

The newcomer introduced himself and proved to be
Hal Spencer, the assistant base superintendent.

"Just had a cable from San Diego. Department of
Commerce's on the warpath and raising holy hell!
They're going to suspend our license if these deaths
aren't explained in a big hurry."

"Dear me, young man, the end of the world won't
come if they do," Dr Dixon mildly remarked.

Spencer glowered. "A suspended license and canceled mail contracts would be a damned serious licking
for T.P.A. The Hongkong Clipper has simply *got* to
take off as scheduled! Do something!" He caught at
North's elbow. "Do something—you've got to——"

"I will if you don't keep your paws off me!"

He in the blue uniform went an angry red. "Listen, mister, I'm telling you, you'd better get some dope on this mess or I'll——"

"You'll what?" Hugh North straightened, rather hoping for an excuse to dot this officious gentleman a couple. He was getting pretty damned fed up; a little workout would be just the thing.

As Trina had said, Spencer had no guts and took a backward step, mumbling, "I—well, I want that plane to take off on time."

"All right." North's voice, while not loud, was effective. "But I'm warning you to not come roaring around like that again. Now listen, Spencer, keep your personnel from talking, go right on as though nothing had happened and let me know the minute Mr Huston gets here."

"Huston coming! When?"

Everyone turned, and North was not a little surprised to discover Mr Paul Swazey standing in the door with an orange-bearded Sikh sergeant at his elbow. North noted several scratches and dull purple bruises about the operations manager's throat.

"Yes, meant to tell you," Spencer said. "He's another old Pan-Am. man. Used to be in Santiago. You must know him. Just got a radio. He's due on the Dollar boat day after tomorrow."

"Of course. Wish you'd told me earlier." Swazey looked distinctly annoyed as he shot young Spencer a quizzical glance. "Where 've you been, Mr Spencer? Tried to reach you at the airport. . . ."

"I stopped at the office a minute," Spencer explained,

then continued, "I guessed you'd come up here, so I dropped in because we'd better talk. The chief's cashing in this way sure has left things in a hell of a mess."

Swazey nodded. "Yes. There'll be a lot to do, especially with Mr Huston due in." Behind their gold-rimmed glasses Paul Swazey's eyes looked sunken and bloodshot as he hurriedly surveyed the evidence awaiting examination, flitted from the stocking to the scribbling and thence to the cigarette butts. "Have you learned anything from these weird-looking clues?"

"No," Dr Dixon grunted, "but we might if you gentlemen will let us get back to work."

At that moment MacAllister returned with a small paper, swearing with more vigor than fluency because he had trod on Kelly's abandoned gum.

"Thanks." North held out a hand for the sugar, but as MacAllister came striding up to the workbench his eye became attracted to a scrap of paper adhering to the A.P. man's sole.

"Some fools don't give a damn where they park their gum," growled the reporter. Reaching down, he pulled loose the scrap of paper and in doing so caused a rift among the clouds darkening Hugh North's comprehension of the case. The Intelligence officer, as he set to work, ran over in his mind every move Patterson had made at the Trans-Pacific Airways office. He saw various fingers numbed with the shock of disaster. There was Trina, leaving with Carleton; again his mental ears registered Patterson's "good night", his retreating footsteps, the way he paused at the head of the stairs as if he had intended to come back. *Why* had he paused?

"Come on, Mr Swazey," Spencer rumbled, "we'll have half an hour to gab before I've got to get back to the airbase. Have to test hop the Hongkong before the 'Diego pulls in. Lindstrom figures she'll come in round two-thirty."

"Be with you in a minute," Swazey replied. "I'm going to stick to the office and keep up the 'business as usual' fiction. The clerks and stenographers look scared to death. Good luck to you, Captain."

"He'll need it!" Spencer cast North a baleful look and disappeared off down the corridor.

Swazey lingered, eyeing the table of evidence with almost pathetic hopefulness.

"Are you making any progress?"

"You asked that before," North reminded.

"Yes, I know. But I'd give a lot to get this mess straightened out before Huston gets here. If you find anything you'll let me know?"

"Of course," North said. Then quite irrelevantly, "Well, Swazey, are you finding spring here as warm as in Chile?"

MacAllister looked up. "What do you mean warm as in Chile? This time of year it's colder down there than organized charity with a deficit."

"My error," North smiled. "Must have been thinking of Colombia."

Swazey nodded. "Good day, gentlemen. I'll keep in touch with you, Captain."

"The guy acts kind of screwy to me," the Hearst man remarked.

"You can't blame him," Dixon explained. "He's the fellow Tipton all but strangled last night."

"Yeh," MacAllister said, "I know. Guess that's why he's packing a gat."

A moment later Kelly reappeared with a pair of hard-boiled eggs and peered hopefully into the beaker containing the alum. Captain North added a teaspoonful of sugar, then some distilled water.

"Always meant to try this stunt before," he remarked as if to himself, "but I guess hell's got a lot of expensive pavement through me."

Selecting a clean pen from a near-by desk, he dipped it into the colorless fluid in the beaker and sketched the neat outline of a mouse upon the egg. Gingerly he placed it in the sunlight and then turned away from it.

"Want to give this a chance to dry," he explained and, murmuring something about a Chinaman and a music lesson, sought a private office in which he rang up Trina Sinclair at Trans-Pacific. She was there and said she had been expecting a call for some time.

"You're all right? You—you haven't been hurt?"

"No. My grandmother always said I was born to be hanged." He asked how she felt, and after learning that breakfast and a cat nap had refreshed her considerably he asked her carefully to examine the vicinity of the office's entrance for a radius of, say, twenty feet.

"Why, of course," she cried, stifling her curiosity with apparent determination.

She was to search for a wad of chewing gum which would be fresh and looking as if something had been pulled away from it.

She chuckled softly. "So the old bloodhound's still on the scent of that gum! Goodness, I'd have thought you'd have forgotten about it. Any suggestions?"

"You're likely to find it behind a picture, under a chair, a handrail or something of the sort. Please take a look now, will you?"

He lit his pipe and during her absence listened to the varyingly pitched voices of Chinese, Indian and English detectives in the corridor outside. On a scratch pad beside him he printed with painstaking neatness, "To discover who murdered Patterson is to learn who has the E.F.F." Beneath this rather didactic bit of prose he listed everyone who had had even the slightest opportunity of seizing the formula.

Then by considering the events of the last few hours he narrowed it considerably. One fact stood out in monumental obviousness: something unforeseen had happened, or the chase would not continue in Hongkong. Had Tashima, Lebov, Martin or Melhorne been in possession they would long since have sped far, far away. *Who the devil had murdered Sam Patterson?*

North dug his pencil point into the paper with vicious force and began to sketch a fearsome and anatomically incorrect skull and bones.

"I found it!" Trina's voice excitedly sounded in the phone. "Almost right away. How did you guess it would b-be behind a p-picture?"

"Tenth sight," he murmured. "Was it near the head of the stairs?"

"Yes, Hugh, and I've an idea I know what it means!" she added with a little flutter of triumph. "After Sam stole the formula he stuck the envelope with gum to the back of that framed poster, then went back and gave the alarm. Of course, when you searched him, you found nothing. But after I left with Carleton I'll bet he went out alone and lingered near the front door a minute. He did, didn't he?"

"Check."

"Well, that pause gave him enough time to pull loose the E.F. formula and clear out with it."

Though deep in conjecture, North admitted the soundness of her explanation. "Now listen, Trina, I'm sending up a detective to shadow you."

"What!"

"And I don't want you to put foot out of that office till I get there."

"Why—why do you say that?" she demanded, and the sibilant intake of her breath was quite audible.

"Because," Hugh North replied slowly and with emphasis, "I'm convinced that right at this moment you're in far greater danger of your life than Swazey ever was. Is Carleton there?"

"No, he hasn't sh-showed up yet."

He bit his lip and said, "Well, have him ring me the minute he does."

"But—but, Hugh, aren't I going to see you? Aren't you coming here?"

"I most certainly am," he reassured her in a lighter tone. "I'm on the ragged edge of the Willies—'less you hear from me, I'll hunt you up around noon."

Her voice was like a satin ribbon unrolling. "Oh, Hugh, come quickly; as soon as you can, won't you? I'm—I'm so afraid for you."

Thoughtfully Hugh North replaced the receiver. Well, that matter of the gum removed his last doubt as to who had removed the formula. Um. That probably meant Patterson had taken it to his room. Had he really been tailed from the office? Was concern for Connie's safety his only reason for refusing to surrender the prize to her? Just what had Connie really done up there?

Sighing, he went back to the laboratory, where he found Dixon and the reporters impatiently eyeing the test egg. The lines he had drawn upon it were dry, had wholly disappeared.

"Well, we live and sometimes we learn," sighed the detective, and amid a hush of breathless expectancy he used a glass stirrer to break, very gently, the egg's innocent-appearing shell. Lips pursed, he then commenced to peel the specimen.

"Look!" gasped Kelly. "Do you——"

Rendered in pale brown on the white glossy surface was the outline of a mouse, flourishing a very gay little tail.

"I should have thought of that." Dr Dixon swore feelingly and said, "Any schoolboy chemist knows albumen reacts to alum."

"But, but . . ." The Hearst man stuttered. "Did you see? The solution absolutely disappeared on the shell's surface; must have been absorbed and passed right through the shell."

Thoughtful little crow's-feet appeared at North's eyes, betraying his great hopes in the original specimen. "The Boche used to use the trick. I remember Bruce Kilgour's speaking of it. It's a smart stunt; you can't doctor that kind of message or read it and pass it on as a trap. Pretty good for a spy in a tight corner too. All he has to do is eat the egg."

Now perhaps he would learn who killed Trans-

Pacific's C.E.O. His supple fingers trembled just a little when he picked up the evidence from Patterson's room and prepared to delicately remove its shell. When he had done so all and sundry could quite distinctly read:

PATRSON: *Take E.F.F. 11 p.m. top floor 507 Upr. Lascar Row.*

"Owe you a feed," MacAllister groaned.

CHAPTER XIX

To look at Hugh North's pleasant brown features none but a clairvoyant could have guessed he was reacting to a sharp surprise and at the same time frantically searching his memory. Lascar Row? Ha! He had it now. Should he go there? He decided in the affirmative; it might, even though deviously, lead to Stag Melhorne, and Melhorne seemed more and more to be the man he wanted to see most of all. The absolute failure of the C.I.D. to locate, to even find a trace of, so striking a figure as the doughty ex-colonel gave one—as the French say—furiously to think.

No matter how one looked at it, the message was not of negligible importance, yet death had overtaken Patterson before he could crack the eggshell. Why? The chief engineering officer had not even been given a chance to obey his instructions.

"Lascar Row," Dr Dixon told him, "is on the edge of the Chinese quarter. The policee wallahs have a hard time there because it's one of those betwixt-and-between neighborhoods. Neither good nor bad. Almost anything can happen there and often does."

"Say, what's that signature thing down there?" inquired the Hearst man. "Chinese?"

"Looks more like a double cross," MacAllister smiled. "What's your guess, Captain?"

"Recognition symbol of some kind, I expect; to me it doesn't look Japanese or Chinese. In fact it looks like a Lorraine cross," he added for MacAllister's benefit.

Every head in the laboratory turned when the door opened and Connie Holden appeared, pallid· save for the scarlet splash of her mouth. She was dressed in a dark tailored cheviot and a black felt hat which boasted a jaunty scarlet-and-white ribbon, matching the vivid color of her lips.

Tragedy, however, lurked among the shadows of her large dark blue eyes. Defiantly she braved Hugh North's glare. For a moment he felt like exploding; the least this infernal girl could do was to obey. Then suddenly he foresaw interesting possibilities in the near future. He smiled broadly and made her welcome.

"Say, aren't you Connie Holden?" demanded the Hearst man.

The girl drew herself to full height and looked both handsome and appealing. "Yes," she admitted with quiet dignity. "I'm here to do what I can to help. My stepfather wouldn't have stayed sniveling at home with Patterson's murder unsolved and the company in difficulties."

Out came reportorial pencils and notebooks. They asked questions, lots of them. She answered patiently, giving Hugh North time to survey the depleted array of unsolved clues. Only the stocking and the scratch pad remained to eat like persistent mice at his peace of mind. He heaved a slow sigh. He'd like to tackle them at once, yet Upper Lascar Row offered tantalizing possibilities.

"So, you see, I—I just can't sit round like a bump on a log," Connie was concluding.

"In that case," North cut in, "we'll leave Dr Dixon to worry over the other evidence, and you'll come along with me."

Once the reporters had departed with their gleanings he slipped out of his smock and pulled on a tweed coat, intrigued to note how interested she was in the silk stocking.

"Where did you get that, Hugh? Looks expensive and kind of exciting."

"Oh, we found it lying around. Isn't one of yours, by any chance?"

Connie flushed. "What made you ask that?"

"It was in Patterson's room."

"Sam's room!" She paled, then blushed a bright scarlet at the implication.

"Yes. Ever seen such a stocking?"

Her rally was remarkable, one of those things with which she continually amazed him. "I've done some crazy things, but really, mister, I haven't begun washing stockings in a water pitcher."

Dr Dixon looked up from collecting the reagents. "Know of any reason why it might have been put there?"

"Big party, maybe," Connie suggested.

A small and devilish smile lit Dr Dixon's face. "That might be it. Once when I was a student in Munich I drank champagne out of a slipper."

North meantime sent for Inspector Yu Shih, who appeared, cheerful as ever, much resembling a duck unexpectedly garbed in an overlarge striped suit. He said he needed three more men—Chinese.

"Yes, tajên, they wait in hall."

"Well, let's go." North started for the door.

Cried Connie, "Hey! Wait for baby."

Her matter-of-fact tone astonished North. Save for a strained look about her outrageously bright mouth there was nothing to indicate her violent bereavement. Once more the Intelligence officer found himself floundering in unhappy debate concerning this girl who sprang so lightly into the double ricksha he summoned. North then gave the address sotto voce and, sighing, settled back on its musty-smelling cushions. Yu Shih and his beady-eyed minions followed in other rickshas.

"You're a darling, Hugh. Can't thank you enough for letting me come along like this. I think I'd go crazy if I had to just sit around."

"I think action's the best pain-killer that's ever been discovered," North stated, taking her hand. "How's the old nerve?"

"Swell! Some breakfast fixed me up good as new," she assured him over the coolie's monotonous shrieks of "Way for the distinguished foreigners!"

Several times they escaped extinction by the narrowest of margins while skimming along Hollywood Road; double-decked streetcars carrying on their sides huge ideographs in black and scarlet bore down like juggernauts, only slightly less fearsome than countless motor busses and trucks.

A victim of rising impatience, North directed the

coolie down a short cut, but soon the narrow street became completely choked by an excited throng of Chinese. More people ran out behind, cutting off retreat, and heads popped out of near-by windows.

"Out of the way! Makee room!" North stormed, trying to see over the wide native hats. "Muchee hurry have got!"

"No use. There's a live-fish peddler ahead." Connie smiled. "Stand up. See that Charley with the big water jars? Well, he's got live fish in those—different sizes worth anywhere from ten to thirty cents apiece. Now look up there." She indicated a balcony on which a fat old man had appeared, bearing a hand line and hook. "See him drop down that twenty-cent piece? Now watch the hawker."

From a fold of newspaper the bony vendor produced a shred of shrimp and fitted it on the customer's hook. A great gabbling arose once the customer lowered his baited line into the nearest pot.

"Ah-h—look the big one!" sighed the crowd. "Fifty cash the yellow one bites! He's worth forty cents."

"No, the blue one is nearer; he's worth more."

Louder grew the uproar, and the old man leaned further out, intent on offering his bait to the largest fish.

Connie excitedly beat North's shoulder. "Bet you a half to two bits the little blue fish gets caught!"

"Taken. That yellow one looks powerful interested."

Six deep about the swimming fish swayed the crowd, silent now and quite oblivious to the angry curses of the ricksha coolies.

"Ho!"

The fisherman had jerked into the air a little blue fish.

As the crowd scattered, talking excitedly, North fished a quarter from his pocket and said severely, "There's skullduggery afoot, young lady. You *knew* that blasted blue fish would bite!"

She flashed him a derisive grin. "Mean to say you can't guess, my great, clever, detective friend?"

"No."

"Elemental, my dear Watson, quite elemental. The hawker feeds all the big fish and starves the little ones. The customers are wise, but they never kick—that's the Chinese of it."

Soon the ricksha re-emerged in the wider reaches of Ladder Street. Presently Captain North thought it wise to dismount. To allow his assistants time to surround Number 507 he and Connie sauntered on through a district in which motor vehicles gave place to wheelbarrows and sedan chairs. By the time they reached the entrance to Lascar Row the air had become redolent of spices—ginger, clove, cinnamon, pepper, in bulk unfamiliar to American nostrils—and pot gardens bloomed on all sides. In this district firecrackers crackled intermittently, and ribby mongrels nosed amid refuse boxes.

An old mandarin, out airing a cageful of songbirds, bowed and gave them a polite, "Have you had your rice today?"

This district, as Dr Dixon had said, was clinging to respectability with but indifferent success. Cheap little shops were beginning to crowd the handsome old Chinese residences whose gateposts still stood like the stubborn survivors of a doomed battalion. Children on clogs trotted past on their way to work.

Number 507 Upper Lascar Row appeared to be an old house converted into an apartment. A gay sign announced that Wong King, Antiquary, did business on the ground floor.

Yu Shih and a big detective he noted in a shop across the street, solemnly dickering for a pair of back-scratchers—lovely little ivory hands mounted in the ends of wands.

"What's the state of the Potomac?" Connie greeted.

Yu Shih blinked unhappily. "Pardon incredible stupidity, Miss Holden. Comprehension escapes this person of no intelligence."

North, on explaining, learned that nothing had happened.

"Well then, let's go," he was saying when the opening of Wong King's door held the detective and his companions in their tracks. A woman was hesitating in the entrance, as if doubtful of the weather, though only the clearest of sunshine was drenching the street in an amber shower bath, but ended by setting off up the sidewalk, a chic figure in white linen suit, wearing a white panama and carrying a stubby white parasol under one arm.

"Why! It's Jill Martin!" Connie cried. "Wonder what she's doing in this part of town?"

Mrs Martin's step was both lithe and vigorous, and at the corner she flashed a look back.

"She wasn't here so early just by accident," Connie said thoughtfully. "She's the laziest white woman I've ever seen about getting up."

That settled it. North detached the big detective
to see if she went anywhere but home and strode over
to the antiquarian's shop. Before entering the man
from G-2 paused before Mr Wong King's shop. Apparently he carried a side line of drugs, for with fictitious
interest he viewed a rhinoceros horn which, powdered,
was warranted to be a sure cure for debility; some
tigers' bones; dust from butterflies' wings; and a particularly repellent collection of dried herbs and roots
tossed in dusty confusion among other weird medica-
ments.

No one was visible inside except a very old spectacled
Chinese from whom North learned that the lady had
been there since early morning. She had been waiting
for someone, Wong King said, gravely pulling the three
long hairs composing his beard. No, he had neither
seen nor heard anything untoward.

With the aspect of the business in hand growing
murkier, North drew himself up. "I'll whistle if I need
you, Yu Shih. Come along, Connie."

"Hugh . . ." Her fingers caught his sleeve once they
found themselves in a dark but very clean hallway. "If
—if anything happens, don't think of me as——"

"Nothing's going to happen," he cut in. "You're to
keep absolutely still and wait down here till I whistle
or call you. And this time you obey orders. Understand?" In his voice was a note she did not recognize.
She nodded hurriedly.

An inspection of a short row of letter boxes, devoid
of markers, told him nothing. Once silence ruled the
vestibule he caught many faint sounds: the frightened
scurry of a mouse under the stairs, the singsong hum

of men talking somewhere. Completing his mental picture of this singular building, the smell of some not inexpensive perfume lingered in the air. It was remarkable, he reflected, how the other senses rallied when a man's sight was hampered.

With the sound of Connie's quick breathing in his ears he started upstairs. Again he silently cursed the loss of his .32; what an ungainly lump the big Webley .38 made in his coat pocket. Nor was it by any means as handy as it would have been in a shoulder holster. Who the dickens would he find up on the third floor?

On the second floor landing he paused, listening, but when no untoward sign met his perceptions he went on up into an ever-increasing gloom. On reaching the third and topmost landing, he again halted, peering at the well-polished knob of a door. This, then, was where Patterson had been told to bring the formula. Um.

All at once he thought he heard a faint sound in the room beyond; a sort of scraping, dragging noise. Beyond cocking the .38, Hugh North made no further preparations, but as he reached for the knob a premonition shut down upon him like a cold and chilling fog. Using the utmost care, he very slowly revolved the knob.

To his surprise the door gave, quietly, easily.

CHAPTER XX

THE INSTANT he opened the door he was greeted by an aura of luxury, feminine in essence and tinctured with expensive perfume, oily, chintzy-smelling upholstery, bath salts and a general atmosphere of warmth and dryness. A rug made of young camel's skin muffled his tread when he crossed the threshold, and overhead an exquisitely delicate Chinese lamp swayed ever so lightly in the draft he created.

Again he heard that dull thump-thumping sound, and though he kept the Webley in his pocket, he threw off the safety catch. Gingerly Hugh North advanced into a room which, though cast into gloom by closed shutters, was nevertheless bright enough to reveal "moderne" furniture skillfully arranged against a décor of light gray, vermilion and buff.

The case had yielded surprises in abundance but none greater than that of beholding Colonel Melhorne lying gagged and securely bound in the center of the apartment's gray-and-black rug with his dress suit badly rumpled. His eyes rolled furiously, sweat beaded his dust-sheathed forehead, which, added to deep furrows in the nap of the rug, attested to the violence of his

efforts to inch over to a desk where lay a dangerous-
looking paper knife.

On a wide divan of vermilion silk the wildly disheveled
figure of Eve Tanqueray lay very quiet; she, too, had
been gagged and pinioned by bands of two-inch adhesive. Her hair ran like an inky waterfall all over the
bright silk, and her legs, protruding from a badly
ripped skirt, looked very long. By this light the metallic green finish on her nails appeared almost luminous
—and decidedly absurd.

Otherwise the apartment was in wild disorder, indicative of a search no less painstaking than that which had
taken place at Shameen Street. After diligently searching the apartment—four rooms and a bath any screen
star might envy—and finding no other callers, Hugh
North returned to the living room.

On again regarding Melhorne, he noticed that a lock
of sparse sand-colored hair had somehow become twisted
into a coy, Kewpie-like tuft so ludicrous that nerves
too rapidly released of tension sent him into spasms
of silent laughter. Great tears rolled down his cheeks,
and he clung to a door, shaking with inane mirth and
watching Stag get madder and madder but absolutely
unable to do anything about it.

From the divan Eve's lustrous dark eyes were begging for relief, so, controlling himself, he sought the
head of the stairs and sent a soft whistling note downwards. Immediately Connie's light footsteps started up,
three steps at a time, and in no time at all she had
appeared in the doorway, pink cheeked, distinctly beautiful in her alert attitude.

"Shut the door," he directed. "We're holding Old Home Week."

With the lithe grace of a deer swinging to an unexpected noise Connie turned and locked the door, then, noticing wet courses traced by his recent tears, she ran over to him, sympathy in every line of her expression. "Oh, my dear, what's gone wrong?"

"Nothing much!" He chuckled, pointing at Melhorne's furious figure. "But would you have recognized this overgrown Kewpie as the hard hombre who stood off a Manchurian division with two hundred men and a few machine guns?"

"So you weren't kidding me last night about his being here! I thought you were only saying it for effect." Connie was too upset to sense North's penetrating evaluation of her reaction.

In blazing indignation she stood above the prostrate Air Oriental man, and for a moment North thought she might take to kicking. "You damned liar, you promised to stay away! What did you mean by coming over here?"

The Intelligence officer mildly pointed out the prisoner's inability to reply as, above his half mask of adhesive, Melhorne's leathery features turned a deeper red. They must be missing some heartfelt if not original profanity, North decided. Connie turned away, her lips became a single red line and she swallowed hard two or three times.

"Now listen." North spoke crisply, in his gray-blue eyes a trenchant gleam. "If I turn you loose you're not to yell or kick up a fuss. Understand?"

Immediately both prisoners nodded with emphasis.

"Ladies first," he murmured, and when he went over to the lovely young woman he knew as Eve Tanqueray he perceived that in her struggles her fragile evening gown had ripped enough to expose a smooth, ivory-tinted thigh, some expensive lingerie and the fact that she had bruised her knee.

After a moment's indecision he decided on precautions in the interest of truth. "Connie, I'm going next door and have a chin with this dear lady. Since listeners overhear little good of themselves, we'll spare Stag's feelings." He jerked his head to the left. "Suppose you tune in something which might interest Stag, such as Patagonian beef prices or the care and feeding of infants? Then you can take off his gag and listen to what he has to tell you."

Once an elaborate radio had begun to bellow fluent Cantonese North gathered up Eve, a fragrant, sense-stirring burden, and carried her to a chaise longue in an adjoining bedroom. Employing considerable delicacy, he detached her gag of adhesive, at the same time noting how badly swollen were her wrists and ankles. Certainly the adhesive had not been recently applied.

"Thank you," Eve mumbled, looking up at him from weary, miserable eyes. "That wasn't much fun. I thought we'd have to wait for Soo-lin, my maid. She doesn't get here till around noon."

"Who tied you up?" he demanded, using her nail scissors to snip at the adhesive.

"Don't know." Then she tenderly tested her jaws and added in a flash of surprising savagery, "But you can bet we're going to find out."

"There." He straightened, once the tape was split, leaving ridiculous patches adhering to wrists and ankles. "I'll let you pull the rest of it off. If you've any alcohol, better use it."

Uncertainly Eve sat up, careless of a shoulder strap's slipping clear to her waist, and began rubbing her reddened ankles.

"Been like this since about eleven-thirty last night," Eve explained in response to a sympathetic glance. Characteristically she didn't complain and looked more angry than frightened. "Mercy, my gown's a wreck! How do you like my panties?"

Powder blue, North assured her while offering a cigarette, had always been a weakness with him. Fiction at ten of the morning, however, was not. Would she bear that in mind while telling him just what had happened?

Colonel Melhorne, she explained, had gone to—er—meet someone at the Pinnacle Hotel.

"Whom did he want to see?"

When Eve looked up from the swab of alcohol with which she was removing the gum from her ankles the faint obliqueness of her eyes became more pronounced. "Patterson. You know it perfectly well, Captain."

"Did he have an appointment?"

"No, he'd hoped to catch the Trans-Pacific man on his way out."

"What happened?"

"Somehow Patterson got out without Stag's reaching him, because when he phoned Sam's room there was no answer. That was why Stag pulled out in such a hurry."

Though North entertained many mental reservations about that explanation, he nodded.

"Since Sam had been given this address and was due for an appointment——"

"Oh, so Stag went up to the Pinnacle just to make sure Sam would find his way to Upper Lascar Row?"

"Yes. We came back here and waited only a little while before somebody rang my bell. Stag got his gun; a lot of people are after Stag, you know."

"Yes, I know."

"Well, it wasn't Patterson; it was a woman with a high fur collar and some glasses. She explained she'd a message for me and walked right in. When Stag turned to grab her a fellow who'd been standing flat against the hallway jammed a gun into Stag's back."

"You saw this man?"

"No, Captain, he wore a mask," Eve replied in such a matter-of-fact voice he felt she was truthful. Then she went on to say that after the first moment the woman also had put on a mask. She doubted whether Stag could have gotten a very careful look at the woman.

"What were they looking for?"

Eve shrugged and gave him a rather derisive look while walking a little uncertainly over to a clothes closet, in the door of which a full-length mirror created the twin North had sighed for. Inside several esoteric garments equipped with dangling garters which ended in mysterious celluloid contrivances met his eye—quite an assortment of them, flesh, white and black.

"You'd better ask Stag about that," Eve said as, with the utter unconcern of an artist's model, she stepped out of her ruined gown. Her figure, North decided, really was superb—mature yet youthful in the resilient line of her breasts. Firmly he turned aside his gaze.

"Did they find what they wanted?"

"No," Eve said, pulling on a saffron-hued Chinese robe heavy with embroidery. "They were very angry. After they had searched the apartment and us they just sat down and waited because, I imagine, they thought Patterson would come." Once more herself, she asked over the blatting of the radio, "I wonder what did happen to him?"

Had Eve been anyone else Hugh North would have credited her with genuine curiosity. "He's dead."

"Dead!" The girl's lovely Bacchanalian features stiffened.

"Yes. He died a little while after you people left the hotel." He leaned forward, a pleasant, appealing sort of man. "It was you who left that egg in Sam's room?"

"What makes you think so, Captain?"

"You just said Sam had your address and orders to come here. Ergo, you knew about the egg upon which that dope appeared."

From her seat before a dressing table dotted with bottles and jars Eve half turned, her profile glowing faintly bronze in the daylight. "You *don't* miss much, it seems. Out of curiosity, why couldn't Stag have left the egg—instead of me?"

"You were on pretty good terms with Patterson," was his rejoinder. "Besides, the airport records show Stag didn't get to Hongkong until 9:55. By then the robbery had taken place; his idea of an alibi, I suppose."

One of her feet lost a slipper, and meditatively Eve

wiggled her toes into the fur of the white bearskin before her dressing table.

"You're right," she admitted, "I did leave it there."

"When?"

"About eight o'clock. After he'd gone to the office——"

"You gave Patterson another egg, didn't you?"

"Yes, as soon as I got word from Stag that everything was set I looked Sam up—around six-thirty."

"Did you write those messages?"

She smiled at him over her shoulder. "Oh no, both of them had been written for days. Stag was very sure Patterson would play ball once he had lined up the Holden girl. Your friend in the next room had poor Sam running in circles, rolling over and playing dead if she batted one eye. To mark the instructions as genuine Stag used a Lorraine cross signature. You see," she added gravely, "we're not alone in our determination to get emergency fuel."

North cast her a quizzical grimace. "Lady, are you telling me?"

She gave him a glamorous smile. "There are pleasanter things I'd like to tell you."

"Thanks. Later, maybe. Let's get on with this. You came here to wait for Patterson. Patterson didn't show up. Two other people came instead, kept you prisoner. How long ago did they pull out?"

"I heard the clocks sounding seven. They were in evening clothes. The woman went away first and came back in a white tailored dress. Then the man went, and when the shops began to open up the woman disappeared. We've been alone ever since."

North heaved himself to his feet with all the grace of a horse arising from slumber, sighed regretfully. "Hate to go, Miss Tanqueray, but I'm going to leave you and Miss Holden to compare notes on early Minoan antimacassars. Feel the urge to talk over old times with my amigo, Melhorne."

"I'll see you again?" she pouted.

"Such is my fond hope," he smiled and went out.

When Connie, in response to his directions, disappeared into Eve's bedroom her manner was subdued. Apparently she and her co-conspirator had been having words warm enough to send an angry flush to her cheeks.

Without delay he freed Melhorne and went right after the subject.

"Well, Stag, did your callers find the formula?"

The big man winced in jerking free the last of the adhesive strips and glared. "Don't be a damn fool! I never had it!"

"Oh, lay off the song and dance. I know damn well you got it when you saw Patterson in his room." He hoped his voice carried more conviction than he was feeling.

Viciously Stag kicked a loose cushion, crossed to a tray of glasses and gulped the remains of a highball ere he growled, "You're all wet! I didn't go to his room. I figured I'd see him go out and tail him down here. When he didn't show up after a reasonable time I phoned and got no answer, so I figured he'd skipped by some side entrance." His brows met, and he seemed to be appraising his companion. "Suppose Eve's told you all that?"

"Yes. And a lot more. You'd better tell the truth."

"I always do." The big man impatiently stripped off his rather tight dress coat, then strode over to a desk, and his fingers had closed over a drawer handle when North said in a suddenly effective voice, "Just leave that be."

The other hesitated, turned slowly. "Just looking for some aspirin. Damn gag has given me a headache."

"Better suffer it a little longer, Stag," North advised.

With a look in his eye like that of a mule getting ready to kick, the other ripped off his dress-shirt collar and swung over to right the cushions of a dainty chintz-covered armchair.

"Some hell's delight, eh, Skipper? By God, that *chinchero* and his gal friend went through poor Eve's place like the grace of God through a camp meeting."

North relaxed in his chair, quietly regarding these hard, leathery features across the room. Certainly Melhorne was in a furious mood, and that triangular shred which was all an H.E. burst had left of one ear looked almost Satanic in this shuttered gloom.

"Hard lines, Stag," condoled the dark-haired man in tweed. "After you went to the bother of knocking off Patterson."

"Patterson's dead?" Deliberately Melhorne stroked his unshaven chin. "No wonder he didn't show up. Who did it?"

"Of course you don't know?"

"No, I don't!" A rasping laugh escaped from Melhorne. "I never saw Patterson after he walked out of my office in Macao!"

"Nuts, Stag! Nuts! You're lying."

The ex-soldier sprang up, and his long lip flattened, rose above irregular, tobacco-stained teeth. "By God, just one more crack like that and old times or no old times, I'll take you apart, see?"

"Try it any time you feel like it," North invited.

Melhorne's bleached blue eyes narrowed, and the two men stared at each other much like terriers debating a fight until some idea modified Melhorne's belligerent attitude and he grinned.

"Help yourself to a skag, Skipper. Should be some in yonder box if that hard hombre hasn't smoked 'em all up."

"Have you any idea who the hard hombre is?"

"No. But I'm going to find out, and he'll wish he'd never been born," Melhorne said. "Listen, Skipper, can you get this through your nut? *I haven't got the formula.*"

"Maybe not now," the man from G-2 conceded, "and that's the main point."

He was up against a stone wall, North realized, and didn't know what to think, so he tried another tack.

"Listen, Stag, we found a girl's stocking in Patterson's room, a stocking with no mate. Did you notice it?"

"No," Stag said and then promptly added, "because I wasn't up there. No, I don't know anything about a stocking." Visibly the ex-soldier's eyes became opaque, uninformative. "What are you driving at, Skipper?"

"We're very anxious to find out about that clue; so far we can't even begin to explain it."

"A stocking, and you haven't any idea why it was there?" Melhorne's interest was flattering. "Where 'd you find it? Under his pillow?"

"No, and you'd never believe me if I told you," North fenced, trying to see beneath the surface of the big man's manner.

"Well, that's one on me, Skipper! Me, I like a stocking better with a leg in it." Air Oriental's manager arose and swung back and forth across the room, absently rubbing his badly swollen wrists. "Listen, Skipper," said he at length, and though he desperately attempted unconcern, he did not quite succeed, "suppose you want to nail the guy who knocked off Patterson the worst way. Is that right?"

North said his assumption was entirely correct.

"Okay, then. If you'll tell me about how you found Patterson and how things were in his room I might be able to give you a lead. There's a Jap I—— Well, how about it?"

A particularly fearsome dilemma leveled its horns; very much did Hugh North want to get this hard-bitten individual talking, but was it worth the revelation of certain more or less important facts? While he debated he could hear the hum of voices in the next room; Connie sounded impatient, irritated, and Eve almost insultingly tolerant. Probably a nice polite cat fight was in progress.

North ended by sketching a picture of Room 423 as he had found it, and Melhorne listened avidly, all the while tracing snaky spirals on the desk top with wet from the bottom of a highball glass.

"So Sam hadn't quite kicked off, eh?"

"No. It takes some time for proponal to kill a man."

"And you said Sam had been writing letters?"

"No, I didn't say that," North corrected and wrote

furiously on his mental scratch pad. "Only that he had
laid out a fresh pen and some paper as if to write. It
blew all about the place, as I described."

The further the conversation progressed, the more
good natured Stag Melhorne became, and at last he
said, "Well, Skipper, I can only say this much. Patterson didn't kill himself; that guy was too much in
love. Men get rough, 'most always. A sleeping powder
sounds to me like some dame was in on the job. If you
want another tip you don't have to look very far to
find who did it; that gal's just a nut for thrills."

"Oh, that reminds me," North said easily. "I was
wondering why you thought it necessary to double-
cross her?"

The bigger man's good humor evaporated into a sort
of sullen wariness. "What do you mean?"

"Didn't you and Connie agree she was to get the
E.F.F. from Patterson and pass it on to you?"

"Sure," Melhorne admitted quite without shame. "I
figured that was my best approach to T.P.A. But she's
too crazy to trust to do anything important. Figured
the whole business would be simpler if I dealt with Patterson direct. You can reason with a man," he added
with a hard smile.

"Yes, I noticed you reasoned with that poor kid.
You sure threw the fear of God into him. Incidentally,
you weren't figuring—as you say—to save that three
hundred and fifty thousand you were going to pay
Connie?"

The other's scarred face contracted in a humorously
solemn wink. "Skipper, you're smart as a he-coon, but

whatever gave you such an idea? I wouldn't dream of it."

He got up but did not pull on his coat. "And now how's about going after some chow. After breakfast you and me can talk about what we can do about the wise buy who horned in and spoiled the game."

"Sure, Stag, that's a good idea." Unbuttoning his coat as he went, North sought the doorway, whistled once and called Yu Shih's name.

Melhorne was across the room in a flash and moving with no trace of his former clumsiness. "Hold on; what's the idea? Who's Yu Shih?"

"Detective friend of mine," came the calm reply. "Much as I'd like to arrest you myself, Stag, I've no official status here in Hongkong. Yu Shih can do the job legally."

"Arrest?" The other stiffened, his pale eyes flickering to right and left. "For what?"

"Compounding a felony. You bribed Patterson to steal something you knew wasn't his. Means around ten years."

"Oh yeah?" Putting all his force behind his fist, the ex-soldier lashed out.

North twitched aside and at the same time drove his left hand into Stag Melhorne's white waistcoat—hard. As the big Air Oriental official gasped, instinctively doubled over, North met his chin coming down with a jolting uppercut.

The whole matter was efficiently transacted so that even before Eve and Connie came running out of the next room Colonel Melhorne was lying on his face and harkening, perchance, to celestial music.

CHAPTER XXI

WHEN INSPECTOR YU SHIH puffed into sight he had with him a saturnine young lieutenant of infantry who did no more than cast a brief glance at Melhorne ere he clicked his heels and saluted. His Excellency, the Governor, said he, presented his compliments and would Captain Hugh North be good enough to call at Government House at his first convenience? Matters of extreme importance were to be discussed.

What now? Why couldn't he be left in peace to work things out? What in hell did they think he was anyway? Only with difficulty did Hugh North stifle a groan and give courteous assent. He'd have given his right hand for half an hour's sleep.

"I'll be in a car downstairs. I'll wait in it—don't want to interfere," the aide said, conquering a curiosity sharpened by Eve Tanqueray's appearance in the background. "You'll hurry?"

Connie, sensing his grinding fatigue, gave him a sympathetic little smile and murmured, "You poor dear. They must think you're made of cast iron! Is there anything I can do?"

Lost in her concern was the last trace of former

arrogance, and shrewdly he deduced that the thorough hoodwinking Stag Melhorne had given her was responsible. A brief deliberation revealed that two ends would simultaneously be served if she awaited him at the police station.

"You'll have Miss Tanqueray and Stag for company," he grinned.

He left Yu Shih and a pair of subordinates working over the unconscious ex-soldier and, blowing softly on his knuckles, clumped downstairs to an official car already drawn up to the curb.

"Sorry," he sighed and, dropping onto the rear seat cushions, went sound asleep.

Luckily the press of traffic was so severe that nearly half an hour passed before the aide gently but firmly prodded him back into consciousness in the shadow of Government House.

Brief as the respite was, it had cleared North's mind surprisingly, and the future seemed no longer to be of unrelieved black. The aide, a rarely tactful fellow, showed him to a lavatory in which the man from G-2 spent a happy, watery five minutes and as a consequence felt mightily refreshed.

"Feel a bit more fit, eh?" smiled the lieutenant, then conducted the guest to a spacious room in which electric fans droned and venetian blinds softened the sun's hot glare. Even as he put foot over the threshold an atmosphere of tension struck North with the force of a cold draft.

Like characters in a musuem display, various figures wearing whites or uniform stood conversing in subdued undertones. Among them North quickly recognized

Sir George Amberson, Paul Swazey and Mr Brundage, the American consul; all of them looking like pages from the Book of Job.

His Excellency, Sir Oliver Harding, Royal Governor of the Crown Colony of Hongkong, was a fine-looking man possessing square shoulders, a gray mustache and rather memorable blue eyes. Next the aide presented the Intelligence officer to a hawk-profiled vice-admiral commanding the Naval Yard and to a plump individual wearing a harassed expression and the dark blue uniform of Imperial Airways. Mr Brundage completed the round by introducing an American rear admiral and a mufti-clad colonel whose expression argued the imminence of doomsday.

In no time Captain North gathered that the official storm occasioned by Patterson's theft was reaching hurricane velocity. London and, more especially, Washington were aghast, utterly dumbfounded to learn that so vital a secret had been intrusted to T.P.A.'s very vulnerable Hongkong base. In twenty-four hours several departments of the United States government had begun to appreciate the overwhelming significance of E.F. 371.

"I won't bother you with these," Brundage sighed and, mopping his forehead, shoved a sheaf of radios and cablegrams into a brief case. "You've got enough to worry over."

North felt sorry for the efficient Mr Brundage; clearly the consul was aware his career would not benefit from this disastrous sequence of mishaps.

Sir Oliver's precise, carefully enunciated accents began, quelling the hum of conversation. "It was most

good of you to interrupt your work and to come here,
Captain. We, however, felt it necessary to get your
views concerning the situation. I hardly need to enlarge
upon the gravity of it. It goes without saying that what
you have to tell us will be reported to our governments
and will determine our course."

In concise sentences Hugh North sketched the record
of his endeavors to date, drew no conclusions. Never
had he been more conscious of observation—it was
though many millions of people were looking through
the few pairs of eyes in the room.

"I think we may be sure of this much. Something
unexpected, unforeseen by those who planned to steal
the E.F. formula has happened."

A bit of gold braid glistened, the fans whined on,
and His Excellency sat with one hand cupped to his
ear.

"If my suppositions are correct, Mr Tashima does
not possess the formula—or didn't early this morning,
as his kidnaping of Miss Holden and myself indicates."
Deliberately his look included the whole semicircle of
tense, perspiring and uniformly intelligent faces. "Nor
do I believe that Commander Tipton embezzled it."

"Might I ask why?" the inspector general demanded
softly, and in the background Paul Swazey's glasses
gleamed with an emphatic nod. "He had every opportunity, and several times his actions yesterday were not
above suspicion."

"The commander was too genuinely upset over the
loss." A grin ghosted across North's expression. "I
think Mr Swazey here will bear me out. Aside from
that, I've uncovered indisputable proof that Patterson

was the actual thief. It eliminated two of the possible suspects."

"Would you mind listing your suspects?" inquired the American colonel.

"Not at all, sir. The list includes anyone who had even a remote opportunity to lay hands on the E.F.F." Without pause he went on. "Now, gentlemen, I'm going to mention some persons who are implicated but who, to the best of my knowledge, do not possess the secret."

"How do you arrive at such conclusions, Captain?" the governor demanded.

"If certain people were in possession of the E.F.F. they wouldn't linger in Hongkong, Your Excellency. First there's Melhorne; though he might have hidden the secret before his rivals showed up and ransacked Miss Tanqueray's flat. There is also an inventor and his wife who are named Martin."

Standing a few feet in front of and facing the governor's desk, North could sense Swazey's surprise rather than see it. "They also just *might* have possession of it. Then there's a gentleman called Lebov, Alexis Lebov, and though I've neither seen nor heard anything concerning him, I have reason to believe he's still in town."

"Why do you think so?" demanded the American consul, frowning.

"I'm almost positive he's a confederate of Melhorne's. You see, it was Lebov who detained Tipton at his office and Melhorne—not Tashima, Martin or any of the others—who took action as soon as he knew the formula was in the office safe. Is that clear?" Apparently it was quite clear.

"That leaves on the list Miss Holden, Miss Sinclair——"

"Miss Sinclair?" Swazey blinked.

North gave no heed to the interruption, went right on. "Miss Valerie what's-her-name, who, I don't think, is really important, Carleton and yourself, Mr Swazey."

There was a stir in the room and a polite craning of necks. As for the operations manager, he caught his breath but as quickly relaxed, smiling. "Under other circumstances I might resent that, Captain; however, you have no choice but to suspect everyone."

"Ye can cross Carleton off yer list, Captain," the inspector general suddenly announced from the depths of an overstuffed chair. "Not an hour gone he was found dead in his room—shot through the heart after-r a terrific struggle."

A long moment North digested this, aware that no one else seemed surprised. "Any clues?"

"None. Except that a' his things had been rummaged."

Strangely enough Carleton's death, as North saw it, changed the situation hardly at all; indeed it rather bore out what he had been maintaining.

Sir Oliver shifted on his chair, commenced absently, gravely, to tap a pencil on the desk's edge. "It's this last murder, Captain, which caps the climax for us. It would be unlucky enough had Patterson, Commander Tipton and the others been British subjects, but this last crime will expose my administration to severe criticism from the Foreign Office. Unless the guilty persons are promptly apprehended and the stolen document recovered the colonial government will undoubtedly suffer a severe censure. Now please tell us frankly just what are the chances of your recovering the stolen document?"

Ere the lean figure before the desk made reply eye sought eye, and expectancy spread over the group like oil over water.

"This much can be said now, Your Excellency. I know who murdered Patterson, and there's better than an even chance the formula can be recovered before"— he hesitated—"before eleven tomorrow morning."

A faint sigh escaped Sir Oliver, and he tried to look confident as he said, "I'm very glad to hear this. I need not remind you that the colonial government is entirely at your service. You have only to ask for any type of help you need."

Buzzing with conjecture, the conclave presently broke up. Sir George Amberson, however, lingered, regarding his colleague with a canny Scottish eye.

"I caught yer signal," he grunted; "not that I wouldna' stayed anyhow. Whatever-r made ye make such an uncommon daft pr-romise?"

"Barring accidents, Sir George, I think it's not so crazy," was his firm reply. "Here's a list. Please see that if any of these people try to leave the island I'm notified at once."

"I will see to it personally." Very bleak was the line of the inspector general's jaw. "I suppose ye'll be going to check up on Carleton's mur-rder?"

The dark-haired American chuckled. "No. I'm going down to the laboratory for a while, and then I'm going to play hooky."

"Hooky?" Sir George lingered on the word as if he suspected the worst.

The gleam of North's teeth was almost boyish. "I'm playing truant, Sir George. A pretty girl and I have a date to go swimming."

"Swimming!" exploded the Scot. "At a time like this? Losh, mon, are ye clean off yer head?"

"It's entirely possible," the American admitted in all seriousness. "I'm told I do queer things on one hour's sleep in forty-eight."

"But ye canna do that! What will His Excellency think?"

"His Excellency thinks it will be quite all right— if that is what Captain North wishes to do," quoth Sir Oliver Harding, reappearing, erect and red of face, in the doorway. "I've always maintained that artists, women and detectives should be allowed to accomplish their ends in their own way," he said, as through the official veneer broke a very likable smile. "Have you ever played hooky with a girl, Sir George?"

"Cer-r-tainly not! I'll have ye remember I'm a married man wi' no time for such nonsense!" The inspector general spoke coldly, then blinked and ended by laughing uncertainly. "Och, Oliver, yer' pulling my leg again."

"Don't apologize, George. It's a blessing they made you into a policeman," laughed His Excellency and offered North his cigar case. "You sounded encouraging just now, Captain. I hope it wasn't just propaganda intended merely to keep up our morale?"

"No. I meant it, sir."

"Good. Come, I'll see you to the door."

In the laboratory at Central Police Station Captain North found Dr Dixon nodding comfortably in a swivel chair, his spectacles slipped low upon his nose, and regretfully awakened him.

"Any luck with the evidence?"

"No. Our cryptographer and I have been trying to make sense out of all those little triangles, but there's nothing to them. Don't mean anything at all."

"Then we disagree, Doctor. I think those scratchings are almost as important as that stocking over there. Have you figured out yet why it was there?"

"Everybody in the station has made a guess, but it's no use."

"In that case the stocking really becomes interesting, because I'm sure it was in Patterson's room for a purpose. Suppose we take a look at it? I'm in need of a lighter touch—something alluringly feminine."

Using a wooden paddle, Hugh North fished the evidence from the water pitcher, placed it upon a length of clean white blotter to dry after a fashion. First he passed the toe, then the heel and lastly the reinforced band at the garment's top beneath the lens of a powerful three-stage microscope.

"I suppose, Captain," Dixon smiled, "you'll soon be telling me her name and address?"

"If I could I'd keep it to myself. Have you noticed the quality of this stocking? It's damned expensive. Incidentally, it's been worn by a woman who fancies garters attached to a belt or, er—one of those foundation things."

Dr Dixon looked impressed, incredulous. "How can you tell?"

"Count the stresses on threads near the top."

The rubicund little man slid onto the stool and, using a glass rod, manipulated the exhibit with mounting excitement.

"You're right! God pity the girl who ever marries you."

"Not necessarily, Doctor. As Yu Shih might say, 'Of great sages love makes the blindest of worms.' How many point of stress can you see? It's important."

"Only two. Why?"

"Because this gal's garters have patented catches."

"How do you know that?"

"See these little triangular impressions in the reinforced fabric? Well, the ordinary catch leaves a round little bump that reappears when the stocking is wet. Faintly, of course, but still, visible. This affair seems to be almost chiffon."

"Tsk! Tsk! Your bachelor's insight amazes me, Captain." Fixedly Dr Dixon gazed into the filmy eyes of a Chinese criminal's severed head lying askew in its alcohol jar. "So round stress marks are usual, eh? Um. And this is an expensive stocking?"

"Yes," the Intelligence officer nodded. "Let's take a look at the other end."

So saying, he turned the limp silk garment inside out and felt of the toe; pursing his lips, he again sought the microscope.

"Look! Here's something. See those smears of red?"

"Yes. What are they? Can't be blood."

"Nail enamel. Gal didn't wait for it to dry."

Dr Dixon, however, was not listening. He had caught up a pair of tweezers and was dislodging a short white hair from the fabric of the toe.

"I say, Captain, this is interesting. It's animal hair, but only an expert would recogni:e the species. Bet your mysterious lady keeps a cat or a spitz which sheds all over her rugs."

Lost in thought, Hugh North straightened. "Maybe so. Well, we're getting somewhere. Now we know that the lady in question paints her toenails, wears a foundation or garter belt equipped with patented catches and presumably keeps a white-haired pet."

"Yes, Captain," sighed the chemist, "but I don't see we're any nearer to finding out why it was found where it was."

A further study of the chiffon stocking yielding no additional information, Hugh North dropped the bit of evidence back into its pitcher, glanced at his watch and learned that it was already twelve.

Yawning, he rubbed eyes which felt as if they had been dropped in hot grit and then put back in place. As he helped Dixon tidy up the workbench he pocketed the scribblings, then said, "Well, guess that's all for now. Thanks a lot. Better get some sleep."

"I could use some. Well, call me if you need me. I'm keen on seeing this come out."

The Intelligence officer sought Connie and found her very sound asleep on a lounge in the chief inspector's office. How young she looked, plunged into this deep sleep; so utterly at rest was she it seemed cruel to rouse her. Meditating on a phone call, he went out into the corridor and all but bumped into Trina Sinclair, who came hurrying down the hall a few paces in advance of Paul Swazey's uncompromisingly erect figure.

That her employer's death was a severe shock to Trina, North had known all along, but now violet shadows made mirrors for her wide-winged brows, and an ineffably weary droop tugged at her mouth corners. Certainly she was feeling the inordinate pressure of events, but when she saw North's sympathetic reaction her expression lighted.

"Oh, Captain! I—we're so glad to catch you in."

"And that's the truth, Captain!" babbled the operations manager. "The Department of Commerce has just suspended our Pacific Division license. They can't do this! It 'll ruin us."

"It's hard lines."

"You're damned right. Looks like T.P.A. needs some house cleaning."

"Here's one employee you w-won't have to w-worry about, Mr Swazey," Trina Sinclair announced in vibrant undertones. "A.W.'s killing himself almost got me. Now Carleton . . . I've had enough!"

Behind their spectacles Swazey's blue eyes widened. "You're not going to leave?"

"Why no—that is, oh dear, the crowd, the people I used to know are dead and e-everything is going wrong!"

Clumsily Swazey tried to comfort her. "It's hard on us all, Miss Sinclair. You know I had a time last night, but I'm not quitting. Getting any nearer to the formula, Captain?"

"Some."

"Well, then I won't pester you. Well, Miss Sinclair, let's be going."

North donned his most winning manner. "Mr Swazey, I wonder if you'd spare Miss Sinclair for a while? I hate lunching alone."

The operations manager blinked his astonishment. "But I need her."

"So do I, Mr Swazey. I need a little relaxation."

"When will you be finished with her?"

Drawled North with a twinkle in his weary eyes, "Maybe in an hour, maybe never. Quién sabe?"

"Oh, Captain!" Trina's expression was little short of ecstatic. "How awfully nice of you."

Swazey smiled, looking down his thin beak of a nose. "Well, turn her loose in time to help me make arrangements for transferring passengers and mail."

Almost jauntily they swung off, leaving Paul Swazey to look after them as if an asylum door had been left open.

"Well, Trina, what do you say to a jaunt over to Repulse Bay? We could have a bite and maybe get a swim later on."

Radiantly Trina cried, "Oh, I'd simply adore to!" She hesitated. "But you'll have to wait while I pick up my swim suit."

"Not on your life," said he firmly. "Time's short and life is fleeting, my girl, so I'll stand you to the scantiest and most fetching suit we can find at Lane, Crawford's!"

Their laughter drew echoes from the grim bulk of Central Police Station.

CHAPTER XXII

AT LANE, CRAWFORD & CO. North remained an amused spectator-critic of Trina's purchase.

"What color do you think should show my fatal beauty off to best advantage?" she demanded, holding before her a bathing suit suggestive of Gunga Din's uniform.

"I've a niggerish weakness for bright red; think your figure can stand it?"

The pretty Eurasian salesgirl produced a miscroscopic garment brave with an embroidered ship's wheel and murmured, "His Honor must be a diplomat."

Unconsciously, perhaps, Trina straightened, a proud, chic figure in well-cut Irish linens. "Of course he is. I'd die now rather than admit I couldn't wear one, so bring on your lions!"

A bathing cap and a pair of gray-and-maroon striped flannel trunks for North completed their shopping. On the threshold he paused.

"Och! So long 's we're playing hooky let's do it right. We'll take along a quart of the best bubbly we can locate!"

"Oh-h, champagney water? That does sound good, mister."

"Then you'll be plied, my good girl."

"Ah plies awful easy," she laughed, brown eyes adance. "I was feeling like one limp rag when you did the Boy Scout act."

"Swazey showing Legree-ish tendencies?"

"Yes. He insisted we go over to Kowloon," she admitted as they struck off down the street. "But I remembered what you'd said and insisted we leave word about the cancellation first."

"Good gal, but let's not talk about anything but what nice people we are. Come along and give me some ideas about champagne."

Trina hesitated, then shook her head. "No. You go. I need some war paint, and besides, I want to put in a phone call. Meet you at the liquor counter."

Once she had hurried off North used the phone himself, then invested in a quart of Bollinger and a box of chocolates garnished with an explosive red bow. Having secured a pirate taxi in the interests of economy, he went for Trina, found her brisk and smiling esoterically. Having also touched up her make-up, she presented a very pleasing vision in gray linens and a jaunty panama sporting a green quill.

Befort starting they dropped in for a quick cocktail at the Metropole's crowded, colorful bar and elbowed aside leather-faced government officers and prosperous tea brokers standing each other to burra pegs and stengahs. Their sidecars were so excellent that it was "only alcohological", as North drawled, to imbibe another.

The sun was warm, and ere the taxi had passed the Naval Yard and started along the Pokfulam Road, skirting the sparkling tides of East Larruma Channel, Trina twitched off her hat and sank back on the rattan-covered seat.

"Trina, you aren't serious about throwing up your job?" North demanded, his long body yielding to the car's motion.

"Yes. When the commander was alive I'd never have dreamed of resigning." She cast him an appealing look. "You know how it is? I've been out of the States a good while now. I—well, I don't want to be a case of 'missing too many boats', as the army people say."

Moodily North studied a neat world cruise liner as it went thrashing by on its way to dock at Kowloon.

"Somehow, my dear, I can't quite imagine you letting your self go, no matter how long you stay out here. What about T.P.A.? Thought you felt your part pretty important?"

The depths of her eyes grew opaque, inscrutable. "I did—when the old crowd was there. The men who did the hard pioneer work are gone—Donaldson, S-Sam and A.W. All of these horrible things happening has changed things," she murmured. "But I wouldn't go, Hugh, if—— We'll talk about that later," she broke off hurriedly. "Oh, what gorgeous flowers!"

A wrinkled old crone in patched blue trousers appeared, hobbling along to town, bent beneath a shoulder basket heavy with violets, jasmines, lilies and great glowing roses.

"*Mahu!* Makee stop!" Brakes screeching, the taxi came to a shuddering, dust-shrouded halt.

"What kind of flowers, O Shadow and Substance of Generosity?"

"They're all beautiful," North declared, "so let's not risk hurting any of their feelings." He would have purchased the whole of the crone's stock and poured it into Trina's lap, but the old woman obdurately refused to sell the last bunch of jasmine.

When North made no effort to persuade her Trina flushed and, looking very pretty, demanded curiously, "Why do you suppose she won't sell that last bunch?"

"If she did she'd have no excuse to go into town and collect gossip."

When the car whirled through the little bay of Aberdeen, picturesque with its festoons of nets, wheeling gulls and gay red and green sampans, a noxious stench of rotten fish lay like a pall along the road. The flowers became utilitarian; Trina buried her fair head in a glowing sheaf of roses, leaving North to hastily sniff a clump of jasmine.

"It's the pleasantest gas mask I've ever worn," he chuckled when the car dashed out of the fishing village's malodorous confines.

After skirting Deep Water Bay he glimpsed Repulse ahead, its smart new hotels and residences pleasantly clean and modern. Stretching along a wide sand beach, dozens of mat sheds were reminiscent of Florida and Long Island cabañas, but North found the local brown thatch cooler and more pleasing to the eye.

Trina's laugh rang out when her muscular companion paused before a shed set at some distance from the main group. Nodding to several rosy-cheeked English children who, with their governesses, were picnicking nearer the club, they entered a tiny veranda on which a luncheon table for two had already been set. Beside it a plump number one boy was enthusiastically shaking hands with himself and bowing low.

"This, my gallant captain, begins to look like a plot," she declared. "Don't know as I'd better step into your parlor."

"Well, then we'll eat at the pavilion. . . ." Very solemn of countenance, Hugh turned as if to leave.

"You wretch! You know perfectly well that if ever a gal was set to enjoy a quiet tête-à-tête she's present and voting aye. To your invitation I bow." She curtsied a very deep curtsy.

The number one boy never batted an eye when Hugh whipped off his hat and bowed from the waist, hand over heart.

Suddenly Trina looked anxious. "I—I hate to mention it, but suppose somebody wants to reach you?"

"They've only to ask at the pavilion. I told 'em where to find me. Now sound another serious note and you get——" Threateningly he held up a broad palm.

"Mercy," Trina dimpled. "Who'd think you entertained such stern ideas?"

"Ah, who would?" he chuckled. "But don't provoke me, gal, till I'm fed. Come on, it's lunchtime, as the tiger said to the martyr."

The meal was such a vast success that the little gold splinters in Trina's brown eyes shone with a new brightness.

"This is better than pounding a typewriter," she sighed and, accepting a cigarette and sinking back in the deck chair, considered a vista of the East Lamma

Channel and the lovely hills of Hanchow Island seen as through blue-green gauze in the distance.

Once the boy, moving on silent feet, had filled their glasses they lit cigarettes, and Trina talked under the stimulus of chilled champagne and his rapt attention. Gradually she disclosed a long, lonely struggle up from a girlhood embittered by the grudging charity of an aunt in Nashville and touched but briefly on poignant disappointments, on minor triumphs and at last on her eventual success and departure for Hongkong. Patterson she barely mentioned but when she did bitter lines aged her face.

Subtly North turned the conversation to a description of a routine day at the Hongkong office.

"Do you often work overtime?"

"No, Commander Tipton was navy enough to get the work done on schedule. Yesterday wasn't normal." Trina colored a trifle. "What with Mr Swazey's arrival and M. Lebov's lateness, there was an awful lot of work to get out. I had to scoot home to change my clothes. You know the rest of what happened that evening."

A grimace tightened the skin over Hugh North's high cheekbones. "Ah, Trina, if only I did, if only I did!" He sat up, stretching hugely. "Lazy . . . Warm, isn't it? But suppose we try a swim? Yonder waters seem to sing a siren song—or is it the champagne?"

Trina sprang lightly up, cast a quick birdlike look down the empty beach and turned, smiling. "Good idea. The body beautiful fairly craves dunking. Vale, vale!"

Once Trina had caught up her parcel and disappeared into one of the bathing compartments North sought the other, very eager to be rid of hot and rather messy clothes. Soon he slid into a pair of trunks and stretched a bronzed body and muscles any college athlete might envy.

Sitting on the mat shed's little veranda with a towel about his neck and looking like anything in the world but a badly troubled man, North draped legs across a deck chair and studied the beach with painstaking attention. Children and a few bathers loafed on the sands, and the area behind the row of mat sheds was untroubled by movement of any sort. Indeed all seemed well, and yet . . . Thoughtfully he fingered a hard lump in the pocket of a toweling bathrobe furnished by the management. Just what would the forthcoming swim tell him?

A small sound made him turn hastily; then his heart skipped a beat. Trina had appeared among the shed's shadows, her loosed hair gleaming with elusive blue-white lights. If, before, Tipton's secretary had been attractive, she was now truly beautiful in this red bathing suit which fitted her figure with greater fidelity than discretion. Gracefully she came over to him on long, ivory-smooth legs, the graceful lines of which blended into rather narrow hips, then swept triumphantly upwards towards high, almost boyish breasts. Under the candid admiration of his inspection she dropped her gaze, turned pink from her scanty red brassière to the roots of her hair.

"Oh dear—what's wrong? You shouldn't have made me wear red! It's a cruel color for blondes."

"Trina! You—why, you—you're gorgeous!" North

burst out, the natural shrewdness of his eyes melted in a sudden rush of admiration. "How did Earl Carroll and George White ever overlook such a bet?"

"You wouldn't kid a poor working gal?"

"No. I mean it. And say, it's nice to see a good-looking pair of legs without ugly garter marks!"

"Knows all, sees all!" Trina chided, sinking onto the deck chair's leg rest. "But I'm glad you think so. Round garters, says I, spoil the set of a gal's stockings and her circulation too. Let's go in, Hugh. I feel stickier than a carrot in an Irish stew!"

Legs flashing, Trina led a race to the water's edge, dove shallow, then struck out expertly for a raft. After he had again scanned the beach and found it deserted save for a distant quartet in cool-looking linens North set out in pursuit, vastly enjoying the water's refreshing coolness. In vain, however, did he attempt to shake off an anxiety which began to corrode his peace of mind. At length the presentiment grew so poignant he turned onto his back and, swimming thus, for a third time examined the beach. All he saw was the row of mat sheds, as deserted as they normally were in the early afternoon.

Um. So Trina never wore round garters? Well, maybe so. Next he considered the question of nail enamel. Um. She'd none on now, but then, a well-trained secretary would only use natural polish on her fingernails, and her toenails betrayed not even a trace of enamel.

When, dripping and breathless, they regained the shore and dropped onto the hot, clean sand North drew his beach robe within easy reach, ostensibly to fish a package of cigarettes from its pocket.

"My kingdom for a color camera," he lamented. "In that scarlet shred they called a bathing suit you certainly do things to an hombre's peace of mind."

Sinuous as a drowsy cat, Trina rolled over onto her back, to lie with lips parted and eyes reflecting the sky's flawless blue.

"How would you have me pose? Like this—La Gatta-like or McClelland Barclay-ish?"

"Either would cause a cardiac crisis. But mine artistic eye tells me we need something to tie the picture together. Say a bandanna and some bright red finger- and toenails?"

"You *would* pick on that," Trina plaintively complained, "knowing that all my beauty lies in a row of bottles in the Pinnacle Hotel." She rolled half over, head pillowed on bent arm, and began to trace a row of pyramids in the sand. North now was surveying her with fresh interest. "Ask me out another day, and my claws will match this swim suit to a T, although I don't generally paint my toenails."

"Another day I will," he began. "Why what's the matter?"

"Look." Trina completed a couple of loops in the sand, then sat up, dusted with particles and very beautiful.

North, turning, felt his heart do a loop the loop on beholding Lebov and Connie Holden drawing near! They were talking so busily that they had not yet appeared to recognize the sun bathers. A stride or two behind walked Mr and Mrs Louis Martin, very smart in their starched linens, which bore no trace of a visit to Upper Lascar Row.

They were less than twenty yards away when Mr Martin glanced up and raised a hand in salutation.

"Hello there," he cried gaily. "What kind of a work day is this?"

An artistic yawn escaped Hugh North as he rolled over to face the oncoming group. "Just a little breathing spell. Is inventing slack too?"

It was Mrs Martin who replied. "Why, my dear captain, this *is* a pleasure—a great pleasure. I was just saying to Louis, 'Here at last I've come across a man with more ideas and originality than you have, my dear.' I'm sure I never thought that day would dawn!"

"But that isn't fair," North protested, aware of Trina's suddenly frigid manner. "I'm told he was up late—or should I say early?"

The ease with which Mrs Martin shed the gibing look he gave her was remarkable. She continued in her flutteriest manner. "Oh, you naughty man, I've heard you were on another party at the Pinnacle last night, and you promised to join us. Was that nice? Why, Miss Sinclair, I didn't recognize you in those dark glasses. How *are* you, my deah? Louis and I have been meaning to look you up for the longest time!"

Behind its glistening eyeglass Lebov's watery eye caressed Trina's bathing suit. "Yes, mon capitaine, such a pleasant surprise."

Summoning an agreeable smile, North got up and shook hands with both men, but his eyes sought Connie, recognized in her temper a crouching storm. Why the devil had she disobeyed orders again? Didn't the little fool realize what she was risking? He thought hard, trying to find a sensible line of conduct.

"Hel-lo, Captain! I'm sure you've earned this little vacation." A suspicious sweetness was in Connie's voice, but a pinched look lurked about her mouth. "I'm sure Miss Sinclair is taking good care of you?"

"Oh yes, we get along famously," North murmured and damned her up and down. Why did she always have to go kicking over the applecart?

"How nice." Connie turned to Mrs Martin. "I was right, wasn't I? Miss Sinclair can't help fascinating interesting men."

"If M. Lebov is as fortunate," smoothly returned the man from G-2, "he will have no complaints."

"Hear! Hear!" Martin cried, his sharp features crinkling into a smile. But somehow he suggested an alert bird of prey as his look wavered between Connie and Trina Sinclair. "We're all lucky, and it's a grand day."

Beneath its white suit Connie's slim figure stiffened, and after treating North to a furious look a suspicious brightness came to her eyes, and her gaze sought a huge Shanghai junk sliding by, its matting sails glistening in the sun.

"Frightfully sorry I—we intruded," Connie said steadily. "Why didn't you tell them at the pavilion you were indulging in a tête-à-tête?"

The secretary tilted her head a little to one side, deliberately surveyed Connie, then said with fingernails in her voice, "How very well your mourning becomes you, Miss Holden. And it's so clever of you to use the Chinese color instead of black."

M. Lebov stepped into the breach before even North could say a word. "It was mos' kind of you, mon capitaine, to be so very tactful and considerate last night."

"A tragic affair," Martin sighed and again fixed his attention on Trina. "And you, Miss Sinclair, have had a wretched time of it, I hear. Has any progress been made towards arresting the guilty party?"

"Why yes, Mr Martin, there has been. Dreadful about poor Tipton, wasn't it?"

"Such a pity!" Lebov's pink countenance contracted in a rueful grimace. "Now for my land we will have to commence negotiations all over again. Besides, Air Oriental have raised their bid."

Privately North asked himself why the this-and-that Connie Holden should be such a fool as to be seen with these, of all people? If she had come in search of him what had been on her mind? From her expression he feared he would probably never know; she seemed utterly outraged to find him with Trina.

"Incidentally, I thought I saw Mr Swazey in the distance," Martin announced. "Seemed to be looking for someone."

All at once Hugh North perceived the one correct maneuver and said, "Oh, yes. Imagine he's looking for Connie." Firmly his look, threatening and pleading at the same time, caught and held hers as he continued. "The Hongkong Clipper's going to leave after all, and he's booked space for you."

"Why, Con-nie," Lebov cried in surprised dismay. "You told us nothing about going!"

For an awful instant North feared Connie was going to indulge in one of her unfathomable fits of independence and so fixed her with a tenpenny nail of a stare until, in response to Mrs Martin's excited babblings, she said a bit sullenly, "Haven't said anything because I didn't know I could get accommodation. It's so damn silly to make a lot of false starts."

"Do you know whether there is any other space left in the clipper?" Martin asked.

The Intelligence officer's bare shoulders glistened in the sun. "Oh, I imagine there will be. All this notoriety hasn't helped Trans-Pacific any."

Trina sat up, gently brushing the sand from her elbow, and flushed at Lebov's lingering look—this time it was not entirely appraising, North thought.

"I don't blame you for wanting to get away, dear Connie," Mrs Martin sighed. "You have been through a lot, haven't you? You aren't going, too, Miss Sinclair? That would be too much."

Deliberately Trina erased her carefully sketched pyramids ere she replied, "I'm not quite sure what I shall do, Mrs Martin. My immediate plans are quite indefinite."

As the party prepared to stroll back down the beach North said, "Sorry to bother you, Miss Holden, but the inspector general wishes to talk to you. You'll look him up before you start packing?"

Connie said she would, then a little defiantly thrust her arm through Lebov's and moved off, calling to the Martins. "Come along, sun's over the yardarm and it's first-drink time."

CHAPTER XXIII

"WAS I A HORRID LITTLE CAT to make that crack about her being in mourning?" Trina demanded contritely.

"No. She asked for it; Connie had no business getting personal about our being here together. Why, what's the matter?"

"I was wondering about Mr Swazey's being here."

"I think it's for the reason I gave."

"Really? I'd a funny idea you made that up about dear little Connie's wanting to get out. I rather envy her." Slowly she let more sand trickle through her fingers and looked fixedly out over the water. "Ugh, that Lebov creature is nauseating, and Mr Martin —well, he's got two of the cruelest eyes I've ever seen."

"Let's forget about him—all of them," he suggested in an effort to recapture their previous mood. "Let's get back to the shed; there's still a tidy ration of Bollinger waiting its doom."

In the bluish shade of the mattings he poured out two brimming glasses and stood towering above her, his crisp black hair showing less gray than usual.

"Well, amiga mía, what shall we drink to?"

"Why not to you?" Stepping quite close, Trina raised her glass and sipped, her fingers ever so slightly atremble.

"Same to you, my dear," he smiled and gravely drunk a little.

"Hugh." She hesitated in setting down her glass, then turned back to him. "I—I—will you help me? I-I've got to make a decision, probably the most important of my life."

Moved by an imp, born perhaps of Connie's illogic, he gently took Trina in wiry brown arms. "What's the matter, little girl? Lost your nerve?" He was amazed by the spasmodic way she clung to him, pressed her head to his chest. Suddenly he kissed her, and for several minutes there was no sound in the mat shed beyond a gentle rustling made by waves on the beach.

At length she whispered. "You l-love me, Hugh— just a little?"

He took her face between his hands, looked down, his damp black hair drawing into little waves. "You're perfectly sweet, Trina, and we do get on. It's such fun, what say we don't hurry matters?"

Pathetically avid of tenderness, she pressed so close that the bathing suit's texture seemed negligible and spoke without looking up. "But I've no patience left, Hugh. Life's tossed me about so much I—I'm not seaworthy any longer. Oh, Hugh dear, *don't* you see? I'm at the end of my tether. As I told you the other n-night, I—I'm tired of fighting the world alone. Honestly, I could have married a dozen different times, but—but none of them, I felt, were top notch—going places."

"But Trina dear." His voice was very deep and

gentle. "You hardly know me or whether you really
feel as you think you do."

"Oh, but I do!" came her flashing reply. "I do!
You're so—so damned understanding, and you've such
a perfectly s-swell sense of humor. Besides, I know
you're not afraid of man, god or d-devil! Oh, I suppose
it's risking everything to talk like this, but I can't help
it." She raised a flushed face, forced a timorous smile.
"I—I wouldn't wear curlers or a boudoir cap ever—
or ask where you've b-been the night before."

Such a scene not having entered into the remotest
of his multiple conjectures, he was for once at a complete loss.

"But Trina, must we decide so soon?"

"Yes, because . . ." She hesitated. "I can't get Sam
out of my mind, and A.W.'s madness. Oh, that was
horrible, ghastly! You hadn't worked day in and day
out with him for three years. Don't you see? I c-can't
stand all these dreadful memories without you as a
s-sort of bulwark. Oh, Hugh, *do* tell me to stay. I'll
help you, encourage you; then when this dreadful investigation's over we can go away together." He felt her
body tighten. "Otherwise, I—I think I'll take the c-clipper home and go on f-fighting, but after I get back
God help anyone who g-gets in my way!"

He was moved, more greatly touched than in years,
as he tilted up her chin and, looking into her eyes, said,
"Trina dear, stop and think. We're both tired, all
jammed up and don't really know how we feel. This
doesn't mean I'm indifferent." His voice deepened.
"God knows I'm not!"

The elasticity went out of Trina's frame, and, turning aside, she replenished their glasses with the last of the champagne.

"I suppose I should be content with that, Hugh." She spoke bravely, but there was heartache in her voice. "It's neck or nothing with me. I'm going to take the c-clipper tomorrow unless—unless you tell me to s-stay. I——"

"Jiggers! Someone's coming."

"It's a good chance for me to t-take the shine off this deplorable beak of mine."

She vanished just an instant before Paul Swazey burst in, coldly outraged.

"You seem to take a lot on yourself——"

"If you'll sit down," North suggested, "and tell me what's wrong perhaps the trouble can be straightened out."

"Spencer called me from Kowloon, asked me to come over for a consultation, but when I went down to the ferry slip a detective came up and told me I was not to leave the island."

"I'm sorry you were inconvenienced," the man from G-2 said. He then went on to deny that the order had been promulgated for the purpose of inconveniencing Mr Spencer and Mr Swazey but to observe the most elementary of precautions. The police had insisted upon it, not unreasonably; surely so shrewd a man as Mr Swazey must understand that? At any rate the embargo would be lifted at midnight.

Swazey's look sharpened. Did that mean Captain North had made more progress?

North said it might mean that.

Swazey then calmed down, even seemed a little shame-faced ere he fixed a shrewd eye on the champagne glasses, on Trina's comb and compact lying on a side table.

If a conference was imperative, North pointed out, Mr Spencer could be reached by telephone.

"I wouldn't have been so annoyed," Swazey said, snipping off the end of a thin cigar, "if you'd warned me. Why didn't you?"

"I had nothing else to do—Mr Swazey. Let's go on the beach; it's pretty hot in here, and there's a breeze out there."

"All right. Where's Miss Sinclair?"

"I believe she's dressing, so we'd better give her a clear field."

Once they were out of earshot North remarked, "Thought you'd like to hear the news, Mr Swazey. The Department of Commerce has reconsidered its decision to revoke T.P.A.'s Pacific Division license. Apparently they came to their senses in time and want the schedule maintained."

"Are you sure about this?" Swazey sat up quite straight.

"Yes. When is the clipper likely to be dispatched?"

"The scheduled take-off was around one-thirty to-morrow morning, Captain. I imagine Spencer will stick to it if weather conditions permit."

North yawned. "One-thirty! What an ungodly hour. Why?"

"Prevailing winds at that hour, I suppose, and it gets the ship into Manila at a convenient time."

"Mr Swazey," North began in a more confidential tone, "I wish you'd reserve four or five seats."

The operations manager uttered a mirthless little laugh. "Oh, there'll be plenty of empty seats, don't worry. We canceled all reservations this noon, so even if we phone the old passengers we're bound to lose a good many. You can't fill up a big ship like that on short notice."

"Too bad," the Intelligence officer sympathized, then added, "If you jump to a phone you could insert a notice in the evening paper, couldn't you?"

"That's not a bad idea, Captain. I'll do it." Paul Swazey pulled out an envelope and prepared to write. "What names on those places?"

"Miss Holden felt she'd better get back ahead to make arrangements for her stepfather's funeral. I understand the remains are to go home on the next clipper."

Swazey registered sharp surprise, then nodded thoughtfully. "Poor old Tipton. Well, I suppose the company does owe him that much. Who else?"

The Intelligence officer dug fingers deep into the warm sand ere he said deliberately, "Miss Sinclair wasn't fooling when she said she'd had enough. I tried to argue her out of it, but she's made up her mind to go home."

It was clear that to Paul Swazey this announcement was both unpleasant and unforeseen and that even after a momentary deliberation he didn't quite know what to make of it. Frowning, he said, "You're positive she wants to quit?"

"Yes. If you're smart you'll let her go without

making it hard for her, because she won't be much use for a long while. She's all broken up—you remember what Tipton was like last night?"

"Do I?" The operations manager's hand crept up subconsciously to finger a throat now marred by reddish-brown fingerprints. "All right, Captain, I'll take your word and have Spencer book her."

"You'll put their names on the passenger list the minute you get back? I don't want any slip-up."

"Okay. I'll phone the airbase right away. Spencer will be tickled to death the schedule isn't to be suspended. Now what about the other places?" Swazey, looking pleased, got up, brushing sand from his trousers.

"Some of the government people may want to run over to Manila."

In a very different mood from that in which he had arrived Paul Swazey departed, straight backed and setting down his feet with precision. Once he was lost to sight Hugh North heaved a little sigh of relief, then, arising, smiled to himself and sought the mat shed.

Trina presently reappeared with ashen hair flowing over her shoulders much as it had that time—ages ago, it seemed—when he had found her working late at the Pinnacle.

"How doth the heathen rage?"

North grinned. "He's calmer now. Lucky he's not fat."

"Poor Mr Swazey's new on the job and has plenty of grief," Trina murmured. "Did I hear him say something about going over to Kowloon?"

"He did—he changed his mind. It's too late now."

"Did he say where he was going?"

"Back to town; and so, I fear, must we."

When Hugh finished dressing he found Trina sitting on the veranda steps, wearing such a woebegone look. He gave her shoulder a small encouraging pat. "There's an end to everything nice; we've one swell memory for today. I have, at any rate."

Blindly she caught his hand, drew it to her cheek. "That's the d-dickens of it. I don't think I've ever b-been happier than I have the last three hours. Oh, Hugh, d-don't let me go on that clipper!" She almost wailed. "As I said, it's a real turning point. . . ."

"Life is full of surprises, dear Trina," came his soft response. "And I do like you the devil of a lot!"

At the Repulse Bay Casino Captain North deserted his rather monosyllabic companion to phone to Sir Oliver at Government House and then the American Consulate. When he had hung up a few minutes later the Hongkong Clipper had been promised clearance. It took no ghost from the grave to tell him that official pressure upon both men had become all but overpowering.

"There goes the girl friend," Trina called from the taxi stand and pointed to a car whirling by with Connie and her party. "Taking it hard, isn't she? It's just like dear little Connie to rush home out of the mess she's made!"

Until their taxi was speeding along towards Hongkong their several thoughts kept him too occupied to talk. At last Trina, pulling off the panama hat, settled lower on the seat with the wind whipping her hair about her forehead.

"If you decide to risk a Mendelssohn with me, Hugh dear," she murmured, "you only have to phone me or find me before the clipper takes off."

"What! You aren't *really* thinking of going on the clipper?" His astonishment was entirely convincing.

She gave him a wan smile, shrugged a little. "Why not? The quicker I leave Hongkong and all its horrible memories, the sooner I'll get over them."

"But Connie 'll be aboard, and you two don't get on."

"I know that, but the clipper's big, and I'll get Moose Hartman to let me sit up in his navigator's cabin. Moose will let me; I know he will."

He slid an arm about her shoulder. "Trina, my dear, I do wish you wouldn't insist on such a quick decision. Must you?"

"Can't help it. That's the way I feel, Hugh," she whispered and let her head come to rest upon his arm.

Again silence ruled the back seat, and the taxi sped on towards Hongkong, past groups of young people bound for relaxation at Repulse. North felt resentful; what a crime one was forced to consider the ugly side of life on such a glorious afternoon. Out on the East Channel gaudy green, yellow and red fishing sampans were heading homewards, and faintly over the water came the discordant singing of coolie women toiling at the sweeps. Above fishermen busy cleaning their catch hundreds of gulls screamed and dropped like ivory plummets in retrieving bits of offal.

Suddenly very aware of Trina's silken hair blowing across his face, he wavered. One could do far worse than to marry such a capable and ambitious young woman;

she'd keep her word, he felt, about asking no questions. Hurriedly he turned to other considerations.

Lord, though, how hopping mad Connie had been! Beneath her icy composure the late Commander Tipton's stepdaughter had been simply livid. Closing his eyes, he attempted to fathom her extraordinary conduct. Was she, he pondered, a bit unbalanced? Else why in the world should she have displayed the extremely bad taste of being seen at Repulse on an afternoon when her stepfather's suicide was yet blazoned across the local headlines? He didn't like her appearing with Lebov, even less with the Martins. Lebov? Bland and polished the White Russian certainly was, but cunning and cruel as well.

Before he knew it the cab was rattling through the sour-sweetish smelling streets of Hongkong, roaring down Queen Street past the garish façades of a hundred Chinese shops.

The question North was preparing to put had been silently debated all the way from Aberdeen, so, oblivious of the grins of passing motorists, he tightened his arm about Trina a little.

"My dear," said he, "while I can't account for it, I've a feeling you're very uneasy about something. Is there anything you want to tell me and perhaps are afraid to?"

He felt a quiver dart through the body, so lithe on the seat beside him.

"Why, Hugh, whatever gave you such a weird hunch?"

"I don't know," North gently replied, "but I—well,

I've met and studied so many persons during the course of my more or less sinful career I fancy I've developed a sort of sixth sense about such matters. If you've anything on your mind please trust me. I—I'm all for you, lock, stock and barrel."

"But not enough to marry me," Trina reminded. She was still after that, and the car covered some three blocks before she drew a long breath and said, "No, Hugh, I'm keeping nothing back. Your sixth sense must have gone a little haywire this time."

Even yet he would not be satisfied. "Think back, my dear," he begged. "See if there's a fact about this case you've forgotten to tell me. Suppose something might have occurred to you just recently? I'd like to hear about it."

"Really, Hugh, you talk very strangely." Her voice, brisk now, was no longer slow and soft, and he wondered whether that little stutter which came to her when she was excited would reappear. "What makes you so sure of your hunch?"

"Oh, several things. Perhaps the way Martin and Lebov looked at you; they seemed to begin wondering after you said it was possible you might go home."

"You're tired, Hugh," she declared with a little laugh. "Your imagination's been w-working overtime. That's all there is to it."

Only then did he abandon the subject, but about his eyes the tired lines were etched more deeply.

Crazily their driver swerved to miss the palanquin of a wealthy Chinese woman, and its bearers cursed vociferously as the car sped onwards. They had turned into Old Bailey Street when the girl beside North asked suddenly, looking up into his face, "Would you think me foolish if I asked the police to send someone to guard me?"

"Why? Are you afraid of anybody? Has anybody threatened you?"

"No-o," she admitted, reaching for her hat, "but after Sam and Carleton, I—I guess I'm just losing my nerve."

"You'll have your guard, Trina," came his prompt assurance. "Two, if you'd feel safer."

"Oh no. One would be plenty, I'm sure." Wistfulness softened her expression. "I wish you could take dinner with me. If it's to be our last night together it would be rather fun."

She brightened when he said he'd do his best. "If I can't you'll understand?"

"I wonder how late the post office stays open?" she queried as the now familiar outlines of the Central Station loomed above the traffic.

"Till six o'clock, I think. Why?"

Deliberately she glanced out at the harbor, then said, "The Dollar boat came today, so there ought to be some mail; thought I'd get my packing done first, then come down and pick it up before it's time to go over to Kowloon."

At the police station North descended and enlisted the services of a tough-looking little cockney to act as guard for Trina Sinclair.

"Except when she's in her room don't let her out of your sight for even a minute," North warned. "And if anything at all suspicious happens take no chances. Get help, then notify me."

"Yes sir." And, whipping on a shapeless and rather dingy panama, Inspector Doling got into the taxi beside the driver.

Trina did not even look up when Hugh North waved her good-by.

CHAPTER XXIV

"Hugh north, of all the crude people I've ever seen, you win the leather medal with palms and stars!" Connie Holden snapped when he entered the office she had previously occupied. "Thought *I* was going to help you. But you go off with that wretched little pencil jockey! Picnicking in a mat shed! Fast worker, isn't she? Who *is* your assistant anyway?"

Head tilted to one side, the spare figure standing before her commenced to pack a pipe so placidly it exasperated her more than a retaliating blast.

"You ought to be ashamed, lying like that! Where 'd you get the idea I'm taking the clipper tonight? Well, I'm not!"

"Come on, Connie; come on!" He smiled. "You look just like a kitten pulled over a rug by its tail, but a lot prettier. There's a good reason back of everything I said or did; so cultivate repose, my sweet, and cease lashing your mental tail."

She took a quick turn up the office, then stopped, glaring at him. "I won't, Hugh North! I won't believe a word you say!"

"Tut, tut, Connie," said he tolerantly. "Come to

think of it, *you're* the one who ought to be getting a good bawling out. What was the idea of disobeying orders? If I weren't so tired I'd take a stab at turning you over my knee. You were supposed to wait here until I came back."

She laughed a brittle little laugh that could not disguise a certain contrition in her eyes. "Oh, so the slave girl was supposed to stew patiently in town while his lordship disported himself with a wench on the seashore?"

His eyebrows climbed a good-humored half inch. "Dear me, Connie, you were sleeping so soundly—even snoring . . ."

"I don't snore!" she blazed.

"Just a small, ladylike snore," he insisted. "If I'd had any idea you craved fresh air so much I'd have detailed someone to take you for an airing."

"Inspector Yu Shih, I suppose!" She was trying hard to stay mad and not succeeding any too well.

"Inspector Yu Shih is very intelligent," North assured her, "and has, I expect, a lot more brains than most of the people you play around with! Now that we've both blown off steam, have a cigarette and let's get down to business."

"Oh, all right. I really *can't* stay mad at you in spite of your callous way of treating me."

"Sometimes it's kind to be cruel," he mocked. "Tell me, Connie, how did you learn where I'd gone?"

Suddenly she began to laugh, good-humoredly this time. "Good Lord, didn't your girl friend tell you?"

"No."

"Well, around noon she called here after trying the

house and woke me up. She told me you were taking her down to Repulse in case I wanted to get in touch with you, the smug louse! I called her a liar."

"And after that ladylike comment what did you say?"

"I'd no idea where you were, so I hung up. Then like a damned fool I called Jill Martin and went down to prove it." Angrily Connie snapped the ash from her cigarette. "Which was just what she wanted."

The Intelligence officer seated himself, leaned towards her on the edge of a leather couch and placed his hand on her wrist.

"Connie, I want you to take that plane tonight."

"Leaving Trina a clear field, I suppose!"

The gaunt figure in brown tweeds grunted his impatience and waved away the suggestion with his pipe stem.

"Please forget about Trina and listen to what I'm saying. If anybody asks tell them you're going home to prepare for your stepfather's funeral."

"Oh." Connie grew markedly quieter. "All right, Hugh."

"Did you call up T.P.A. and make your reservation?"

"Yes," she said, "although I'd no idea why you wanted me to."

"Good gal. You need only pack one bag."

"I get more than that on the baggage allowance. Why only one?"

"Can you keep a secret to yourself?"

Her manner grew more serious still. "Of course. I'm not a fool all the time."

"Well then—the Hongkong Clipper is going, but you're not."

"Not going!" she gasped. "Are you cuckoo or am I?"

"Neither of us. But it's the truth."

"Why, why . . . What's the idea?"

"That, my dear Connie, I can't tell even to you, my lovely little mutineer. I nearly had a stroke when I saw you on the beach with those people." Somehow he managed to inject a particularly sobering quality to his next remark. "I wonder if you realize, Connie, you very likely wouldn't be sitting here if that little stunt of your going on the Hongkong Clipper hadn't suggested itself?"

"Why—why no. Why?"

"You can believe me or not, but if they hadn't thought they saw a better opportunity they would have put the B on you—just as Hsing tried to."

At that Connie's eyes grew troubled and quite round. "But they didn't, Hugh."

"No. Because they weren't sure they could break you down, and they figured if you really were clearing out you'd take the E.F.F. with you. Get it?"

Connie's neat head inclined. "All right, I'll do as you say, really I will, and I'll even be nice to Trina if she shows up."

"A real penance," he smiled. "Yu Shih is at your home, and he'll stay with you till you come over to Kowloon Airport. Vaya!"

She got up, straightened her skirt with a quick twist of narrow-hips and, delightfully wrinkling her nose at him, said, "You have a pretty brisk way of giving orders, my lad, so just to show you I'm still independent, I'm not going to go for another five minutes—unless you bribe me!"

He wavered just a split second, then suddenly pounced upon her and despite outraged scuffles spanked her twice, then kissed her on the cheek with more force than dignity and propelled her to the door.

"Go along wid yez!" he chaffed. " 'Tis heaps of work I've got to do before the clipper takes off."

Once he had seen Connie off in a police car he sought Sir George Amberson's office and was not surprised to encounter a number of messengers in the act of entering and leaving. Sir George, it seemed, was taking literally North's plea that none of the suspects leave the island.

The governor's aide emerged just as Captain North drew near, and hurried out, mopping his forehead. He nodded worriedly and clumped off down the passage in a big hurry. Then Chief Inspector Duveen brushed by with a curt nod, to disappear behind a ground-glass door uncompromisingly marked, "C.I.D. Division No Admittance."

Once the man from G-2 had sent in his name a general exodus of various secretaries and subordinates preluded the appearance of the inspector general himself.

"Come in, Captain." He stepped back, then in an excitedly calm tone demanded, "Weel, and how fares this sorry business?"

"Too early to tell yet, Sir George, but we're making some progress," he stated evenly.

"Only 'some progress'?"

"Yes. To put it in broad terms I'm staking everything on one interpretation of the situation. If I'm wrong, well, I'm wrong."

Wearily the inspector general dropped into a chair beneath an oil portrait of Governor Sir William des Veoux, a rather sardonic-appearing gentleman, and motioned North to a seat opposite. Brows knitted, Sir George shoved aside a heap of telegraph and cable forms, selected a cheroot from a case which he did not offer and lighted it. Heaving a long slow sigh, the inspector general settled back in his chair and began talking to his cigar.

"Ye disappoint me, Captain. We've given you every help, and I thought ye'd have got more results by this time. Something definite, like an arrest."

The dark-haired man said nothing, merely stared at a bright lance of sunshine stabbing at the office's badly worn carpet.

"Government House, your consulate, T.P.A. and Imperial Airways have been snapping at me like a pack of hounds. Duveen is insisting that he take over the case himself. He was not pleased to hear ye'd gone romancing at the seaside."

"I'd good reason to go there," North interjected, feeling so tired he thought he would be gray before sundown.

"No doot, no doot," the Scot said mechanically. "Then there's yer State Department. They're making some verra pointed comments about the death of those three airmen. Yer Navy Department's already shipped a man off from Manila."

"Thoughtful of them," was the Intelligence officer's unconcerned comment as he finished loading his short-stemmed pipe. "By the way, here's the automatic you lent me. Got an idea now why your C.I.D.s so seldom go armed. I wouldn't either if I had to carry such mountain guns around with me. I've been walking crooked with the infernal thing, and I'd rather get shot than carry it any longer."

At this sudden levity the Scot's face turned the color of raw salmon, but suddenly a twinkle shone beneath his shaggy brows. "And where are the bullets? There were twelve."

Silently North released the magazine's contents, felt in his pockets and ranged the cartridges in a triple column of fours. "I may have worn a little lead off one of them."

"If ye have we'll no' charge ye for it," grinned the Scotsman, and, reaching into the drawer, he produced an object which North immediately recognized.

Not noticing his reaction, Sir George said, "We're rather puzzled about this."

"Why?"

"It's the gun wi' which Carleton was mur-rdered. For some reason the killer left it on the scene."

"I don't know what his reason was, but I can tell you whose gun it is," the Intelligence officer stated. "It's mine."

"Yours!" Had a live mermaid come flapping into the room the inspector general could not have looked more astounded.

"Yes. It's mine, all right. Notice the cut-down frame, the thin handle. I can even give you the serial number if you wish."

Dazedly Sir George stared at the blunt blue-black

weapon before him. "I see. This is the gun that fellow Hsing took away from you?"

"Yes."

"In that case," the inspector general said, "we'll know who should be credited with yon ugly bit of work."

"We know," politely corrected North, "*but we can't prove*, that Mr Tashima, having made one wrong guess, has made another."

"We'll prove it, all right, if we can lay hands on Hsing, and it shouldn't take long. His description's been broadcast from one end of the island to the other, and there's no' a ferry or a boat leaves without its being carefully looked over."

North was reaching for the .32 when Sir George interrupted very seriously.

"Is it no' the custom in America to pay a reward for the return of lost articles?"

"Sorry, Sir George," grinned North, tossing a three-penny bit onto the desk. "Here's a contribution to your retirement fund." Pocketing his cherished Smith & Wesson, he went on without change of voice or manner. "I've found out who owns that stocking we found in Patterson's room."

"Ye *have?*" The ash fell from Sir George's cheroot, and in mounting agitation he arose but sat down again and snatched a stub of a pencil from his waistcoat pocket. "Now yer' getting somewhere! Whose is it?"

"It belongs to a woman who paints her toenails for evening wear; I could tell that because a smear made by wet enamel was in the toe of an evening-weight stocking. She is given to wearing a girdle with two garters to a leg—something rather unusual."

"Girdle?" From Sir George's expression one might have inferred that such an article formed an obscure unit in a Dyak witch-doctor's regalia.

"It's a flapper cousin to what was once known as a corset, Sir George."

"Yes, yes. Get on wi' it, mon, get on wi' it!"

"The last and most important clue we got was the presence of an animal hair in the stocking's toe. . . . By the way, Dr Dixon deserves credit for that find."

"Aye, he's no' so dense as most Englishmen."

"Well, although no single one of these clues is in itself important," North was speaking slowly, impressively, now, "the sum of them is. Bearing those three leads in mind, I suggest we consider the women known to have been intimate with Patterson.

"Connie Holden, I know, paints her toenails, because I noticed the fact when I—er—dropped in at her flat last night. But on the other hand, round garters were lying on a chair, and when Hsing and his men were going through her bureau drawers I don't recall seeing any girdles tossed about. Last, and most important, she keeps no pets."

"That gives her one yes and two nos." Sir George glanced up from his writing.

"Next we must consider Patterson's ex-fiancée."

"Ye mean the Sinclair girl who wor-rked for Tipton?"

"Yes. Well, it was to settle some of these points that I took her swimming," North said but characteristically made no reference to Duveen's unwarranted criticism. "There were no marks on her legs, and she further assured me she never wears round garters."

"One mark against," Sir George grunted. "What about the hair ye mention?"

"Once I saw her wear moccasins trimmed with white rabbit's fur."

"Um. Sounds as if it's her stocking. Am I right?" Despite the inspector general's suddenly narrowed lids sunlight wrought two bright little spots on his eyeballs.

"Perhaps. But here comes an objection. Trina was very firm about not liking to paint her toenails. Another point. On a secretary's salary could she afford so expensive a stocking as the one in evidence?"

Sir George grunted his annoyance and nodded. "Well then, Captain, whose do you say it is?"

"Miss Evelyn Tanqueray's," Hugh North replied briskly. "She rates a plus on all three questions. When she opened the door of her bedroom closet I couldn't help noticing several very fancy garter belts and foundations. Besides, a woman of Eve's subtlety and profession dresses too carefully to risk lumpy round garters and the impressions they might make. Second, she undoubtedly is very skillful with the use of nail enamel; third, there's a big polar-bearskin lying before her dressing table."

"Seems plain enough," the Scot said, on reviewing his tally. "Does this mean you are prepared to charge Miss Tanqueray wi' the murder?"

"Not yet. Here's the odd part of the situation. These same three women *all* were in the hotel at ten-twenty last night."

Sir George wanted to know what ten-twenty had to do with the question, whereupon he learned that according to Dr Dixon's estimate the fatal draft of proponal

must have been administered to Patterson about that
time.

"What! Do you mean to say the Holden girl was
there?"

"Yes. It was proved she was in his room at least once
before she arrived the time you saw her."

"I don't understand." The inspector general was all
attention now, and his cheroot went out from neglect.

"Do you recall the circular impression we found on
one of the cigarettes we found in Patterson's room? We
commented on it at the time. Well, it was made by the
pressure of an arm or lever in the cigarette case intended to hold the cigarettes in place. Not by a holder
as we"—tactfully he used the plural—"had previously
supposed."

"And Trina Sinclair was in the hotel too?"

"Naturally. She lives there."

"What about Eve Tanqueray?"

In detail North described her part in Melhorne's
plans, how she had dined at the Pinnacle after giving
Patterson his instructions. Sir George had risen and
was trampling the waning sunbeam underfoot.

"Well, now that ye've learned whose stocking it is
what do ye propose to do about it?"

CHAPTER XXV

THE ROAR OF TRAFFIC, homeward bound and impatient, beat in through the window while Captain North deliberated. "There are further tests to be made on the stocking. But first, do you mind . . . ?"

He crossed to the telephone, rang up the T.P.A. office and, identifying himself, requested a reading of the Hongkong Clipper's passenger list up to date. When the booking clerk obliged in distinctly awed tones, North invited him to repeat the list for Sir George's benefit and passed over the receiver ere repairing to a window from which point of vantage he watched for the tall Scot's reaction. He was disappointed, however. Sir George only copied the list, replaced the receiver in grim silence and remarked that while he supposed Captain North knew what he was about, he, personally, was unco' damned if he could understand this nonsense about permitting the clipper to take off.

"Yer' not really sending Eve Tanqueray off on yon plane?"

"Not on your life!" grunted the American. "*I* put her name on the list. I presume you noticed Tashima's booked, along with the Martins?"

"Aye, but where's Monseer Lebov?"

301

North looked unhappy. "Don't know. Maybe he's smelled a rat. That's what is bothering me. Yes, and there are a couple of other people I'd like to find showing more interest in air travel."

And now suppose they looked further into the matter of the stocking? Sir George nodded, so for a third time —and the last, North fervently prayed—they sought the laboratory. Though Dr Dixon was absent, the man from G-2 seemed unperturbed.

"I don't know why I didn't think of this before," he commented, picking up the clean pen and eyeing it. "Somehow I'd an idea it was put there by the hotel people and that he'd never used it. Of course if I'd looked more carefully I'd have seen there was no dust on it."

"Of course ye'd nothing else to occupy ye," Sir George commented drily.

"Thanks—but that's no excuse. However, it did strike me from the start that *one* stocking was a lot harder to explain than two, and ever since we found it I've been trying to figure out why that stocking was in a water pitcher. Later I came to wonder why a half a glass of water should be standing on the writing desk. Also there were these." He pointed to the dozen odd sheets of paper. "Can you see anything on them?"

The inspector general couldn't, he admitted after examining them with minute attention. "What are ye driving at?"

"Well, Sir George, as we say back in the States, I may be barking at a knot, but I've a queer hunch that this stocking served the same purpose as Lincoln Trebitch's neckties and collars."

"Trebitch? Lincoln Trebitch?" Audibly Sir George considered in the depths of his throat, seemed to retire into a mental study. "Ah yes! He was the German agent they caught in London back in '15."

"Yes. Does that case suggest anything?"

"Ou—aye. Lincoln Trebitch. Seems to me the fellow soaked his collars, or maybe 'twas his handkerchiefs, in some colorless ink the Boche gave him."

"Right. Recall how Trebitch transmitted his information? He simply soaked his collars in plain water and dissolved the ink, then he used a clean pen and wrote his data across the face of an innocent-appearing letter."

"Aye. I remember," the Scot muttered.

"I suggest we try writing with water from Patterson's pitcher and see what happens."

Five minutes later Hugh North was blowing on a line of colorless characters and watching the inevitable "Now is the time for all good men to come to the aid of the party" fade from sight as they dried. Certainly that fluid moistening the stocking left no trace or odor.

"Until this bit of evidence proved to be Eve's stocking," North explained while switching on an electric oven, "the secret ink idea never occurred to me. Should have thought of it sooner, though; clean pens are unusual."

When the inspector general expressed uncertainty concerning the tests to be attempted North essayed to relieve his mind. "Since mild heat acts as a reagent for a great majority of sympathetic inks we'll start off with that. Then if nothing happens we'll take a whirl at standard reagents such as ammonium sulphide, ferri-chloride, ferrous sulphate and iodine. One of them ought to do the trick because the stocking very likely was impregnated with some basic chemical ink such as chloride of cobalt or protochloride of iron *if* it's been used as we suspect."

The Scot snorted disagreement. "Those are verra elemental types—too simple."

While admitting the truth of Sir George's observation, North still maintained that under the conditions a simple ink had most likely been employed. This was not wartime when everybody was on the qui vive for traces of sympathetic ink.

After glancing at the oven's thermometer North regulated it downwards, took a fresh grip on his nerves and cast a half-humorous, prayerful look at his companion ere he slipped his sample sheet into the oven. For all of a minute and a half he and Sir George solemnly discussed the merits of the Fan Ling golf course and then deplored the ball-losing proclivities of Chinese caddies. It was very hard to assume a proper nonchalance, North found, when he raised the oven's door latch, but he had to because the inspector general had studiously lost himself in a contemplation of the neatly ranged evidence. Quickly he jerked out a sheet of slightly yellowed paper—and found it blank.

Swallowing a heartfelt "damn", he hurriedly flipped it over. "Now is the time for all good men . . . ," he read, written large in his own handwriting. Now but one question remained; it was, however, very pertinent. Had Patterson been given time to write anything?

The collaborators fed sheet after sheet of note paper into the oven's maw; but just as often the note paper

emerged crisp, slightly browned, unmarked. Much as
fire creeps underground on a forest floor and smolders
ere breaking into scorching flame, so North's disappointed ire spread and waxed.

"I'm sorry for ye, Captain. Ye desairved better
luck," Sir George condoled when but four remained and
the clocks of the city commenced a straggling announcement of six o'clock.

Hopelessly the Intelligence officer was removing the
third from the last specimen when the inspector general
bent forward and, snatching out the monocle he wore at
the end of a narrow black ribbon, jammed it in his eye
ere catching up the still hot sheet.

"Losh, mon! Yer' overlooking something." His
gnarled forefinger indicated a dim line of scratches executed in the palest of pale buff. "We've not heated the
evidence long enough."

North jerked a hopeful nod. "Time's right to avoid
scorching, but Patterson must have mixed the solution
too dilute. The pitcher was half full of water, remember?"

"Aye."

In no time the sheet was back in the oven, with North
frowning over his watch and trying to forget the tattoo
his heart was beating. At the end of two minutes he
drew forth the evidence and both of them bent low and
read:

10 p.m. June 29

To the police:
*People have been following me ever since I got back
from Macao and I found the door to my room unlocked.*

Somebody's been poking about my things. I've a feeling something's going to happen pretty soon, and I'm right worried, so I'm writing to tell you I swiped the E.F. formula all right, but I'm only trying in my dumb way to help the chief. Honest I am.

Even after the Donaldson business A.W. simply couldn't or wouldn't understand how badly Air Oriental wanted to get hold of the E.F.F. Today I learned they have to have it or go bust, so I figured to out-fox them, but I guess I should stick to motors and engineering. Right now I don't know what to do, and I'm scared stiff. Connie was waiting here when I got in from the office, but I wouldn't give her the E.F.F. She isn't hep to what kind of a poisonous snake Melhorne really is. I think he's going to try to double-X me, so I'm writing this letter. He won't get me without a fight, though. I feel sure he's going to try to jump me. If he doesn't I'm watching out for that Martin guy. There's something fishy about him. There was nothing at all to that invention of his, but he's smart, though. Lebov too.

Hope you dope out this invisible ink. North ought to get it. When I was playing round with Eve Tanqueray she gave it to me when she went over to Canton one time and I wanted to write her on the q.t. Reckon she never figured I'd use it like this, though.

If anything happens tell the chief I'm trying to help him. Think I hear Connie at the door again, but I'm not going to give it to her.

Away down the street firecrackers crackled and spat in a magnificent uproar, and the discordant wails of a native band heading some *taipan's* funeral procession would have set North's teeth on edge had he not been so wholly absorbed in rereading the note.

"Don't know what yer about, Captain," Sir George remarked delicately, "but to my mind this clinches it. 'Twas giddy Holden girl did for Patterson. Can you not see her flying off the handle when the boy refused to make good his promise?"

North, sighing, admitted he could, all too easily. He himself had never been wholly convinced as to her attitude at any time. On the other hand, he thought Sir George must know that Trina Sinclair had been almost fanatically devoted to the company. At the office she had learned firsthand of Patterson's possible, nay almost probable, guilt.

"Devoted to the company? Then, Captain, why has she given notice?"

"I should have said Miss Sinclair's loyalty was rather to Tipton than to the Trans-Pacific Airways," North amplified. "She greatly admired her employer."

"But not enough to return the secret if she took it from young Patterson, and there's nothing to prove that she did."

He wondered how Trina was faring now. Poor girl, she'd seemed pretty wretched at their parting. Funny, her worrying about her mail. North's eyes wandered over the evidence table.

"What would you say about Miss Tanqueray?"

The Scot wrinkled his brow over Patterson's sprawling, rather characterless writing, then said without looking up, "A verra good bet too. She and Melhorne make a slippery couple. What are you frowning over?"

"I was just thinking this letter about ends our theory

that the stocking's owner and the murderer are necessarily the same person. Pathetic letter, isn't it?" the American asked solemnly. "Like the cat who chased the rat over the family's best china, poor Patterson meant well. Must have been pretty scared—to write like that."

At length the inspector general put away his monocle and stood very straight beside his desk, one shaggy eyebrow slightly elevated.

"Well, what now, Captain?"

"First I'm going to catch forty winks—I'm really dead for sleep. Then around twelve suppose you and I go over to Kowloon and watch the Hongkong Clipper take off?"

CHAPTER XXVI

THE SLUMBER from which Captain North of G-2 was aroused by a sympathetic young constable had freed his spirits of many weights, and once more his mind seemed able to function without an undue grinding of gears. Hunched on the edge of that same divan upon which Connie had napped, the Intelligence officer rubbed his eyes and stretched luxuriously while running back over the case. What a bizarre pattern the fates had woven since that first encounter in Connie's flat on Shameen Street. Patterson's peaceful death, Tipton's madness and—grinning sleepily, he recalled the famous poker game. He knew he'd never forget the picture of Connie sitting in that smoky cabin with her pile of winnings before her. Lord, but she'd worried him! Some letdown!

Yawning, he went out and washed before seeking a belated supper in a near-by restaurant. It was going on eleven, he noted. Funny how the streets here were all but deserted; at eleven the downtown of Peking or Shanghai would be ablaze and the sidewalks jammed.

Good thing Stag Melhorne was under lock and key, he thought as he tranquilly finished his meal. Things would be so very different were that hard-bitten individual at large. What would the Air Oriental people in Macao be thinking? Had someone else taken over? Would a possible successor persist in attempting to seize the emergency fuel formula? He paid his bill, comforted in the thought that if he could recover the E.F.F. neither they nor anyone else would get a second chance at it. Lucky the E.F.F. ingredients were not entirely identifiable when mixed.

His pipe lit and drawing freely, Hugh North started back to the Central Station, all the while formulating plans and very mindful that even a minor miscalculation might well permit his quarry to vanish into that vast hiding place which was China. Um. By all the rules a distinctly memorable scene should be enacted somewhere near the Hongkong Clipper's landing float. He found himself suddenly impatient to see the great airbase upon which this whole grim business turned. Probably it would prove to be no more than a typical Trans-Pacific terminal; the usual hangars, personnel quarters, floodlights, chemical wagon, gas tank outlets, tenders and illuminated buoys.

How strange so very much could take place in little over twenty-four hours. Yet if one considered the significance of the matter at stake it was understandable. In the rush of events, North reflected, he hadn't taken time fully to appreciate the E.F.F.'s colossal importance, and he found it disconcerting to realize that the course of a hundred million lives could be affected by what soon might chance in Kowloon.

In this great sleeping city not over fifty people were aware of Destiny's bated breath, but then probably even fewer persons in Sarajevo had guessed what impended when, on that June night, Gabrio Prinzip began studying Franz Ferdinand's route. Dizzying, appalling flights of fancy invited his imagination. France, Japan, Germany, England, America—all would be pitted tonight.

Sternly he ordered his thoughts back to earth. Um. Once he got to the airbase how could his men be disposed to best advantage? He yearned for those trained assistants still hastening down from Shanghai and Peking as a sudden fear etched deep lines across his forehead. Suppose Duveen and Sir George had been ordered to intervene or had taken such a step on their own initiative? Lord knew, they had every legal right.

It was eleven-thirty by the time he reached the police station where for fully half an hour he perfected his plans after memorizing the airbase's ground plan. There must be *no* slip-up! At length he pushed a bell and directed a stolid policeman to bring up Colonel Melhorne. No chances were to be taken.

He wondered whether Connie could this time be depended upon. What a strong, uncontrolled nature was hers! Perhaps—— He straightened, on hearing footsteps in the hall an instant before the door opened and Colonel Melhorne appeared, flanked by a pair of burly constables. The ex-soldier had sent out for some clothes, because he was no longer in evening dress and wore a tweed suit of rather hectic design.

"Come in, Stag," North invited. "Glad to see you looking so well. I gather your nap did you good?"

Direfully the prisoner surveyed that lean figure

before the desk ere he crossed the threshold. "Go to
hell! I owe you a couple for that sock."

"It's all right," North told the constables. "I'll phone
when I want you to come back."

After he had locked the door and pocketed the key
he gestured his companion to a chair. "Sorry you're
peeved about that punch on the jaw; but you took a
poke at me, you know."

Over the ex-soldier's battered countenance crept a
shamefaced grin. "Forget it. Only thing got my goat
was your bending my new bridgework." He seated himself on the edge of a chair, warily. "Funny, your sending for me, Skipper. All day I've been trying to get hold
of you, but those limey cops wouldn't carry any messages."

"What's up?"

Picking a bit of lint from his cuff, the bigger man
said, "I've had time to do some thinking about you . . ."

North seated himself on the edge of the desk and,
one leg dangling, prepared to give polite attention.
"I'm flattered you'd waste valuable thought on me."

The other hesitated, his pale eyes shrewdly regarding
his vis-à-vis. "Remember what I said, Skipper, about
my being a businessman now? How'd you like to come
in on a deal—a good sound deal?"

"You haven't lost your sense of humor, I see. An Intelligence officer and a sort of trigger man for a foreign
air line would make an amusing team."

"Oh yeah? Well, I've seen queerer combinations clean
up a pile of money, Skipper."

When the dark-haired Intelligence officer merely
tugged at his mustache Melhorne talked on, all the while

striding up and down the borrowed office. "Remember that time we were hiding in the jungle above Matagalpa?"

North nodded; he wouldn't in a hurry forget the way General Lopez's *macheteros* had combed that hill.

"And we talked about life?"

"That was a long time back, but let's see, now . . . You said something about money being the only real force in the world. Money and enough nerve to grab it any way one could."

"You and the elephants! Well, here's what I wanted to say, Skipper. I figger there's some important jack in this E.F.F. business. The Japs, the Germans and the Russkys, not to mention the French would dig deep for a look at that formula——"

"If?" quietly suggested the seated figure.

"If? Nuts! You and me together can rout out that formula before sunup." The bigger man paused, studying the effect of his words. Presently he continued. "And would we rake in a stack of blue chips!"

North shook his head. "You should know better than to talk like that, Stag."

The well-groomed figure looked pained, raised a protesting hand. "Wait. Keep your pants on. There's no law says we can't sell the secret back to the Airways or the U. S. *if* they'll pay high enough. Of course if you want to go on playing Holy Willie you needn't take your share. You'll have done your job by recovering the secret, see?"

"What about Air Oriental?"

"Nuts to them if we get a higher bid! Like I said that time, it's money that really settles things."

It was a more subtle appeal than North had thought Melhorne capable of. Um. Too bad Melhorne was slippery and his bare word not worth a sneeze in a gale of wind. This might prove a short cut to victory. He was sorely tempted. '

"Think it over," Melhorne urged, plainly determined to be conciliatory. "If you're willing to pool what we know about this business we'd go to town! I've got Lebov, and he's nobody's fool in case you didn't know it. Knows everybody worth while in Canton and Shanghai. I tell you, between us we can bring plenty of guns to bear."

Very serious of mien, North leaned forward. "Maybe I'll throw in with you, Stag."

"Swell! Now you're talking."

"On one condition."

"Well?"

"Will you agree to sell the E.F.F. back to Trans-Pacific *and to no one else?*"

"Not if anybody else raises the ante," grunted Melhorne, reddening. "Business is business. And don't start flag waving. What have the States done for me? Nothing. Kicked me out of West Point for hazing—broke my old man's heart."

"Sorry, Stag, I can't see a deal if the secret doesn't go back to Trans-Pacific for what they will pay."

Melhorne fumbled with his bright yellow tie, looked nonplused and a little awed. "Don't be a damn fool. What's this Intelligence work going to get you? A bullet in the butt some day, and if you should pull through, a pension which wouldn't keep a cuckoo clock in birdseed. Get wise, Skipper, get wise!" Like a me-

nagerie beast prowling behind the bars of its cage, Melhorne ranged up and down over the office's gritty floor.
"You're a swell guy, North, but you're growing no
younger fast. None of us are. God! If I'd had half your
brains I'd have retired ten years back. Think it over
and don't forget I've been round this neck of the woods
for months. I may be in choky right now, but I know
plenty of people on the outside who'd rub out a wise-
guy detective and never bat an eye." The ex-soldier's
manner was becoming staccato, prompted by the impatience of one who is accustomed to instant and implicit
obedience, of one who, having made up his mind, ruthlessly batters down any and all opposition.

Stag, the gaunt captain knew, was not jesting about
the "rubbing out." Far from baseless were the reports
that, in Manchuria, he had with his own hands machine-
gunned the officers of a disobedient battalion.

North's look did not waver. "One good tip deserves
another. Don't get tough, Stag, or I'll wind up your
clock in short order. You see, I don't worry too much
about idle morality and legal technicalities when handling an hombre of your caliber."

The two stood eyeing each other, as slowly a wave of
red rose and receded above Melhorne's collar. The latter ended by shrugging and cocking his big head a little
to one side. "Okay. Now it's your spiel. Why did you
have me brought up here?"

"Wanted to ask you about that woman who came to
the door of Eve's flat last night."

"Yes?" A metallic glint shone in the depths of Melhorne's eyes. "Just wait till I get my claws on that
dame!"

"So you think you'd know her?"

"Would I!" snapped the other. "Say, the one good look I got at her when she came in was enough; and if that boy friend of hers figgers his mask is going to save him, he's all wet!"

The Intelligence officer pulled out a cigarette case, thumbed its lock.

"Oh, so you'd know him too?"

"Sure! You dicks aren't the only ones who notice details. That bird's about five foot ten, weighs a hundred and seventy, his ears haven't free lobes, and he's got a mole on his chin I could spot twenty yards away. On the back of his left hand he's got a hook-shaped scar; saw it when he was tying me up." Melhorne broke off to rub a nose broken at some remote date. "Why? Want me to identify him for you?"

"I might," North said, blinking in the glare of the lights overhead. "Might even want you to come along over to Kowloon. I think your pals of last night are going to try to skip on the Hongkong Clipper. If you behave I'll see what can be done about getting you off easy on the compounding charge. Are you on?"

"On? Sure!" Melhorne's teeth glinted in a tight smile. "Let's have one of those skags."

"Sure," North said, held out the cigarette case, and just a split second late he saw his error. In a lightning grab Melhorne had him by the wrist and was jerking him forward, off balance. In a flash the man from G-2 lay sprawling, his head a fair target for Melhorne's vicious kick.

Amid a grand blaze of illumination North lost consciousness.

CHAPTER XXVII

At first Hugh North thought Melhorne must still be kicking his forehead, so painful was its throbbing, but gradually the impact lessened until he was aware of his error. Weak beyond all understanding, he simply lay where he was, struggling to resist nausea prompted by the wild heaving of the floor—or was it a deck? At length he summoned enough strength to reach up and test a great raw bump above his right temple and then tried to straighten his legs but could not. All at once he became panic-stricken; his eyes were open, and he couldn't see! Had he gone blind? Perspiration stung at his forehead. Faugh! How bad the air was in here!

An awful possibility suggested itself to his reeling imagination; he had been thought dead. He was buried alive! Fear restored his strength enough to grope about, and he uttered a little relieved sigh. Rubbers, a walking stick and a mackintosh didn't belong in well-regulated coffins! Swallowing hard, he looked up to see a small spark of light glowing miles above him, it seemed. Instinctively he guessed it must be a keyhole.

Then like the rush of a mill race memory came flooding back, and with the first violent spring of an over-wound toy he jumped up, only to stand swaying, fighting down rending nausea. Leaning against the door panel, he commenced weakly to pound.

What an utter, inexcusable lop-eared jackass he'd been to grant Stag Melhorne even half a chance! *What time was it?* A look at the luminous dial of his watch doused him in an icy bath of despair. Great God, it was just past one o'clock!

Frantically he yelled, kept up his hammering at the door until, aeons later, a passing constable heard him. More precious time slipped away while the policeman hunted a passkey to the office and then ran back for another fitting the closet.

It was one-fifteen when, green-faced from the closet's foul air, Hugh North burst out of his prison. Ye gods! Fifteen scant minutes later the clipper should take off from Kowloon and, roaring out over the China Sea, go winging off on her course to the Philippines, bearing with her—— No time now to spread his elaborate dragnet, but perhaps he could prevent the flying boat's departure. Raging, he darted to a phone and, on ringing the airbase, got a busy signal!

Sickened, he pounded down a passage filled with staring, half-dressed police and detectives. "Got to get—Kowloon—fifteen minutes! Get me—car! Quick! Phone for speedboat! Someone call airbase—tell 'em to delay plane!"

"Fifteen minutes, sir?" protested a phlegmatic desk sergeant. "Why, we couldn't get you there in under half an hour."

"Shut up, you goddamn dunderhead! Do as I say!

You"—he beckoned an intelligent-looking young detective—"come along!"

While clattering down the Central Station's steps he learned that no one had noticed Melhorne's departure, so there was no telling whether he'd headed for Kowloon or for safety in Macao. North searched his soul for curses at his own unwariness. Connie! Good God! Right now she'd be aboard the Hongkong Clipper, unprotected if Yu Shih, his assignment completed, had gone ashore. Should the crisis develop no one would be there to step in.

Hatless and with a thread of blood crawling down his cheek, he jumped into the police car beside its driver.

"Don't care how many laws you break. For God's sake, get moving!"

Probably the chauffeur was driving with all speed, but to the Intelligence officer his progress made cold molasses seem fluent. Brakes screeching, tires whining, the police car sped down Old Bailey Street, ignoring protesting curses of British and Chinese citizens until, on a freshly watered length of road, the car went into a nerve-crisping skid and ended by slamming against the curb with such force as to break one of the headlights.

When the chauffeur could not pull himself together Hugh North shoved the fellow aside, took the wheel himself and raced on towards the water front, picking an erratic course through a maze of traffic. Though he tried to collect his scattered thoughts, the situation's various elements remained confused, fragmentary, like the scenes of a cinema being unreeled too fast.

Someone at the police station had used his head; a long gray speedboat lay sputtering beside a float at the foot of Gilman Street. If only that greenish-white minute hand would cease its inexorable descent! Not even delaying to set his vehicle's emergency brake, North hurdled out of the car, scrambled down to the float and into the launch.

"Trans-Pacific Airport!" he rasped, without hesitation, abandoning his assistant who had waited to check the car. "How soon can you get me there?"

"Not rough, sir," the Chinese engineer replied and opened his throttle with a jerk which made the motorboat surge ahead with the speed of a speared dolphin. "Mebbe ten, fi'teen minutes."

"Drive her! Get every bit of speed you can."

Of the furious cruise across the harbor North later recalled little beyond the thuttering sound made by hard-flung spray, the racket of roaring exhausts and the searchlight's restless groping. Good thing the launch was a fast one—intended for the pursuit of those smugglers who made life miserable for the Victoria Police. It grew quite cold, and though North turned up his collar, the wind felt good on his throbbing scalp. What a hell of a kick Melhorne had given him! Where was that big devil anyhow? The air tore at his hair, filled his eyes with tears as gradually the radiance of a fan-shaped glare ahead assumed more intensity while behind, the glowing triangle formed by the lights on the Peak grew dimmer. Triangles?

He thought of those scribblings, then of Connie. God! What if she'd fooled him after all? It was far from impossible. Mental snapshots of the actors in the problem flashed across his imagination. Tashima, Hsing, Trina, Connie, the Martins and all the rest; sometimes in characteristic poses, sometimes as caricatures.

Feeling somewhat stronger but increasingly apprehensive, North steadied himself against the police boat's plunges and by the half light of a waning moon searched the roadstead for a possible glimpse of Melhorne. He took himself sharply in hand at that. If Stag *had* gone to Kowloon he must long since have reached the airbase.

"Which side's the airport?" he demanded of the English steersman beside him.

"Over there—right of the peninsula beyond Honghom, sir. That's their floodlights ahead."

Ignoring a lookout's frenzied curses, they cut across the bows of a lumbering Chinese freighter, the Ching Mu, and the motorboat heeled like a Star boat in a breeze. The nearer lights glimmered on the mainland, the higher seethed Hugh North's doubts. A little shiver ran down his spine because somewhere ahead an airplane's motors began to crackle and roar. Too late? He cast a despairing glance at the Chinese engineer, but that worthy grimaced his helplessness to raise more speed. Presently, however, the launch commenced to skirt the Kowloon water front, rushing past the sterns of several great steamers which, lying tranquilly in their berths, were sending their breath skywards in attenuated smoke pillars.

The glow of floodlights had become dazzling as a long mole of newly dressed stone materialized with a minor beacon blinking some signal at its end. A measure of North's anxiety dissipated when he made out the Hongkong Clipper's huge silver-painted hull, overshadowing both tenders and a landing stage swaying beneath the weight of a small throng of stay-at-homes. In the harsh glare of a searchlight fixed atop a huge hangar he could see lines yet to be cast off and even picked out the company's leaping sailfish insignia on the flying boat's bow.

Just as Hugh North was preparing to jump ashore an abrupt additional radiance cast hangar and incompleted administration building into sharp relief and drew highlights from the spars of near-by vessels. What the devil was going on? He had secured a firmer grip on his presence of mind when with a little bump the launch pulled in to a slip near the tip of the mole.

Mopping his face, Hugh North ran towards the flying boat and was somewhat perturbed to see a pair of shadowy figures move promptly in his direction. They were detectives, however, posted there by Chief Inspector Duveen.

"What was that light just now?"

"Photographers taking pictures, sir. Plane's been held up for the official mail sack. I guess that's it now."

The fellow pointed to a truck rumbling down across a great concrete apron past the tractor and cradle designed to draw flying boats from the water to the hangar. This, then, was the background—glaring lights, jet water, bold shadows—by chance an uncannily theatrical setting for the drama so sure to follow.

Her cabin lights ablaze, the Hongkong Clipper appeared enormous, a streamlined, porpoise-shaped creation, all silvery in the moonlight. Standing in the navigation compartment, North could see the chief pilot and the navigation officer looking down and calling out some direction to the postal employees. Bright silvery riffles caused by idling propellers marred the otherwise polished ebony of the water, and on the short sea wings a junior flight officer was squatting to address a young woman. Rapidly the Intelligence officer's look took in the scene in its entirety—the big ship and the people swarming antlike around it.

"Please line up," somebody began calling over the motor's sleepy drone. "We're going to take another shot——"

Out of breath, hatless and coatless, North wiped the dried blood from his cheek while circling the outskirts of the crowd to that point where Sir George and Chief Inspector Duveen stood aside in glum and uneasy isolation, like conspirators in a Victorian drama. Just beyond them lingered a small knot of detectives who should long since have been posted around the limits of the airbase.

"Figured a swell caption for this shot," he heard MacAllister saying. " 'T.P.A. Official's Daughter Defies Company Jinx. Takes Off For Manila.' "

Sir George Amberson saw North come up and treated him to a look of anger mixed with contempt. "I'm thinking ye've a strange way of doing things, Captain. Where 've ye been? Down to Repulse again? What's the meaning o' this?"

The man from G-2 choked down his resentment while running an eye over a group of some fifteen passengers noisily engaged in lining up in front of the clipper. "Explain later," he gasped. Almost a typical crowd, North decided, usual number of well-fed, faintly uneasy business men, giggling young women and seasoned travelers. Laughing and grinning in the peculiarly inane fashion of departing voyagers, they permitted the camera men to line them up.

Hurriedly Hugh North counted noses. There were the Martins, she with a corsage and looking very bright eyed and gay; he restless, complying with only mechanical good grace. Mr Tashima stood a little further down the line, showing all his teeth and towering above a fat little man unwisely dressed in plus-fours. Where was Connie? His heart skipped a beat, then he saw her, straight as a young pine in her black suit and waving to someone in the crowd. Further on Inspector Yu Shih's chunky figure stood among the shadows with its big blunt head swinging in slow semicircles. He was not missing much.

"Okay, Mr Swazey, you get in this one too," Mac-Allister cried, and to the operations manager's obvious irritation caught him by the arm as he passed.

"But I'm not a passenger," the T.P.A. man protested.

"Oh come on," Connie hailed. "This is an occasion. You, too, Alex." Out from a group of spectators she dragged the White Russian and clung to his arm as he stood blinking in the unreal glare of the searchlights.

Was anyone still missing?

"Stop bawling me out!" North warned the resentful chief inspector who had kept pace with him. "I didn't get this goose egg playing post office. . . . Seen anything of Melhorne?"

"Melhorne!"

"Yes. He got away. Better call your men and tell 'em to keep their eyes skinned!"

Again he silently made a roll call; somebody wasn't

there on the float. Who? As the shutters clacked and the flashlights blazed again Hugh North desperately ran down his mental list until he came to Trina Sinclair. Trina! Where was she? Cheekbones very prominent, he hurried over to a neat young officer of T.P.A.'s passenger division who held a clip board in his hand.

"Has Miss Sinclair appeared?"

At the Intelligence officer's disheveled appearance and sweaty features the uniformed youth gaped an instant ere he jerked a nod.

"Yes sir. She's here. Saw her talking to Moose Hartman just a few minutes ago."

A glance over his shoulder told North the reporters were taking brief interviews, getting names to accompany the photographs. Connie seemed the focus of their attention. He caught the passenger agent's gold-braided cuff and detained him.

"Have the passengers been aboard yet?"

They had been, the agent informed him; some of them for over an hour. They had only recently disembarked to please the photographers.

"Well, keep them out here another five minutes," North directed in a compelling tone. "I don't care what the excuse. That's a police order!"

While mounting a short flight of steps leading to the clipper's gangway he cast a last look at the crowd, a restless black and silver pattern seen by the searchlights. Lebov, he knew, had seen him; Tashima also. Further away Sir George was craning his long neck as Swazey talked, pointed out something, and in the far background hovered the silent figures of the C.I.D. men— watchful but uninformed. No Melhorne yet. Maybe he hadn't come to Kowloon. Or was he lurking somewhere on this broad stage, merely biding his time?

Where the devil was Trina? He stepped into the hull's green-tinted interior and, finding himself opposite a space marked "Cloakroom", turned right down a corridor. In number 1 compartment he found no one sitting on its comfortable-looking green and gold upholstery, though coats, mufflers, hats and other articles of apparel littered the seats.

"Trina!" he called.

In the lounge a deserted cigarette butt smoldered disagreeably, but only a few scattered magazines and newspapers kept it company.

In compartment number 3 a white-jacketed steward was picking up a rather wilted corsage of violets. Smiling a courteous Trans-Pacific Airways smile, he inquired, "You're looking for someone, sir?"

"Yes. A Miss Sinclair. It's most important I find her at once. Please see if there's anybody in the lavatory."

As a rising wind moans louder about the eaves of an exposed house, so Hugh North's misgivings increased. *Where* the devil had Trina gone? Suddenly he recalled her remarks anent the navigating officers' cabin and was debating an ascent to the god of gadget's lair when the rattle of a hand truck delivering the belated mail pouches drew his attention to the front of the ship and he again noticed the compartment marked, "Cloakroom."

When he pushed open its door a queer little croak escaped him, and he froze into immobility. Amid a tangle of fallen raincoats Trina Sinclair was lying, huddled and motionless. At a glance he could tell that she was unconscious, a red bruise shedding a drop or two of blood over her forehead. Her handbag lay open and obviously rifled beside her, with its compact, lipstick and mirror scattered far and wide over the coatroom floor.

Captain North wheeled and burst past a startled employee of His Britannic Majesty's post office but hesitated on the ladder, raking the throng outside. He glimpsed someone moving away from the float and delayed not an instant longer.

CHAPTER XXVIII

FAINTLY TO HIS EARS came Connie's startled, "Oh, Hugh! Where *have* you been?", Mr Martin's startled "Mon Dieu!" and the hiss of Mr Tashima's sharply drawn breath, but with eyes darting in all directions he drove a path through the crowd standing silhouetted against the flying boat's silver background. Yu Shih moved closer to Connie and, being Chinese, devoted most of his attention to Mr Tashima.

"Got to get back to the office. They interrupted me, and I left the receiver off the phone," Mr Swazey was informing the inspector general as they moved away from the float. "You'll stop in before you leave, Sir George? I'd like to show you about."

"Verra well." The inspector general nodded vaguely. "By the bye, Mr Swazey, we can give ye a lift back to town if ye like."

The operations manager nodded his thanks and had turned away when North hailed, "Just a minute, Mr Swazey."

The Trans-Pacific man, however, did not appear to hear him and only increased the length of his stride up the hangar's apron.

"Hey! Wait! Come back. There's——"

The operations manager began to run.

"Stop him!" yelled North as Swazey dashed past the knot of detectives. He, too, began to run, but the fugitive had got a good start and was running like the very devil towards an automobile waiting on the driveway. When the car sped to meet him North halted, pulled out the .32 and, erasing all consequences from his mind, sighted and fired.

Even as the automatic's flat, dry report made the hangar resound, the operations manager staggered in mid-stride, clapped a hand to his back, half turned and fell heavily, rolling over and over like a shot rabbit. He was game, however, and, cursing in fluent German, twisted sidewise in an effort to extricate a weapon from his coat pocket. North came up, stepped on his wrist and wrenched away the pistol.

"That will do," said he.

The car's driver, sensing disaster, instead of slowing, merely continued his circuit of the drive and dashed off into the night.

"Ach du lieber Gott!" Swazey was panting like some animal run down on a road, writhing dreadfully. "In my legs I feel nothing! My back is broken!"

North said nothing but, aware of a ring of C.I.D. men closing in, felt reassured enough to kneel, search his inner coat pocket. He found nothing there so, disregarding Paul Swazey's weak attempts to beat him off, looked until, between the wounded man's belt and clammy belly, he encountered three envelopes. His heart gave a mighty upward surge, and he had commenced to scan them when a hand closed on his shoulder.

"I say, Captain, what's the meaning of this?" rasped Chief Inspector Duveen. "If you've made a mistake you'll have to answer for it!"

North paid him not the least attention but dashed sweat from his eyes and, trembling like an ague patient, held his discoveries to the light. Shoes clattered on the concrete, voices called out, and Swazey kept up a breathless strain of profanity, but the gaunt American was aware of nothing save the fact that all letters were addressed to Katrina Sinclair. All three of them bore American postmarks, but there was no letter addressed in a feminine hand stamped with a Hongkong stamp and dated June thirtieth. What had become of it—or was it camouflaged within one of these other letters?

An odd buzzing sensation manifested itself in North's bones when he hooked a finger beneath the flap, wrenched open the first of the captured missives. No luck—the glare of the floodlights revealed no lines of chemical symbols.

"You Americans are too ready wi' yer guns," Sir George growled, pushing his way through the crowd, his craggy features forbidding. "What's that?"

"The E.F. formula. Should be in one of these covers."

Duveen gaped in loose-mouthed confusion. "I don't understand how Swazey could have recovered it. Kindly explain why you have shot this man?"

"Because he isn't Swazey. He's a German," the American snapped, throwing on the .32's safety catch and placing it on the ground beside him, tore open the second letter. *Still no luck!*

"German?"

"Yes. It will be interesting to find out what's hap-

pened to the real Swazey." He bent above the prostrate
figure. "Where's Swazey?"

Outlined against pale concrete, the impostor glared
up an instant, then shrugged. "He's being held in Canton. I was sent to meet him on the steamer coming over
from Manila."

"You were sent?" Sir George queried, then ordered
the C.I.D. men to force back the crowd.

"Yes. I take my orders same as you." The wounded
man stifled a groan and then turned, peered curiously
up at North. "Ach. I thought my acting was perfect.
When did you begin to suspect?"

"Fairly early," the American quietly replied and,
fearful of another disappointment, hesitated ere ripping
open the third envelope. "Anyone who's been to Chile
knows that spring comes down there in November. After
that break I noticed your signet ring—its heraldry is
German."

"Ah, so that was it! I felt you might have seen that
imperial eagle on my chest. Ach, what a foolish cadet's
trick that was."

"Yes, I smelled a rat then, but even before, I wondered
why, if you were making a perfectly ordinary call on
Tipton, you'd wear crepe rubber shoes on a wet night.
That was absurd in the face of it and so was the story
you told."

The man they had known as Swazey bit his lips and
sucked hard on the cigarette. "No need to open that
last letter, friend North; what you are looking for will
be in it."

"Who are you really?" Sir George demanded, bending over the fallen figure.

North meanwhile thrust the last precious letter close to his skin and rebuttoned his shirt.

"Oberst Max von Schniewind of the Army Intelligence. Herr Hauptmann North, my congratulations. I am sorry about Miss Sinclair, but this game is not for those afraid of getting hurt, eh?"

North drew a deep breath. Someday, reason warned, he, too, must lie like that, helpless, finished. Von Schniewind's voice broke in.

"Please, this concrete is very cold . . . Ah." He had sighted a pair of attendants hurrying up with a stretcher from the crash wagon.

The inspector general cleared his throat as they hurried down to the great silver flying boat and said, "My error. What led ye to think of Miss Sinclair?"

"Process of elimination. There were three essential clues—the torn pocket, the coat buttoned womanwise and that scribbling. Anyone could have torn the pocket, probably any of the three women could have made that mistake about the coat, but only one person would scribble the same way while thinking hard. There were triangles and circles on that scratch pad. Well, I saw Connie scribble crosses and Melhorne draw snaky spirals on a wet table top, but Trina, down at Repulse, drew pyramids and loops in the sand when she was thinking. People subconsciously generally repeat such designs, you know. Incidentally, I'd appreciate your having Mr and Mrs Martin arrested on a charge of illegal entry; later I believe we can charge Mrs Martin with attempted murder."

The inspector general looked mystified. "What do ye mean?"

"Just this," North said as they hurried back, neared the Hongkong Clipper's gangway. "Some charming young thing took a pot shot at me right after the robbery was discovered, and I'm pretty sure it was Mrs Martin. The whereabouts of the three other women who might have done it are all accounted for."

Under the cyclopean wing of the flying boat Sir George hesitated.

"I'd best get to a phone and ease His Excellency's mind, but if ye wish me to go wi' ye, I can wait."

North deliberated a brief instant, then, spying Yu Shih's solid little bulk detach itself from the dark swarm of people crowding about the false Mr Swazey's ambulance, he shook his head. Besides, he yearned privately to examine that last letter.

"No, Sir George. I'm just going to look over the ship. The Sinclair girl is aboard, knocked cold."

"The Sinclair girl?" The inspector general looked his astonishment. "It's a tall feather ye've put in yer cap tonight, Captain. Weel, I'm off."

As Sir George swung briskly away Yu Shih came up, a troubled look marring the bronze moon of his face.

"What's wrong?" North demanded sharply.

"This unworthy creature's attention briefly distracted by shooting here. Pleasing aspect of Miss Holden not visible anywhere, tajên."

"She's probably in the crowd there with everybody else," North sighed. Long ago he'd ceased to do more than hope Connie would follow instructions. Peering sidewise at the Hongkong Clipper, he saw the great flying boat, huge, ghostly and apparently deserted, floating restlessly on jet waters which, under the force of a rising wind, had begun to slap at pier and apron with increasing noisiness. "Crew go ashore?"

"Yes, tajên. At time shooting began most officers in administration building for final instructions; rest of crew came out carrying pistols. They have not yet returned."

Um. North lengthened his stride. It was a bit grim to think of poor Trina lying there utterly alone. Where the devil had Connie betaken herself? All at once he fished into the front of his shirt and snatched out the last letter taken from the man who had posed as Paul Swazey. Great God above! Here was no chemical formula, only a long, typewritten, personal letter. How had Swazey managed to trick him? Or had he? Maybe Swazey, too, had been fooled. With a despairing sense of futility he grabbed at Yu Shih's wrist.

"Quick! Go back, get some men and quietly throw a cordon about the plane!"

The little Chinese cast him a swift, white-eyed look ere scuttling off towards the hangar beyond which people milled and shifted under the floodlights in the inimitable manner of crowds.

North raced for the clipper in a towering, consuming rage at himself. Why had he dared jump to such an absurd conclusion that the pseudo Swazey had of necessity won the formula! The backs of his hands tingling, he plunged into the Hongkong Clipper's hull, and even before he thrust open the baggage-compartment door he suffered a sickening presentiment.

On the floor lay a few bright drops of blood, Trina Sinclair's bag, lipstick and compact. Even the soft gray hat she had worn remained among the tumbled luggage, but of Trina herself there was no trace. Aware that several moments must pass before Yu Shih could summon and dispose his men, North hurriedly searched the passenger compartment and even cast a glance into the crew's quarters in the clipper's tail.

Had Trina gotten away? Of course! It would be very simple to drop into the waters alongside and swim quietly away. But to reach the water she would either have to climb through a window below or escape through the navigator's cabin above. Obviously the regular entrance was too risky even with the distraction of a gun fight. On seeing no open windows on this deck, he pocketed his .32 and scrambled up a ladder into the god of gadget's lair. Did another ladder exist towards this great ship's stern? Climbing, he wondered.

In semidarkness and beset by all manner of complicated gears, gauges and placards, he had started forward towards the pilot's cockpit. A little sound made him wheel about in time to behold a figure materialize in wraithlike silence from amid the shadows beneath a small chart table.

It was Trina, who stood not six feet away, leveling a small automatic. Her hair, he could see by the half light, had tumbled down about the shoulders of a dark tailored jacket, and a small smear of blood marred her face from the corner of her suddenly tigerish mouth to the point of her chin.

"T-Too bad you checked those letters," she gasped over the slap-slapping of waves against the hull. "You l-leave me n-no choice . . ."

That this hard-eyed girl meant to kill him he knew, and at this range she could hardly miss. To make matters worse, the noise of feet pattering down the pier gave her a desperate incentive. He gathered himself, bracing for the tearing impact of her bullet. One thing was sure: even if she shot him through the heart he'd hang on; she must not get away.

Even as he surged forward towards the girl's blazing eyes and rigid mask of a face her right shoulder sagged under a blow delivered from behind, and her arm flew violently sidewise under some involuntary nervous reaction. For all the world like a blocking back, North took Trina "out" and though she tried to bite him, he took away her gun.

"Let me go, you f-fool! Let me go—t-tell you where —E.F. is if you will . . ." she pleaded as they rolled about on the floor, but when involuntarily her left hand flickered towards the bosom of her dress North almost savagely tore at the buttons and fabric until his fingers closed over an oblong of paper warmed by body heat.

"Let me go, you d-devil! Let me g-go!" Trina began beating futilely at his face, at the same time gasping exasperated profanities.

Deliberately pinioning the squirming girl beneath one knee, North thrust the letter into a shaft of light from below. At once he recognized a Hongkong postmark and Trina's writing!

"An interesting pose, Captain," Connie's deep tones commented. "Looks like a companion piece for 'Civic Virtue.' Or is it 'The Sophomore's Love-Making'?"

Hugh North, busy with the envelope's flap, grunted but made no further reply.

Still grasping a brass fire extinguisher, Connie stepped from the navigator's cabin, a bit disheveled and breathless, but otherwise calm and faintly sardonic.

"Why, if it isn't dear little Trina playing with the boys again." Connie chuckled, but her stance was alert. "Rough, isn't he? Tsk, tsk! Hugh! Who'd ever dream you'd go in for the caveman stuff?"

Satisfied that this time he indeed had possession of the E.F.F., Hugh North arose, a slow grin widening over his face like a ripple over a still pool.

"Merely a change of pace, my dear. Besides, I didn't notice you erring on the side of tenderness just now." His look conveyed volumes of appreciation as he said, "I was becoming afraid you'd got temperamental again."

"Not a chance," came her grim reassurance. "I just loved sticking to dear Trina."

Trina sat up, fumbling angrily at her ripped blouse front. "Well, what's next?" she snapped. "Get on with it."

North dabbed at a scratch she had given him and shrugged. "If it were up to me, Trina, I'd call quits, but the English will probably charge you with Sam Patterson's murder."

"It wasn't m-murder! I swear to God I d-didn't m-mean to k-kill him. It was an accident." Trina's bravura evaporated, leaving her to shake violently. "I d-didn't mean to kill S-Sam, only put him to s-sleep long enough to get the f-formula."

"You *knew* he was going to take it?" Connie suggested above the scrape of feet advancing over the cement apron below.

"No!" Trina's face crumpled, and she dropped heavily on the radio operator's seat. "I only knew that S-Sam and A.W. had the combination. No one else. I

c-couldn't suspect A.W.—no matter what his stepdaughter was," she added with a sudden flicker of spirit.
"If you think I p-plotted to s-steal the formula you're
wrong. I didn't. But when it was missed I guessed S-Sam
had it, so gave him some proponal I'd bought to kill
myself with when—when S-Sam and I broke up."
Mechanically she pushed a strand of hair from her eyes,
looked dully at North standing before her. "I wanted
to give you the f-formula—even c-called your club
twice, but when I learned Sam was dead I got too s-scared
to say anything more. After I got to thinking I figured
the formula could make me rich for life, so I decided I'd
better hang onto it."

She was infinitely tragic in that pose, and her tone
was bitter. "I knew you were my worst danger," she
went on, "s-so I thought I could k-kid you into falling
for me." She tried to shrug but ended by rubbing the
shoulder Connie had injured with the fire extinguisher.
"It—it wasn't hard, Hugh, to play up to you. You're a
pretty swell guy even if you are a detective." Trina bit
her lip. "What a laugh that would have been—to be escorted with the E.F.F. out of Hongkong by the great
Hugh North himself! Funny, I really thought you were
falling and never guessed you suspected."

"That, my dear Trina, was your first mistake," North
said, switching on the radio room lights. "All along I
couldn't figure out why, at that hour of the night and
under those circumstances, you went back to your room
and took time to write a letter to someone in Hongkong."

"How did you know it was Hongkong? I hid the address."

"I saw a penny ha'penny stamp so knew it must be a

local address. In itself that was unimportant, but it attracted my curiosity." Wearily he wiped away the
perspiration evoked by the gleam of Trina's pistol
barrel.

"Tajên," Yu Shih hailed from below. "What have got
up there?"

"Two queens—hearts and spades."

"And an ace," Connie amplified with a serene smile.